When he turned to go, Sabrina caught his forearm

Her fingers felt warm through the material of his dress shirt. "Will you think about the interview?"

Her face was open and seemingly sincere. But Noah knew how easy it was to fake emotions for the camera or, in this case, the potential interviewee. "Yes." He let her hand remain on his arm a moment longer then nodded. "Have a nice day, Sabrina."

"You, too, Mr. Mayor."

"It's Noah." He didn't know why he said it. If she wanted to call him by his title, as so many in town did, he shouldn't care. Didn't care. He attempted to cover his verbal hiccup. "Most people call me Noah."

"I'm not most people."

She was standing only a couple of inches away. The breeze caught her hair, tugged the strands toward him. They whispered across his cheek, just as soft as they looked. Noah exhaled slowly. "I've noticed."

Dear Reader,

The summer I turned thirteen, I attended a family reunion in a small town. Up to this point, I'd never experienced small-town life: a hotel that had a grand total of four rooms, a single thoroughfare aptly named Main Street, and residents who not only knew each other by name, but were versed in all the tiny details of each other's lives. I've always wondered what it would be like to grow up in that kind of close-knit community and what might make a person leave or stay.

Noah Barnes never considered living anywhere but the small town he calls home, while Sabrina Ryan hoped never to return. But when their lives connect, they start to see that maybe home isn't a place, but a person.

I loved writing *This Just In...* and hope you enjoy it. If you're curious about the music I played and the actors I pictured while writing the book, visit my website, www.jennifermckenzie.com.

Happy reading,

Jennifer McKenzie

JENNIFER McKENZIE

This Just In...

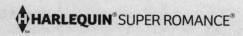
HARLEQUIN® SUPER ROMANCE®

Recycling programs
for this product may
not exist in your area.

ISBN-13: 978-0-373-60864-5

THIS JUST IN…

Printed in U.S.A.

www.Harlequin.com

ABOUT THE AUTHOR

Jennifer McKenzie lives in Vancouver, Canada, where she enjoys being able to ski and surf in the same day— not that she ever does either of those things. After years of working as a communications professional and spending her days writing for everyone else, she traded in the world of watercoolers, cubicles and high heels to write for herself and wear pajamas all day. When she's not writing, she's reading, eating chocolate, trying to talk herself into working off said chocolate on the treadmill or spending time with her husband.

Books by Jennifer McKenzie

HARLEQUIN SUPERROMANCE

Other titles by this author available in ebook format.

For my dear friend Jenn who always cheers me on, offers support when I need it and laughs at my jokes. Just for you, the P-word is nowhere to be found in this book.

CHAPTER ONE

SABRINA RYAN HAD NEVER planned to return home.

Not that Wheaton, British Columbia, the small town where she'd grown up—population: 4500, number of ATVs: 600, movie theater: 1—was home anymore. Not for the past nine years, at least. So finding herself there, for more than just a quick weekend visit, was a real kick in the teeth.

"What can I get you?" she asked the teenager at the front counter of her parents' coffeehouse. Yes, that's right. After living on her own and making her way in the world as a Vancouver newspaper columnist, becoming semi-well-known for her celebrity interviews in the process, she'd been reduced to working as a barista. In Wheaton.

She got irritated just thinking about it.

The teenager requested a latte and Sabrina set to work steaming the milk. At least he didn't try to strike up a conversation, ask her what had brought her back and try to share all of his own life's little details with her. Not like the previous ten people she'd served. And the ten people before them. And the ten people before them. And, really, everyone who'd made their way into the cozy coffee shop in the two weeks since her return.

So different than Vancouver, where a person could lose herself in the masses. Where a sudden appearance after years away brought no more than a single raised eyebrow, if anyone noticed at all. Sabrina sighed and watched as the milk began to froth. But anonymity was an anathema to small-town residents. Something she'd cheerfully forgotten in her years away because she hadn't planned to come back. Ever.

She turned her attention to pulling the espresso shot, ignoring the pinch of her high-heeled boots around her right pinky toe. Considering she was going to be on her feet for the next seven hours, heels might not have been the most sensible choice, but it was bad enough that she'd had to leave her fabulous city life, amazing job and cultured friends behind. She wasn't giving up her style, as well.

She rolled the milk to create a smooth, glossy surface and then poured it into the coffee with a couple of added wrist flicks and shakes to create a perfectly presented leaf. A latte that any Vancouverite would be proud to sip. Or take a photo of to share online.

Sabrina handed over the beverage, smiling through the pain in her foot and reminding herself that her visit was only that. A visit. A way station in her journey of life. Just as soon as she was able, she'd be on her way back to the city and Wheaton would be nothing more than a speck in her rearview mirror.

She made three more lattes, two espressos, eight plain black coffees and one hot chocolate in the next thirty minutes. She was asked about her return seven times during the same period, but though her answer remained the same—"Why am I back? My newspaper wants me to write a book about the celebrity interviews I've done over the years"—her smile began to feel strained. She might not have visited Wheaton since she was eighteen, but it still felt wrong lying to people. Even her parents didn't know the real reason for her return. It was simply too embarrassing to admit she'd been fired. Too embarrassing to admit that she'd blown through her savings in less than six months and, with no cash to pay for food or rent or any other necessity, had been forced back here.

Sabrina inhaled slowly and concentrated on masking the shame with a cheerful smile. As far as she was concerned, no one would ever know. One day soon, she was sure her former boss and editor would greet her regular phone check-in with the news that she'd been forgiven her little gaffe and was needed back at the office immediately.

So far, no one had questioned her story. Not even Trish Mason, the editor of the *Wheaton Digest,* who'd agreed to hire her on part-time while she was in town. It felt like the first bit of good luck she'd had in ages.

Well, it had felt that way until Trish handed over her first assignment: interview the two candidates running for mayor this November.

The assignment itself wasn't the problem. Although it was only May and the election wouldn't take place until the third week in November, the fact that there was an actual race had caused big interest in Wheaton. Sabrina had already scheduled an interview with the challenger, Pete Peters, who'd been only too happy to agree to a sit-down interview, photo session and whatever else would get him into the local paper.

But the incumbent was a slippery sort. She'd tried calling and had even popped into his office last Friday to try to talk to him in person, but so far Noah Barnes had evaded her.

And Sabrina knew why.

Too bad for him, she wasn't so easily dissuaded. Even though writing articles on a pair of small-town politicians angling for the mayor title was far below her usual celebrity subject matter and though the paper had a circulation in the thousands as opposed to over a million, she'd write to the best of her ability. Not just because the editor of the paper was a close family friend, but to prove to herself that she was still an excellent reporter.

Excellent enough to recognize the mayor when

he walked into the coffee shop with the jangle of an overhead bell.

Noah Barnes. This time, she didn't have to fake her smile.

Sabrina eyed him as he joined the line, noting his broad shoulders and golden hair. She remembered him from when she'd lived here before, but as she was four years younger they hadn't run in the same circles. He was a good-looking man, as handsome as many of the actors she'd interviewed and taller. In his charcoal pants and green golf shirt, he looked like the kind of guy who spent his downtime rescuing cats from trees and mowing his elderly neighbor's lawn. From what she'd been able to uncover about him, that guess probably wasn't too far off.

As well as being the town's current mayor, Noah owned a successful car dealership, which currently employed twenty residents. He sponsored the local hockey team, chaired the town's annual festival and could be called upon in any sort of emergency.

He was also the brother of her ex-boyfriend.

"Mr. Mayor," she said when he finally reached the counter. "Just the man I've been looking for." She felt the curious gazes turn their way, heard the low hum of conversation hush as everyone strained to hear, and she planned to use it to her advantage. The practically perfect mayor wouldn't turn her down with all his constituents listening, right?

"Good morning." His tone was friendly as he placed his order. One double shot espresso, a box of coffee to go and an assortment of fresh pastries.

She keyed the items into the register. "Could I have a moment of your time?" She was so sure that he'd nod and smile, she was already planning what she would say to convince him that a little bit of family drama shouldn't take precedence over his mayoral campaign.

Instead, Noah offered a polite frown. "I'm afraid I'm in a bit of a rush this morning, but call my assistant and she'll book you in."

Sabrina blinked at him. She'd called his assistant three times last week and each time she'd been shot down with the excuse that the mayor was away from the office or in a meeting and unable to be disturbed. She'd believed her the first two times, but by the third it was beginning to look more than a little circumspect. Still, it wouldn't do to accuse him of such behavior in front of everyone. Sabrina might not have been around in a long time, but she remembered small-town loyalties and they would all lie with the mayor. She forced a civil nod. "I'll do that. But maybe you could give me a moment now? While you wait for your order."

His smiled tightened, but he seemed to realize there was no gracious way to deny her request. "All right then."

She launched into her spiel. How the interview

would be an opportunity to lay some groundwork for his future campaign. How his opponent had already agreed. How it might look to potential voters if he chose not to participate. She poured a small glass of sparkling water and handed it to him as she finished.

He looked down at water. "What's this?"

"To cleanse the palate." Her favorite coffeehouse in Vancouver always served one with the espresso and she thought she'd bring the practice to Wheaton. But it was probably too sophisticated. "You don't have to drink it."

His fingers wrapped around the glass. "No, it's a nice touch."

A flicker of pleasure tickled the base of her neck. So maybe not everyone in town was a lost cause. "What do you think? Can I schedule your interview for later this week?"

"Call my assistant." A reiteration that Sabrina understood completely: thanks, but no thanks.

She kept her smile in place. Mr. Mayor might think he'd successfully brushed her off, but then he didn't know her very well. She finished his order and then pulled off the green apron that doubled as a uniform and asked her coworker to handle the few people remaining in line.

Most customers had left, on their way to work or school, and there wouldn't be another rush until the teenagers got out of class. No reason she couldn't take a few minutes to pursue her assignment. She came around the side of the counter to where Noah stood. "I'll give you a hand out."

His blue eyes were cool. "I've got it."

"It's no problem." She scooped up the box of pastries before he could. "I'm due for a break anyway."

She waited until he picked up the coffee and then led him to the door.

NOAH WATCHED AS Sabrina Ryan picked her way through the crowd that still lingered in the coffee shop. He hadn't seen her in close to fifteen years. Back then he'd been a senior and she a lowly freshman. He had a vague recollection of a pretty but young girl. Far too young for his seventeen-year-old sensibilities with his hockey scholarship to attend university in Michigan already in place.

He sure as hell knew she hadn't looked like this. All huge green eyes, flowing dark hair and pouty mouth. He tamped down the flash of interest that sparked. She wasn't to be trusted. Not only had she told his family's story to the world when it was no one's business but theirs, she'd also been Kyle's high school girlfriend. Totally, completely, 100 percent off-limits. No matter how gorgeous she was.

Still, Noah appreciated the changes she'd made to the general uniform at the coffee shop. Most employees wore a plain white golf shirt with black pants and running shoes. But Sabrina's white button-down shirt was tight and accentuated her curves. Her jeans were even tighter and he eyed them approvingly.

He followed behind her, easily handling the box of coffee and his own espresso. Noah really didn't need the help out to his car, but forcing her to hand over the box of pastries was likely to cause a scene. Instead, he reached out to push the front door open for her and caught a whiff of her perfume. Something spicy and sweet mixed with the heady aroma of coffee.

The flash tried to sputter to life again. He drowned it with a large inhalation of clear, crisp air, and turned toward the back lot where his car was parked. "So what's this about?" He kept his voice controlled and polite. Sabrina did not.

"Let's cut to the chase. You're putting me off."

"Pardon?" He turned the full force of his feigned politeness on her. The look his mother called his mayoral face, used to convey sincerity, express concern and occasionally to put people off.

"The interview. You're sidestepping my request. And I know why."

Noah lifted an eyebrow but said nothing. He led her to a practical black sedan near the entrance and pressed his fob to unlock the doors.

"It's because of the article I wrote about Kyle."

At the mention of his younger half brother, Noah

felt his facade slip but only for a moment. He regrouped and opened the back door on the driver's side. "I think it's a reasonable concern."

Sabrina sighed. "Not really. It was almost a decade ago."

Almost a decade since she'd announced to the town and the province that his baby brother had not only wrecked his back and his future NHL career, but that he'd gotten his teenage girlfriend knocked up. It wasn't so easy to forget. "I don't think you're the best fit. Now if someone else were to do the interview, we wouldn't have a problem." Because he could trust the paper's other reporter not to skewer him publicly.

"Is this payback?" She refused to hand over the box of pastries when he reached for them, placing them behind her back. "Because it seems a little petty."

No, petty was lambasting your former boyfriend and your best friend in public, but Noah didn't mention that. "Then let's just say I think there's too much history. A reporter should be unbiased."

Sabrina narrowed her eyes at him. Even so, he couldn't help noticing the way her shirt was stretched across her chest.

"May I have the pastries?" So he could get out of here before he took another peek at her cleavage.

"No, you may not." She took a step back, like she thought Noah was going to tackle her for them.

He wouldn't, but he also wouldn't make the same mistake his brother had: trusting Sabrina Ryan. Sure, Kyle and Marissa were happily married with four kids, but Sabrina's words had followed them. He still heard the rare comment from someone about how Kyle had "done the right thing." He didn't intend to let her write anything that might follow him the same way.

She tilted her head to look at him. Her long dark ponytail spilled across the bright white of her shirt. Noah wondered if the strands would feel as smooth as her skin looked. Probably. He told himself he wasn't really interested, that he was merely indulging in idle speculation.

"What can I do to convince you it's a good idea?"

Nothing. There was no convincing to be done here. This was a simple question and response, and his response would be the same every time: no. "I really need to run." Noah held out his hand for the pastries. He had a staff meeting at the dealership and they'd be eagerly awaiting his arrival and the sweets.

"Then let's set a time and you can be on your way."

"Not today."

Her eyebrows drew together. "Look, I'm not planning to write some hard-hitting exposé. Just a couple of softball pieces on the mayoral candidates."

Noah would have liked to believe her. "Is that what you told Kyle and Marissa?"

She jerked back. "Ouch."

Perhaps, but it was a fair question. He waited for her response.

Her ponytail swished as she shook her head. "That was different."

"Different how?"

"It just was." He thought he glimpsed regret on Sabrina's face, but then it was gone and she was back to watching him with those big green eyes. "Look, this is my first assignment for the paper. If you say no, Trish won't give me another one. I'll have to go back to pushing caffeine on the masses."

He glanced at the shop behind them. No one had worked up the nerve to follow them outside, but Noah knew it would only be a matter of time. Small towns. Where people thought they had a right to know everyone else's business.

"Please." Sabrina's voice drew him back. "It's important."

Noah looked at the downward tilt to her eyes. She really did think it was important. Either that or she was a hell of an actress. He inhaled another lungful of cold air. Her point that it might look bad for him if only Pete's interview ran was valid. But wouldn't it be worse if she wrote a less than flattering portrayal of him?

Yes. Unequivocally and undeniably.

She appeared to think his silence meant he was considering her offer. Her face brightened. "I promise not to tell any of your deep dark secrets."

Which only reminded him again of how she'd already done that to his family. Fool him once, shame on her. Fool him twice…

"I don't have any deep dark secrets." There were no secret babies, no hidden marriages, no arrests or youthful indiscretions. Just that his birth mother had died when he was an infant. That he and his father had moved to Wheaton when he was four and his dad had married Ellen. That when his dad had died a year later in a freak car accident, Ellen, with a brand-new baby to care for, had adopted Noah. Which everyone in town already knew.

"Really? Doesn't every politician need a deep dark secret or two?"

"Not this one." He kept his voice steady. Even as a teenager when most kids were out too late, stealing from their parents' liquor cabinets or just testing boundaries, Noah had been a model son. He got good grades, worked hard to earn a hockey scholarship to a Michigan university and never stayed out past his curfew. And he hadn't been that way only for his mother. He'd seen it as his chance to show the whole town that although he hadn't been born within town limits, he was one of them.

"Okay, but if you did—" Sabrina's eyes caught his and held "—I wouldn't write about it. I wouldn't write anything that could be considered inappropriate."

He'd like to believe her, like to give her the benefit of the doubt, but he couldn't. Not when there was so much at stake. An article that she might look at as something to entertain the readers could derail his political career. And then who would he be?

Noah placed a hand on her arm, the one still holding his pastries hostage and tugged until they were between them. "I'll think about it," he told her as he plucked the box from her grip.

She let the box go without a fight, but when he turned to leave, she caught his forearm. Her fingers felt warm through the material of his dress shirt. "Will you?"

Her face was open and seemingly sincere. But Noah knew how easy it was to fake emotions for the camera or, in this case, the potential interviewee. "Yes." He let her hand remain on his arm a moment longer then nodded. "Have a nice day, Sabrina."

"You, too, Mr. Mayor."

"It's Noah." He didn't know why he said it. If she wanted to call him by his title, as so many in town did, he shouldn't care. Didn't care. He attempted to cover his verbal hiccup. "Most people call me Noah."

"I'm not most people."

She was standing only a couple of inches from him. The breeze caught her hair, tugged the strands toward him. They whispered across his cheek, just as soft as they looked. Noah exhaled slowly. "I've noticed."

CHAPTER TWO

NOAH CLIMBED OUT of his car in the driveway that led to the attractive blue house with its white front door and beds of flowers lining the pathway up to the porch. The house wasn't his.

"Uncle Noah!" His only niece, Daisy, raced out the front door and into his arms. He switched the bag he was holding to his other arm and scooped her up, then swung her around until she shrieked.

He'd needed some family time after this morning's run-in with Sabrina. Not that anything bad had happened or would happen, but it had unsettled him. He carried Daisy up the stairs and back into the house.

"Mommy, Mommy. Uncle Noah's here." Daisy wriggled to be let down.

Noah sent her off with a pat and made his way to the kitchen where he could smell whatever Marissa was cooking for dinner. The scent made his mouth water and reminded him that other than the half scone he'd managed at the morning meeting, he'd had nothing but coffee today.

"Uncle Noah's here," Daisy said again before

darting out the kitchen door and into the backyard. The door slammed shut behind her.

Marissa sighed and wiped her hands on a dish towel. "Noah." She came forward to give him a peck on the cheek. "To what do we owe the surprise?"

"Just thought I'd drop in." His stomach grumbled, giving him away.

She laughed and pulled down another plate. "Put this on the table."

He did, feeling guilty now that he'd barged in on them. He spent a lot of time at Kyle and Marissa's house, but sometimes he worried that he was an intrusion on their life. "I brought dessert." He offered the cardboard box containing cupcakes that he'd bought at the bakery before heading over.

"You didn't have to do that." But she looked pleased and accepted the gift. "Kyle's out back with the kids."

Noah could hear them all in the backyard. Five-year-old Daisy screeching at the top of her lungs and eight-year-old Paul trying to talk over her. He glanced out and saw Scotty, who'd just turned two, running with them, his little legs pumping to keep up. Kyle stood at the edge of the patio keeping an eye on his brood while the baby, Timmy, slept on his shoulder.

Noah opened the back door and stepped out. Daisy spotted him and let loose another loud cry of happiness before hurtling toward him, hell-bent on hugging him or taking him out at the knees. He picked her up before she could do any real damage. He rarely had trouble with the old knee injury he'd sustained in college hockey, but a determined five-year-old moving at full speed wasn't a risk he wanted to take.

Kyle grinned when he saw him. "Heard you were here."

"I wonder who from." Noah jiggled Daisy until she laughed and then plopped her back down on the grass and moved to stand beside his brother. They were almost the same height and coloring and looked more alike than most siblings.

They watched as the kids tore around the grass. Paul dribbling a soccer ball, sending a gentle pass Daisy's way. She missed the ball, but cheerfully ran after it, Scotty trailing behind her.

"I talked to Sabrina Ryan today." Noah broached the subject casually. Though his brother worked at the dealership and Noah could have pulled him aside at any time during the day, it hadn't felt appropriate. This was a personal matter and should be treated as such. "She wants to interview me."

"Really?" Kyle turned an interested face toward him. No sign of any discontent or distrust, but then Kyle was like that, friendly and forgiving, like an overgrown puppy. "What for?"

"She's interviewing the candidates for mayor."

"Nice." Kyle clapped him on the shoulder. "When?"

"I didn't say yes." Noah ran a hand through his hair and looked to his brother's face for clues, but found only idle curiosity. "What happened when she interviewed you?"

Although Noah had read the article, they'd never discussed the details. Noah hadn't wanted to press and Kyle hadn't seem interested in analyzing it.

"Nothing as exciting as you think." Kyle shifted Timmy to his other arm. "She called and asked if I'd be willing to talk to her. She said she was try-ing to make an impression on her boss at the paper. Something about trying to get promoted from in-tern to a paid position. Apparently, my failure to return to training camp was of interest. So she came out and I told her that I wasn't going back to camp, but was staying in Wheaton with Marissa." He patted his infant son's back.

"Did she know about you two before she got here?"

"Ah, no." Kyle winced and looked away. "We should have told her before she arrived. It's not like Sabrina and I were still together. We'd broken up months earlier, but I don't know. It felt weird. Tell-ing my ex that I was marrying her best friend."

Noah thought it was weirder that Kyle hadn't foreseen how things might turn out, but that was all in the past. And despite the fact that Sabrina had blasted his family publicly, Noah felt a pang of sympathy for what must have felt like a betrayal.

It was no excuse for splashing their personal business all over the *Vancouver Tribune,* but it helped Noah understand why she might have done it. "Do you think she's still mad at you?"

"Sabrina?" Kyle frowned as though the thought had never crossed his mind. "I don't think so." He looked up. "You should do the interview."

"I'm thinking about it." But every time he started to lean one way, a new thought crept in, made him reconsider.

Marissa cleared her throat behind them. "I wouldn't be so sure about that. Sabrina didn't need to throw us under the bus to do her job." Her blue eyes were frosty. "I'm not saying she'll do the same to you, Noah, but you should keep it in mind."

He was, which was why he'd yet to commit.

Marissa looked tired as she waved the kids in. "I just want you to really think about it before you agree. I don't know what she told you about her reasons for the article, but I can assure you, she's got an angle."

"Marissa." Kyle looked pained. "It was a long time ago."

She nodded and looked at Noah. "Just be careful around her. Now, can you two handle the kids and their hand-washing?" She took Timmy from Kyle and walked back inside.

Noah was left with his thoughts and a dirty niece and a couple of dirty nephews to wash up.

Sabrina pulled into her parents' driveway smelling of coffee grounds, sugar and the milky tea Mrs. Thompson had spilled on her table and then on Sabrina when she'd arrived with a cloth to wipe up the mess.

The spill had been an obvious ploy to ask Sabrina what she thought of their town's venerable mayor. Apparently, everyone thought their little meeting outside had some romantic overtones and no one had believed her when she'd told them it was a business discussion. Finally, just to shut Mrs. Thompson up, Sabrina had told her that the mayor had a nice butt. Which she'd noticed when he'd bent over to put the coffee in his car.

Only she'd forgotten how quickly a statement like that would spread and she'd spent the rest of the day fielding questions about what other parts of Noah's body met her approval. Mrs. Thompson had been texting away before Sabrina had even finished wiping up the spill. No doubt the entire town had heard about her appreciation for Mr. Mayor's butt by now.

And yes, there was her mother coming out the front door with her hands on her hips. "Did you tell Linda Thompson that the mayor has a nice rear?" She asked as soon as Sabrina hopped out of the SUV she'd borrowed from her parents while she was here.

Sabrina found it worked best to deal with these

kinds of things directly and succinctly. Some of her former interviewees would have done well to practice that. "Have you taken a good look at it?" She locked the door behind her and tossed the keys into her purse. "Spectacular."

"Really, Sabrina."

"Yes, really." Her feet hurt, her clothes stank, and the last thing she wanted was to have a long and involved discussion about Mr. Mayor's finer features with her mother. Her heels clacked against the cement driveway, drowning out the sounds of nature. The whine of mosquitoes, bird calls, the rustle of wind through the trees. Sabrina missed the sounds of the urban jungle. Honking cabs, the whoosh of the electric bus, the constant chatter of people on their phones.

Her mother sighed and followed her into the house. "How was the rest of your day?"

"Fine." Sabrina unzipped her boots and dropped them in a tangle by the front door, grateful to feel the blood rushing back into her toes. She wriggled them a few times to speed the process. All she wanted to do was get clean in a nice, hot bath.

Her mother had other ideas. "Anything interesting happen?"

Besides the fact that it was now a known fact she'd checked out the town's mayor? "Not really." Sabrina rolled her neck, letting the ache ease from her shoulders. She was used to sitting in front of a computer all day; standing on her feet, reaching and pulling on the coffee machines worked a whole different set of muscles and she felt the burn. She knew her mother had missed her and just wanted to bond, but she just wasn't up for it. Not smelling like old tea and dried sugar. "Can we talk later? I need to change."

"Of course, sweetheart." Her mother stepped forward to give her a quick hug, but stopped short, her nose wrinkling. "What is that smell?"

"Mrs. Thompson's tea." She headed up the stairs, already untucking her shirt. The blood was rushing back into her feet now and the throb worsened with each step. She winced. Apparently, heels weren't meant to be worn for standing eight hours straight.

Sabrina stripped off her dirty clothes and dropped them in the hamper of her old bedroom. Nothing had changed since she'd left nine years earlier. The same white wainscoting and camel-colored walls. The same white bedspread and bright blue accent chair. The same green topiary on the oak nightstand. She'd even found her old red cowboy boots in the closet.

Of course she'd tried them on. Just to see if they still fit. They did. That was the great thing about shoes. Almost a decade later and they still fit the same way. Her old prom dress? Not so much.

Clad in only her underwear, she pulled her ratty

old terry-cloth robe out of the closet. Her chic black silk one with gold embroidery hung beside it, but Sabrina was chilled. Summer temperatures had yet to arrive in Wheaton and her coastal blood was no longer used to the cooler days and nights. She wrapped the old robe tightly around her. It still fit, too. Though nothing else in town did.

Sabrina sank down to the end of her bed and fished her cell phone out of her purse. Time for her weekly call to the Vancouver newspaper. Though she had little hope that this time would be different, that her editor would tell her everything was fixed and that she was to haul her ass back to the city immediately, she called anyway.

Really, the whole thing was ridiculous. She'd written a short article on Jackson James, son of a wealthy developer. She hadn't wanted to. Although she did interview local celebrities, she didn't think Jackson qualified, but Jackson's father was an advertiser—a big advertiser—and her editor had insisted.

Only Big Daddy hadn't liked it when her article painted his son in a less than golden light. Please, his son was a wannabe playboy with rocks between his ears and Big Daddy's insistence otherwise was an embarrassment. The whole thing should have just blown over, like other articles she'd written, showcasing her subject in an unflattering light, interest died down quickly and everyone got on with their lives. Except that wasn't good enough for Big Daddy.

He believed that she'd sullied the family's good name with innuendos and half truths and he wanted her to pay with her job. Since the paper wanted to keep him happy, a compromise was reached. His dollars were in and she was out.

Sabrina pushed the disappointment away. Just a few more months and either the paper would see the light or Big Daddy would finally ease up. They had to.

The phone rang a couple of times before her editor's voice mail picked up. She left a message. The same message she always did. Just checking in. Let me know when things change. Call my cell phone.

Her stomach hurt. The first couple of months after her firing, her editor had been quick to take her calls. But lately, she was lucky to get a return phone call. And when she did, the information was always the same. A terse response that there was nothing new to report. She was beginning to worry there never would be.

She pulled her robe around her more tightly. If she didn't get her job back, then what? Stay here? Shilling coffee and covering small-town politics for the rest of her life? Her parents would be thrilled, but she would not. She was meant for more than this.

She'd only been away for fourteen days and already she craved the late-night clubs, restaurants on every corner, and constant change and movement. People in the city tried new things, new looks, new music.

Residents in Wheaton seemed to have been caught in a time warp. But not the same one. There was no overarching style that permeated the town, so it didn't look like a throwback to any specific era. Instead, people remained trapped in whatever look had been current at the time of their high school graduation. Sabrina was pretty sure she saw an old classmate wearing the same Ugg boots she'd worn all through high school. Her own mother was still known to rock the big pageant hair of the '80s for special events. Mrs. Thompson had been wearing the same baby-blue sweater set she'd worn when she was Sabrina's third-grade teacher.

Sabrina pushed herself off the bed and padded down the hall to the guest washroom that had been hers when she was growing up. Not much had changed in Wheaton since she'd been gone and not much had changed in the bathroom, either, including the potpourri her mother favored. She considered throwing it away, but the dried petals would no doubt flutter all over the tile and then she'd be on her hands and knees picking them up one by one.

Instead, she turned on the faucet, adjusted the temperature until she was happy and let the tub fill up. When the water neared the top she twisted her hair into a knot on top of her head, slipped off her robe and underwear, and slid beneath the surface, a sigh sliding out from her lips. This might be the one thing she'd missed. In the city, her apartment bathrooms had either a shower alone or an old tub that even she, at five feet four and a half inches, couldn't fit in comfortably.

Sabrina stretched, letting the water sluice over her and feeling her muscles unkink. She still needed to figure out how to convince Noah Barnes that she only wanted to interview him, not make a federal case. But apparently the Barnes family was still holding on to old grudges.

Wasn't there a statute of limitations on these things? It was nine years ago, for God's sake. She shoved down the bubble of guilt that tried to rise. One more reason to get out of here. No one in Vancouver made her feel guilty or as though she'd done something wrong when all she'd done was report the truth.

The whole thing had started out so innocently. Sabrina had been taking journalism classes at the University of British Columbia and trying to find a way to finagle an internship at the *Vancouver Tribune,* the city's broadsheet. But a university freshman with a few articles written for her local hometown paper the previous year was hardly the kind of student they were looking to groom.

Until Kyle, an early-round draft pick in the NHL's draft, had injured his back at practice and herniated a disc. He'd been sent for surgery and then permitted to go home for recuperation and physiotherapy. Except Kyle had never come back.

Normally, an early-round player who crapped out before ever playing a game at the pro level wouldn't do more than cause a brief mention on one of the morning talk shows. But Kyle had been drafted to Vancouver and he was a B.C. boy, so fans were interested. And Sabrina knew she could get the inside scoop.

Though she and Kyle hadn't kept in touch after their breakup, she knew he'd agree to her interview and he had, willingly. No arm-twisting required. She'd flown home, expecting to find that Kyle, who'd been a naturally gifted athlete if a somewhat lackadaisical player, had simply decided he wasn't interested in the work necessary to rehab his back to professional-sport caliber. Or he'd been one of the unlucky ones for whom the surgery didn't mean full recovery.

She'd never expected that he was staying in Wheaton for Marissa. Or that her best friend was already pregnant with his baby. Her best friend and her ex-boyfriend. Together.

Sabrina hadn't cared that Kyle had moved on. They'd never been anything serious. But Marissa? Her best friend since they'd met in ballet class as three-year-olds? The one who'd come to visit her for a few days over the holidays before they'd flown home together to spend Christmas with their families in Wheaton? That had stabbed.

So she'd let all her feelings seep onto the page. Snotty and snarky and cutting. How sad that Kyle had given up a promising career. What a shame the whole situation was. She'd never explicitly stated that Marissa was expecting, but anyone with half a brain could read between the lines.

She'd meant to hurt and she'd been successful. By the time her mad wore off and she wondered if she'd taken things too far, the choice had no longer been in her hands. The editor at the paper loved it, ran it as the cover article in the sports section and Sabrina was hired on part-time.

Sabrina shook the old memory off. That was the past and she couldn't change things now. And right now, she just wanted to enjoy her soak.

She wet a washcloth and laid it across her eyes, sinking down until the water touched her chin. Her eyes shut and her mind quieted. It felt good.

Sabrina was sure she'd only just closed her eyes when a knock startled them open. She pulled the washcloth off, blinking away the wetness on her eyelashes. "Yes?"

"Dinner's almost ready, sweetheart."

"Thanks, Mom." Sabrina climbed out of the tub, noting the water was far cooler than when she'd entered, and toweled off. Back in her room, she pulled on a pair of cute yoga pants and matching hoodie. Just because she was in the boonies was no reason to look like it.

She glanced at her cell phone as she pulled on a pair of warm socks, but she had no new messages. Tucking away the hurt that no one had called her—not her editor, not her friends, not even the mayor—she put the phone back on the nightstand. They were busy, that was all. Unlike her, they still had vibrant lives.

It was probably too much to hope for a call from the mayor's office anyway. Even though he'd seemed to be considering her proposal, Sabrina didn't think he was the type to make a snap decision. She resolved to call him first thing tomorrow morning. She couldn't fix the mess back in Vancouver, but she could get her interview with Noah Barnes. Surely he could see that the interview would benefit him as much as her. And if not, she'd tell him.

Feeling marginally positive that things would soon be going her way, she headed downstairs to dinner with her parents.

CHAPTER THREE

THE MAYOR WAS being difficult. Luckily, Sabrina had worked with difficult interviewees before. The hockey player who'd cancelled three times before she'd finally shown up outside the arena after practice like a groupie and done the interview while his hair was still wet. The singer who'd appeared an hour late, hung over from the night before and answering most of her questions with requests for a cigarette. The actor who'd insisted on staying in character, accent included. All had ended in successful columns for Sabrina.

She knew how to get what she wanted. And she wanted this interview.

Since their meeting in the parking lot on Monday, she'd had two other opportunities to talk to Noah in person, both instances as she was making his espresso. On each occasion, he'd nodded politely and told her he would get back to her. The four times she'd called his office, she hadn't even managed to get him on the phone. His assistant had acted as a gatekeeper and brushed her off with the now familiar story that he was in a meeting or out of the office.

But Sabrina was pretty sure he couldn't avoid her if she showed up on his doorstep. Not that she was turning into some creepy stalker who would wait outside his house and pounce the minute he showed his face. No, she had more couth than that. She was moving in across the hall. Far less creepy.

She'd known her parents owned an income property, half of a pretty little duplex in town, but she hadn't known Mr. Mayor called the other half home and, upon learning this tidbit, she'd convinced them—okay, there might have been a teensy-weensy bit of begging involved—to let her move in. Their previous tenants had moved out a couple of months earlier and the apartment had been sitting vacant. Sabrina didn't believe in astrology or fate, but her stars? Those were aligned.

She wondered if Mr. Mayor was a briefs or boxers man. Really, it was the kind of investigative journalism that readers would want to know. Her cheeks warmed.

"What are you thinking about, sweetheart?" Her dad interrupted her thoughts.

"Just excited to be getting my own space." She rolled down the window. Mr. Mayor wasn't even her type. She preferred the slightly dangerous bad boys. The ones who demanded rather than asked and kissed a woman so hard that she popped right out of her shoes.

"You haven't even seen the inside yet."

Although it was now Friday and she'd talked them into letting her use the apartment on Monday, she hadn't had a chance to come out until now. The coffee shop had been busy all week as tourists began spilling into town for the start of the summer rush. Sabrina had worked two double shifts already and in the few hours she'd had off, she'd been at the newspaper office getting to know the staff and preparing for her interview with Pete.

But she didn't need to see the inside to know the apartment was going to be perfect. Already, she could picture curling up in a cozy corner with a book, setting up her computer somewhere other than her bedroom and lingering over a cup of coffee on her mornings off without interruption.

At her parents' house, she sat at the same dining chair that had been hers since she was old enough to scramble up on it, slept in the same twin bed that she'd graduated to after toddlerhood and had to share the remote for the TV.

It wasn't that she didn't love her parents. She did. A lot. But she'd lived on her own for the past nine years—except that one period when she'd had a roommate who spent the entire six months on the couch leaving crumbs on the cushions and smoking a bong. Never again. Sabrina was used to having privacy, playing the music she liked and watching various iterations of Real Housewives without having to justify herself to anyone.

Her father smiled as they cruised through town. Probably because he and her mother were now certain that Sabrina would be staying in Wheaton long-term. She'd heard them talk about it through the wall in her bedroom last night. Apparently, her fib about writing that book hadn't fooled them. But there was another more important reason to get out and into her own place. The discussion about her future hadn't been the only thing she'd heard from her parents' room last night.

Logically, Sabrina knew they were still young and vibrant and sexually active, but she really didn't need proof of that fact. Ever. Again.

"Here we are." Her father pulled into a long driveway and parked in front of the house. "Ready?"

Ready? Sabrina was already out of the car and heading up the stairs that led to the long wraparound porch and front door. She hadn't seen the place in over a decade but it was just as cute as she remembered. From the front it appeared to be a single dwelling with three steps that led to the blue front door.

Matching sets of French doors, one on either side of the main door, opened to the porch, as well. In its original state, the house had been built for one family and the doors led to a pair of sitting rooms and could be opened to catch the summer breeze. Now they provided porch access for each apartment occupant without needing to go through the entry and front door.

They were missing the artful iron vines she was used to seeing on large glass doors and windows in the city, but then security wasn't such a concern here. Sabrina had been shocked to find her parents still didn't lock their doors. And not just during the day when they happened to be at home. All the time, day, night, in or out.

Petty crime—or non-petty crime—wasn't something she needed to worry about in Wheaton. No one was going to snatch her purse off her shoulder or kick in her window to steal her valuables.

Someone had planted shrubs along the sides of the house and in front of the porch. Probably her mother. They were well-tended, with small white flowers starting to bud.

There wasn't any outdoor furniture, but Sabrina figured she could borrow some from her parents. She'd already requisitioned a coffee table and the floor lamp with a pink shade and '20s fringe from her mom's sewing room. What were a couple of outdoor lounge chairs, a small table, maybe some oversized pots of brightly colored flowers added to her tally?

Sabrina had loved her tubs of blooms on her

balcony in Yaletown. Well, loved them until the tenant below her complained that they were making a mess on his balcony. One measly bud had fluttered onto his ugly wicker chair, but he'd acted like she'd purposely defaced his property. Her boot heels clacked a little louder. Please, her flower had done more to improve his decor than a mountain of furniture. Which she'd told her landlord, but he'd merely pointed to the clause in the contract that stated she needed permission to put anything on her balcony and she hadn't bothered to get it.

But there weren't any balconies here and Sabrina doubted Mr. Mayor would get crabby about flowers. People in Wheaton were friendlier, more agreeable. He would understand that her decor improved his space, as well. Assuming he even noticed.

She tried to peek through his curtain-free French doors while she waited for her dad to finish fiddling with the car and join her, but the glare from the sun prevented her from seeing much. She squinted, but couldn't make out anything more than a couple of blobby shapes.

There was always the possibility that they'd become friends and he'd actually invite her inside. So far, her old friends had made themselves scarce. She hadn't even seen Marissa or Kyle. Not that she'd expected to.

Her dad finally finished whatever he was doing

and unlocked the front door. The entry was plain but neat. An overhead chandelier, original to the house, sparkled under the afternoon sun. Wood floors were polished to a golden gleam. A well-used Turkish-style rug lay in the center of the room beneath a round oak table that had a bowl of pot-pourri on it.

Sabrina wrinkled her nose. "Potpourri, Dad? This isn't the '80s." Which was exactly what she'd told her mother when she'd spotted it in the guest bathroom.

He shrugged. "Your mother said it would smell nice."

Yes, if people wanted their homes to smell like an old lady's underwear drawer. Sabrina made a mental note to take the bowl and all the dried flowers with her when they left.

Her father walked past the offending decor without a glance and stuck his key into the interior door on the left. Men. Sabrina lingered, noting the cheerful welcome mat in front of the mayor's door. There was a small nail beneath the peephole. Probably to hang a wreath at Christmas.

"Sabrina?" her father called.

She sent one last look at the door, not that it told her anything, and headed to what would become her new home. She imagined plain white walls, simple wood floors polished to the same gloss as the entry and maybe some architectural features

found in older homes that gave them such character. Crystal doorknobs, paneled doors and thick
crown molding.

What she found would have caused her mouth
to fall open in a gasp of horror had she not trained
herself out of the habit years ago when one of her
university friends told her it made her look like
a rube.

"What do you think?" Her dad was practically
rubbing his hands together.

Sabrina wondered if they were seeing the same
thing because what she saw was that the bowl of
potpourri wasn't the only thing left from the '80s.
The walls of the duplex were pastel stripes. Yes.
Pastel. Stripes. In four colors. Lilac and mint and
blush and sunshine shown off in all their glory
because there wasn't any furniture to distract from
it.

She prayed it wasn't wallpaper. Oh, God. She
did not relish stripping thirty-year-old paper from
the walls. She'd done that in an apartment once.
The paper had practically fused to the drywall and
it had taken her days of hard labor, one of those
scoring tools, fabric softener and finally the rental
of a steamer to get it off.

There was one lonely rug that the previous tenant
had left behind. A fringed circle of lemon yellow—
and not the cute and sexy fringe like her lamp. No,

this was the thick yarn type. She didn't bother to disguise her shudder.

But the wood floors appeared to be in good shape and the fireplace was nice. A simple, traditional wood frame that just needed a fresh coat of white paint to bring it back to life. The kitchen was all right, too, if she avoided looking at the walls, which had been sponge painted.

The appliances were standard white, but clean and carried no leftover odors. She'd once moved into a place where the previous tenant hadn't bothered cleaning out anything ever. After scrubbing the fridge and scrubbing and scrubbing and scrubbing some more, Sabrina had insisted her landlord replace it. He'd been irritated and pissy. Apparently, he'd hoped she'd just grow used to the stench. The counters were a neutral beige. Nothing to get excited about but most definitely livable. The pink ruffled curtains, not so much. They would be coming down first thing.

"It needs some upgrades," she said.

"Now, Sabrina. Don't go getting any ideas about granite and marble and stainless-steel appliances. I'm already covering the costs of shipping your furniture from Vancouver. Why did you ever put it in storage? Waste of money when we can store it for you in our basement."

"Because I'm going back." She'd already explained this, but her father chose not to hear it.

He waved off her statement as he'd done the previous two times she'd told him. "Or you could stay."

"Now you sound like Mom." Sabrina sloughed off the idea without another thought because she wasn't staying any longer than necessary. But until that day arrived, getting the apartment into the new millennium would be a good project for her. Something to fill the long evening hours when Wheaton shut down for the night. Her current obsession of checking email, text and social networking sites was not working for her. At all.

"Don't you want to come back home?" her dad asked. For the hundredth time, she considered telling him the truth. That she wasn't back to write a book about her experiences interviewing celebrities, filling the pages with all the tidbits that hadn't fit into her articles. That she'd been fired and that it wasn't looking like she'd ever get her job back.

Once again, she swallowed the words and smiled. "It doesn't feel like home anymore, Dad. It's been a long time since I lived here and I love the city." With its late-night burger joints, extensive shoe stores and Opera Guy, a local gentleman who strolled around the neighborhood singing opera at the top of his lungs, Vancouver was the place she longed for. "But I promise to come and visit more, okay?"

When she saw the downturn of her father's lips,

guilt snuck into her cheerful attitude. It had just been easier for her parents to come to her. First because she worked at the paper through the holidays. Low person in the chain of command. Then it had just become habit.

"Oh, come on." Sabrina elbowed him lightly. "Cheer up. I'm here now. You've got me doing slave labor at the coffee shop." Even with what she hoped would be an increased workload at the local paper, she'd continue to work most mornings at the coffee shop. "And I'm going to fix up this place for free."

"Does this mean it's not going to cost me anything?" The edges of his eyes crinkled.

"My labor is free," she clarified. "Which we all know is the majority of cost. I'm giving you a deal."

She could see the finished project in her mind. A pale pink on the walls, like the inside of a rose, to play up the reds and pinks in the large throw rug she had. Maybe she could search out an old wrought iron chandelier to hang over the coffee table. Antiques shops would just be opening for the summer season and would not yet be picked over. Her parents had a grandfather clock in their entryway that was too large for the space, but it would be perfect against the wall in here. Pillows on her oatmeal-colored couch, throws on her ivory chairs, flowers in crystal vases on the end table.

She had a small series of sculptures that would look fabulous on the fireplace mantel.

Sabrina was still thinking about it as they exited the suite. Until she saw the monstrosity of a potpourri bowl and hurried over to dispose of it. An act of compassion, really, putting the hideous thing out of its misery.

She was sweeping some of the dried blooms that had fallen onto the table back into the bowl when the front door opened. Her senses went on high alert. If she was at the table and she could still hear her father locking up the apartment, then the front door could only be opened by one person.

"Mr. Mayor." Sabrina put down the bowl. And felt her insides wobble when she turned and got a look at him.

Gone was the nerdy golf shirt and dress pants combo, exchanged for a pair of jeans and a plain white T-shirt that did wonderful things for the muscles in his arms. In his more casual attire and without that polished veneer, Noah didn't look like the same man. She felt something warm unfurl in her. Her fingers itched, wanting to touch.

"Hello." Noah glanced from her to her father, a line of confusion between his eyes. "Just checking up on the place?"

"Hi, Noah." Her father turned from the door and handed the keys to Sabrina. "You won't have this old place to yourself much longer. Sabrina is moving in."

"Moving in?" Noah's eyes darted back to her.

"Pretty soon you'll be inundated with loud music and singing. Hope you have earplugs."

"Dad." Sabrina rolled her eyes as she stuffed the keys into her pocket and focused on Noah. "I'm not that loud," she told him.

"You can be," her dad said. "I'll be outside." He pulled the door closed with a click and silence filled the space.

Sabrina smiled. "Hello, neighbor."

Noah rubbed the back of his neck as his eyes flicked over her. Were her eyes deceiving her or was he checking her out? She twirled a lock of hair around her finger before letting it slip and trail down her cleavage. Yes, she was a shameless hussy. She saw his gaze drop down, following that lock of hair, before shooting back up to her face and giving her a guilty glance. Yes, that's right, her eyes were up there.

He cleared his throat. "Neighbors. Welcome then." He put on his fake politician smile. Sabrina was well-versed in that smile. Every celebrity, pseudo or otherwise, had their own version of it. Some were bright, others mysterious, but they all indicated the same thing: an unwillingness to share a person's real self. She hated that smile.

"Thanks, and for the record, I sing in key. No earplugs required."

Noah's smile warmed, edging toward reality. "I'll hold you to that."

She felt a flicker of heat waft through her. "Please do." Or just hold her. Wait, what? Now she was having dirty fantasies about the mayor? Shameless, shameless hussy. No upstanding citizen would do such a thing. Luckily she was neither a citizen of Wheaton or particularly upstanding. "Well, I should be going. My dad's waiting." She picked up the bowl of dried flowers.

"Sabrina." She looked into his eyes, so soft and blue like the blanket she used to carry around as a toddler and that her mother still had stored in a box somewhere. Good ol' wubbie. "When are you moving in?"

"Tomorrow." Just as soon as her furniture arrived. She'd considered sleeping on the floor of the apartment just to avoid accidentally overhearing her parents' bedsprings again, but common sense won out. She had an iPod. And earbuds. "Why? You want to help?"

She didn't expect him to say yes. No doubt he had better things to do than help her move. Particularly as he didn't even seem to like her enough to give her that interview. Yet.

"Sure."

Sabrina blinked. "Seriously?" She couldn't even

get him on the phone and now he was willing to spend hours with her?

His smile widened. "Seriously."

She wasn't one to question her good fortune a second time. "Then I'd love to have your help."

And love to watch him work. All sweaty and hot. Bare arms. Carrying her bed. Her throat felt dry. She clutched the bowl in her hands more tightly and wished for a glass of water. Really any liquid would do. *A drop of sweat running down Noah's chest.* Perhaps there was a way she could convince him to go shirtless and then snap a few pictures. For the paper, of course, not personal use.

Really, she'd be doing it for the readers.

CHAPTER FOUR

NOAH WASN'T SURE what had made him agree to help Sabrina move. Neighborly assistance? Manners? Something else? Her pretty green eyes?

Maybe because it's what was expected of him, what he expected of himself. When people in Wheaton needed help, he stepped in. Even when he shouldn't.

He sighed. Wasn't that always the way, though? He had deadlines to meet, budget concerns to deal with, council meetings to attend, new staff to train, but he still made time for whatever someone else needed. Some days it meant leaving the house before seven and not returning until ten. Other days it meant skipping meals and breaks. Driving all over town to attend to whatever had cropped up this time.

Usually, he enjoyed doing it. Giving something back to the town and the people. They hadn't had to accept him, but they had. Opened their arms and their hearts and allowed him to come of age in a place that was safe and loving. Noah had only left them once in his life and even then only long enough to get his business degree.

There had never been any question in his mind about leaving permanently. And upon his return, he'd thrown himself into town life. Eight years later, he still didn't regret it. Well, maybe he wouldn't mind a weekend or two to himself. An afternoon to sit by the lake with his fishing pole and no one else. An evening where he turned off his cell phone and wasn't interrupted. But that wasn't his life.

Noah poured a cup of coffee and seated himself in front of his computer to do some work before the movers showed up. Sabrina had left him a message that she'd be by around ten to prepare for the movers and until then Noah had plenty of things to keep him busy and not think about what it might mean to have the attractive reporter living across the hall from him.

He started by examining the sales numbers for his two car dealerships, sent an email to the talent booked for this year's Northern Lights festival and then reviewed the council minutes that were to be posted online on Monday.

He'd just emailed his assistant to approve the minutes when he heard the crunch of wheels turning into the driveway. A moment later, a knock sounded at the door and he rose to answer.

Noah didn't expect his pulse to hammer when he opened the door. Although he'd seen her multiple times now—five, if he included this one—

his attraction to Sabrina still caught him off guard. He wasn't used to having feelings that snuck up on him or hit him over the head or did anything but stay in the neat little box he'd designed for them.

Bad enough that he wasn't sure if he could trust Sabrina to interview him. But when he added this spark of attraction, things became tricky. She'd dated his younger brother and though that had been over for years and Kyle was long since happily married, it still created an awkwardness. She'd been with his brother. She had a broken friendship with his sister-in-law. Two of the people closest in the world to him.

"Hi." She pushed a cup of coffee into his hands.

"Good morning." Probably best that he just stick to being her neighbor. Help her move her furniture and boxes in and then excuse himself and get back to his own life.

"I can't tell you how much I appreciate this." Sabrina's eyes were bright and her hair, tugged back into a high ponytail, swirled around her shoulders as she spoke. Summer had arrived suddenly, going from jeans to cut-offs weather practically overnight, and the thin tank top she wore beneath a pink hoodie and a tiny pair of shorts left little to his imagination. His fingers bit into the sides of the coffee. "It all happened sort of fast. Anyway, I'm grateful."

"No problem." Noah took a sip from the steaming takeaway cup. Espresso. Double shot. His favorite. The fact that she remembered and had gone to the trouble to pick it up this morning when she was likely juggling a number of other things touched him. Some residents didn't even remember that he liked coffee, offering tea or another beverage when he was at their homes cleaning gutters, shoveling snow or mowing the lawn.

She turned and headed across the entry to unlock the door to her place. Noah found himself watching the wiggle of her hips as she went. It wasn't as though he planned to, but the shorts were vibrant red and demanded attention. Who was he to deny them their right? He sipped his coffee and enjoyed the moment.

Soon enough he'd be back to himself, mayor, employer, helper, but for a moment he was simply a guy enjoying a woman walking in front of him.

Sabrina pushed the door open and glanced back at him. "Come on in. Enjoy the dated decor."

Noah pushed himself away from the door frame, closing the door behind him and followed her inside. She wasn't lying about the apartment's styling, but he'd already known that. The former tenants, an elderly couple, had often requested his help for small jobs: changing light bulbs, unclogging drains, dusting the corners of the ceiling. So he was well-versed in the pastel shades that they'd seemed to enjoy.

Sabrina stood with her hands on her hips. "Hideous, isn't it. I'll have to do something about it and quick. This stuff will give me nightmares." She picked at the edge of a piece of wallpaper that had come loose. "How long do you think it will take me to get this off?"

"I have no idea."

"Hours, probably." She sighed. "Guess you wouldn't want to help with this, too, would you?"

Noah pressed his lips together just in case his tongue got the idea to agree against his better judgment.

When she looked over her shoulder at him, she laughed. "I was only kidding. You're already doing more than enough."

The breath caught in his chest loosened. Sabrina hadn't gotten upset or given him a look that said he'd disappointed her. His shoulders relaxed. Soon they were chatting about furniture placement and which items would go in which rooms. He was practically enjoying himself. "When is the truck arriving?"

She pulled her phone out of her pocket and glanced at the front door. "Any minute. Actually, I've got some boxes I brought over from my parents' place in the car. Maybe we should grab those now. Get them out of the way."

Noah followed her outside to the SUV parked beside the detached garage. She popped the back, exposing a stack of labeled and taped boxes. When she reached forward, her shorts pulled tight. He allowed himself to enjoy the view.

The rumble of a large engine drew his attention from the pretty sight. A box truck pulled into the driveway, followed by a gray sedan that he knew to be her parents' because he'd sold it to them.

"Fantastic." She shut the door, leaving the boxes inside and grinned up at him. "Sure you don't want to back out? You've still got time."

But suddenly, the idea of spending the day working alongside Sabrina sounded much more appealing than hanging out at the lake alone. Even with his fishing pole. "I'm happy to be here." And he was.

Even four hours later, once she'd directed him to put the couch in four different places and the sweat was running down his back, Noah was still enjoying himself.

"Are you sure?" he asked. "You said it was perfect by the window."

"I was wrong." She shrugged. "Plus, I like seeing your muscles in action." She winked.

A low heat swirled through him. Noah was pretty sure she was flirting with him. Had been for a while now. Ever since the movers had finished up and she'd sent her parents on their way about an hour ago. He moved the couch to her chosen location. "Good?"

Sabrina came around from behind the kitchen counter where she'd been unpacking utensils and cocked her head. "Yes. I think that's the spot."

"You realize that was the first spot."

"I didn't know that was the right spot until I saw the couch in other places." She smiled up at him. "So thank you for hauling it around." She went back to the kitchen, which opened onto the main room. "So tell me, Mr. Mayor. If you weren't allowing me to appreciate the fine labor of your muscles, what would you be doing today?"

Noah lifted the hem of his shirt to wipe his brow. The day had warmed up, the sun now beating through her open windows. He could hear the hum of a nearby mower, the scent of freshly cut grass tickling his nose. What would he be doing? Working on the computer, babysitting his niece or nephews, heading into the office, answering requests from residents. "I'm not sure."

"Really?" She unwrapped a large plastic spoon and added it to the canister that seemed to be full of them already. "No hot date?"

"No." He rarely dated. Didn't have time for it. Which was a sad statement on his life. "Why? Are you asking me out?"

She blinked and her mouth opened slightly. Then she laughed. "Mr. Mayor, look at you flirting with me."

Noah's cheeks burned. He didn't flirt. It wasn't

appropriate for a man in his position. He knew that. And yet, his guard had slipped around her. He needed to watch out for that. "Sorry."

"Why would you apologize?" Sabrina plunked another spoon in the canister. "You're a handsome guy. You must have lots of women wanting to go out with you."

He studied her, unsure if this was more of her casual banter or if she was fishing for information to put in her article. If he answered wrong, she could use his words against him, twist them to make him look like some sort of sex pervert, which he might become if she wore those red shorts very often. So he didn't answer at all, simply picked up a box labeled Bathroom and carried it in there.

When Noah came back out, he felt more in control. "How long will you be living here?"

"Not forever. Just until I write my book. Then it's back to the city." She sounded a bit sad, like she wasn't sure that was where she wanted to be.

Noah could relate, but he didn't ask for details. That would be inviting personal questions about his own life. "So I've just moved your couch four times for fun?"

"No, that was all part of my plan to see you flex your muscles." The sad tilt to her eyes lifted. "Actually, I just need my own space while I'm here. My parents let me have the apartment because they want me to move back permanently."

"Seems like a lot of work to move in all your things if you're just turning around and leaving." He didn't understand why anyone would bother. Was there something more that she wasn't sharing?

"Okay, that's not the only reason." Sabrina put down yet another plastic spoon. "I also moved in because I found out you lived across the hall."

Noah's chest suddenly felt heavy like someone had laid a wet blanket over it. He sucked in a breath. "Oh."

"No, don't get like that." She stepped around the counter and over to him. "I'm not going to force you to do anything you don't want to do. I just hoped that if we were neighbors and you got to know me better, you might see that I'm not so bad."

"And give you the interview."

"Well, yeah." She stopped in front of him. She'd pulled the hoodie off some time ago and the skinny tank top showed off her curves. "I know you're worried because of what happened with Kyle, but this isn't the same type of interview." She reached a hand out and laid it on his arm.

A spark fizzed through him.

"I haven't always made the best decisions when it comes to my columns. If you read them, you'll see that I wasn't always nice."

And this was supposed to convince him to say yes? "I think you need to work on your pitch." But he didn't step back or shake off her touch.

"Probably, but I'm being honest with you. Your interview and the article I write aren't going to be like that. It's not what the readers of this town want. It's not what I want."

"So you and your readers want something else in Vancouver?"

The side of her mouth lifted in an effort to smile, but ended up looking sad. "Yes. They did and I did. But this is something else." She took her hand off his arm to run it through her hair. Noah missed the contact. "You don't need to decide this second. I'm interviewing Pete on Tuesday and his article will run in next weekend's paper. Wait. Read it and then make your decision."

"So you're not going to push me now?" He felt off-balance. Now was the perfect time for her to push. They'd been having a good time, working as a team. Sabrina had done an excellent job of forging a bond to convince him to trust her. Only she wasn't capitalizing on it. He studied her more closely. Was that part of her plan?

"If you want to say yes right now, I won't turn you down." Her eyes stared into his. Such a bright and cheerful green, like grass in summer. "But no, I'm not going to push. You're helping me move. Really, you've suffered enough."

Noah laughed and the weight in his lungs eased. She seemed genuine and she'd given him the free-dom to confirm her sincerity by waiting for Pete's article to run first. He couldn't expect more. "All right then. What else do we need to move?"

"I'm so glad you asked."

His muscles ached when they were done, but it was a good ache. The kind that spoke of a job well-done and a rest well earned.

Sabrina flopped onto the couch. "I'm beat. What do you want on your pizza?"

"Pizza?" He looked longingly at the couch, but didn't sit. His mother had taught him too well for that. His shirt stuck to his back and his shorts looked like he'd been swimming in them. He wasn't about to sit on her nice couch and drip sweat all over it.

"And beer. Isn't that the standard gift for helping someone move?"

"You don't have to feed me."

"Of course I do. You helped me move. You don't think I know the rules of payment for moving?" She patted the couch beside her. "Sit down. You've worked your butt off."

The little shorts rode even higher as she reached over to pull her cell phone from the pocket of her hoodie, which had been left on the floor. Noah swallowed. "I should shower." A long, cold one.

She grinned up at him. "Mr. Mayor, are you flirting again?"

"No. I didn't mean it like that."

"Too bad." She stood up and Noah watched the

shorts shift as she moved. He shook his head to clear it of the image of Sabrina in the shower.

She was teasing him, toying with him. The careless flirting probably meant nothing to her.

"Why don't we sit outside then? It's cooler." She walked over to the French doors that had been left open to catch any breeze that might come through. The day had been still, but the temperature was a few degrees cooler outside.

Noah followed her out and lowered himself to the porch step where there was no worry about leaving a sweat outline behind. He leaned his elbows back and inhaled the cool air. Just as good as a shower. Well, not if the shower included Sabrina. He shoved the thought away. Clearly she'd been joking.

He heard the fall of her steps as she headed back inside and let his eyes close. It would be nice to have a neighbor again, to know there was another warm body in the house. He'd never asked his previous neighbors for anything, but he'd liked knowing they were around. He'd like knowing Sabrina was around, too. Watching TV, singing in the kitchen, standing in the shower. A long, hot shower with soap and scrubbing that would leave her skin pink all over.

Noah jumped when cold glass pressed against the back of his neck.

Sabrina laughed and handed the bottle to him.

Condensation dripped down the sides, cooling his fingers and some of his distracted thoughts. Imagining his reporter naked in the shower was nothing like imagining the audience in their underwear when he was about to give a speech. Not even close. He shifted and took a long pull from the bottle. It didn't lower his body temperature.

"I ordered the pizza. They said forty-five minutes." She sat down on the step beside him, her thigh brushing his. Her skin was soft, silky-looking. His fingers wanted to touch. Noah curled them around the bottle instead.

"So tell me what you'd normally do for fun on a Saturday night." She stretched her legs out in front of her. Her skin brushed his again, stirring his nerve endings.

He called on his mayoral face, but he was having trouble bringing it to the surface. Really, he just wanted to look at her. "Sometimes there's an event where I need to make an appearance. But often I have work from the week I need to catch up on."

Sabrina nodded and sipped her beer. He watched the smooth glide of her neck as she swallowed. The pulse point just below her ear that thrummed a steady rhythm. "Those are things you do for other people. What about you?"

Concern spiked through him. "I thought we weren't doing an interview."

She remained reclined in her loose pose. "We're not. I'm just curious about you."

He swallowed. This was not good. He still wasn't sure about her. She seemed sincere, but how well did he know her? And now, sitting on the porch like a couple, her spicy-sweet scent mingling with the grassy smell from the neighbor's lawn. He looked away. Dinner. Together. And beer. When he was already filled with confusing push-me-pull-you thoughts. This was not a good idea. He cleared his throat. "I just remembered, I can't stay."

Her mouth opened and then closed. "You sure?"

"Yeah." Noah set the beer down, barely touched. Fantasies of her naked in his bed rolled through his mind, followed by the worry that this sparking attraction would make him do something he'd regret. No, he definitely couldn't stay. Not tonight. Not when his mind was in a whirl. "I promised Kyle and Marissa I'd babysit." He hadn't, but they were always happy for the extra hands.

Sabrina nodded, but he couldn't tell if she believed him. "You do that a lot, don't you? Babysit."

He felt something icy and irritable slide down his spine. "They're family." Why shouldn't he babysit? He loved his family. He loved helping them.

She sat up and put a hand on his arm. "I think it's great." Her eyes bored into him, reading him. "You do a lot for other people."

"No, I don't." Noah hated it when people talked

about him like that. He didn't want them to notice, just to know that they could count on him to be there. "Anyone would do the same."

"No, Noah. They wouldn't." Her hand was warm, comforting.

He reminded himself that he didn't know who she was, what she wanted. He pushed himself into a standing position. "Right. Well. Thanks for the beer."

Sabrina lifted her bottle to him in a toast. "Anytime. We'll rain check dinner."

Noah knew he should correct her. Tell her that dinner wasn't necessary, that he hadn't agreed to help her for any reason other than it had seemed like a good idea at the time. But he didn't.

And he beat it out of there before desire could overwhelm common sense.

But he didn't feel any better once he arrived on Kyle and Marissa's doorstep.

"Hey, bro." Kyle welcomed him in with a slap on the shoulder. "What brings you here?"

"Kyle?" Marissa came into the entry. "Noah, hi. We weren't expecting you."

He could hear the rumble of kids. "I should have called first. Sorry." He hadn't brought anything with him. Hadn't even taken that much-needed shower. Just climbed into his car and driven straight over.

"It's not a problem." Kyle turned to the kitchen. "Want a beer?"

"Yes, that'd be great."

"What were you doing?" Marissa plucked at his shirt, which was still stuck to his skin as they turned to follow Kyle. "You look like you've been chopping wood."

Close enough. "I was helping someone move." Kyle pulled a pair of bottles out of the fridge. "Who? You should have called me. I could have helped."

But Marissa, always more astute than her husband, didn't wait for his answer. "Sabrina, right?" She shook her head when he didn't respond to her query. "What else did she want?"

"Nothing. She didn't want anything." He twisted the beer cap. No, he was the one who wanted something. Something that he couldn't have.

"Are you sure?" Marissa asked.

"She's my new neighbor. That's all." Sabrina didn't want anything else. He didn't think. Well, except the interview, but she'd been perfectly up-front about that. No, he was the one with the wicked thoughts of her naked body. Damn her little tank top and littler shorts.

"Noah." But whatever Marissa had been about to say was interrupted by his noisy niece, who burst into the room singing and dancing.

Daisy flung herself at his legs when she saw

him. "Hi, Uncle Noah." Then she launched into a story about some tights with a hole in the knee.

He picked up his niece, suddenly wildly interested in the case of the striped tights.

"Mommy threw them away." Her tiny face was set in a picture-perfect expression of outrage. "And she won't buy me more. Will you buy me a pair?"

"Yes," Noah said just as Marissa said, "Absolutely not."

Marissa plucked Daisy from Noah's grip and set her down with a pat. "I need to talk to your uncle. Go see what your brothers are doing."

"I don't wanna." Daisy crossed her arms and stamped her foot.

"Daisy." The warning note in her mother's voice was clear.

Daisy looked from her mother to her father, and stuck out her chin. "Uncle Noah will buy me tights. He loves me. Right, Uncle Noah?" She grabbed his leg.

"Don't manipulate your uncle, Daisy. Go and play with your brothers."

Daisy responded by wrapping her arms more tightly around Noah's thigh and clinging like a monkey. "No!"

Noah sighed, used to these exchanges. He'd learned to simply stand by and let Marissa handle her daughter as things inevitably ended more quickly and with less screeching.

"Daisy, I swear." Marissa attempted to pry her daughter's fingers loose, but Daisy was a girl on a mission.

"No. No. You can't make me." She tried to wrap her legs around Noah's shin.

Marissa tugged on her daughter's arm. "Yes, I can." She pried her daughter free. "Off to find your brothers or you won't get dessert."

Daisy seemed to consider that, then nodded. "Okay. Bye, Uncle Noah."

So much for his three-foot savior. Marissa was now bearing down on him with a gleam in her eye that looked remarkably like the one Daisy often wore. "I can't believe Sabrina moved in beside you. You need to be careful."

"Why?" Noah honestly wanted to know. Was it really such a big deal? It's not as if they were co-habitating.

Marissa's eyebrow lifted. "People already think there's something going on because of that talk the two of you had in the parking lot. Do you want the whole town talking about you?"

Noah's stomach rolled. He did not want the whole town talking about him.

"This is ridiculous." Kyle piped up with a snort. "What are they going to say? That he helped some-one move? That they're neighbors?"

The roll slowed. His brother had a point. Living

next to each other wasn't scandalous. "We're just neighbors. I hardly know her."

"I've been thinking a lot about the interview. I don't think you should do it," Marissa insisted.

Just when he was thinking that he should.

"Marissa." Kyle draped an arm around her shoulder. "Don't you think that's a little harsh?"

Marissa's face was set in a hard line. She glanced at her husband. "Have you forgotten what it was like here after she wrote that article about you?"

Kyle nodded. "I remember, babe." He wrapped his arm more tightly around her. "But that doesn't mean it'll be the same for Noah."

Noah watched the tension seep out of his sister-in-law. "I know. I just worry." She looked at him, brackets of that worry around her mouth.

He was deeply touched. "It'll be fine. She's not going to write anything horrible about me." Her openness today had convinced him of that. She was telling the truth about what people in Wheaton wanted. A blistering exposé on him was not it.

"I know her better than you." She turned her head and looked at her husband. "Better than both of you."

"You knew her better *before*," Kyle said. He ran a hand up and down Marissa's arm. "Maybe she's changed."

Marissa sighed. "Maybe. But I'm going on record now that I am not in love with this idea."

"I haven't even said I'll do it." Noah told them. He would wait to see how Sabrina's article on Pete turned out before making a final decision. "But even if I agree, it's only one interview. I've handled reporters plenty of times. I know how to stay on message."

If Sabrina asked him a question he didn't want to answer, all he had to do was respond with a piece of information he did want to share. Simple.

And there wasn't much that was off-limits. His life wasn't exciting enough for that. Look how he was spending his Saturday night. Hanging out with his younger brother and family instead of drinking beer and eating pizza with his sexy new neighbor. He bashed the thought down.

Marissa frowned. "She's not some small-town reporter who's going to ask what your favorite pie is. She's a professional, and she's good."

He raised an eyebrow. "You sound almost complimentary."

"Well, I don't mean to." But a ghost of a smile drifted across her face.

Noah smiled, too. "It'll be fine." Sabrina was welcome to ask about his childhood and how that had shaped him. How being the only kid in school who didn't have a biological parent had impressed upon him the need for community spirit, how a person could forge family bonds with anyone they loved, blood-relation or not and how giving back fulfilled him.

He wouldn't have to share that he still felt as if he was trying to achieve "local" status, how he often felt that he didn't fit in, that if he stopped giving back, the residents might eventually lose interest in having him.

Those were his own private demons and not for public consumption.

CHAPTER FIVE

EVEN BEFORE SHE met Pete Peters in person, Sabrina knew she wouldn't like him. In their phone conversations, he'd called her darling twice and joked about women in the construction business as if women couldn't swing hammers and saw wood with any hope of competency.

The interview did nothing to change her initial opinion. But as she'd told Noah, these articles weren't about snarking on the candidates. So she wrote as polite an article as possible about Pete, leaving out his rampant chauvinism and highlighting his family instead.

She was proud of her work. Really, it had been difficult not to let her distaste of the subject creep through, but she'd done it. Since the article had run three days ago, she'd received multiple compliments on it.

In the city, Sabrina had often wondered if people read her work at all.

But she wasn't in the city right now, she reminded herself. She looked at her newly bare walls, ignoring the pile of hideous Easter-egg-colored wallpaper piled in the corner. The walls were in decent shape, requiring only a bit of patching.

She hadn't seen much of Noah since he'd helped her move a little over a week ago. She'd thought he might come knocking on her door this morning, or pop into the coffee shop to schedule that interview, but she hadn't seen him at all.

Sabrina hoped he'd read the article. If not, she had an extra copy sitting on her coffee table that she could personally deliver.

She patched the nail holes and the intermittent dents in the walls. Once the putty dried, she could sand and paint. She stepped back and dusted her hands on the seat of her shorts. Might as well go get the paint now. Tuesday evening was bound to be quiet at the hardware store and she didn't have anything better to do.

Sad, but true. In her old life she'd be on her way out for dinner and drinks on a patio, maybe heading to a club for some live music. Or having a barbecue on the beach with friends. Here? She was watching home-decorating shows and stripping wallpaper. Such a glamorous life she led.

Sabrina grabbed her purse from her bedroom and glanced at her footwear in the open closet. Her old red cowboy boots stared back at her, bright and cheerful and a memento of bygone days. She'd had some good times in those boots.

Being named Miss Northern Lights at the town's

annual festival for the second year in a row. Getting caught smoking and drinking behind one of the tents at same festival and being uncrowned. High school graduation day. Graduation night.

She remembered the day she bought them. She and Marissa had been shopping for Marissa's sweet-sixteen party when she'd seen them sitting on top of a pedestal, practically glowing at her. Like fire. She'd snatched them up and held them to her chest, ready to do battle if necessary and looked over to find Marissa doing the same thing to a pair in cotton-candy-pink. They hadn't stopped laughing until they'd left the store wearing the boots. They'd been the talk of the party. But then, they always were.

Sabrina still hadn't seen Marissa. Since there were only a few thousand people who called the town home and Sabrina was confident she'd seen every one of them multiple times, she could only assume that it was a purposeful snub. She'd hoped they could say hello, maybe have a chat. A little ache worked its way into her heart. What was it her mother always said? *New friends are silver but old friends are gold.*

In her case, friends were nonexistent. Both new and old.

She slipped the boots on. Maybe she didn't still have her friendships, but she still had her boots.

As expected, the hardware store was empty except for Ed, the owner, working behind the register, and her. He scowled when she brought up her paint. Probably still angry with her for that missing parking sign from a decade ago.

But what had he expected? He'd installed a special custom-made parking sign in front of his store, reserving the space for his newly restored 'Vette. He'd even gotten Marissa ticketed for parking there once, which was ridiculous and would never have happened had the sheriff not been his brother. So one night they'd crawled up the post, removed the personalized sign and hung it in Marissa's room. Sabrina wondered if she still had it.

She paid without engaging Ed in a chat and carried her purchases out to her vehicle, cranking the radio as she drove back home and indulging in the cheerful twang of the country song spilling from the speakers. In Vancouver, she rarely listened to the songs of her youth, worried that they'd highlight her humble beginnings.

Maybe she should crank the tunes when she got home, too. Perhaps that would draw Noah out. She could casually point to the paper and ask if he'd had a chance to read her article, then book his interview on the spot. And if she were completely honest, she wouldn't mind spending some time with him, either.

He might try to hide it behind his preppy haircut and collared shirts, but Mr. Mayor was a sexy beast. She remembered in high school all the girls, her included, thinking Kyle Barnes was the hottest guy in Wheaton and quite possibly the country. But after spending a bit of time with Noah? Kyle wasn't even in the running.

And she was due for a little fun in her life. She turned into the driveway. A fling with the mayor sounded pretty fun indeed.

Sabrina was so busy singing and thinking about a potential fling that it took a moment to notice the mess on her formerly pristine front porch.

NOAH JUST WANTED to get home. The day had been longer and more eventful than he would have liked. He'd had to drive to his dealership in a town an hour away when the manager there had up and quit without notice. Once he'd calmed the staff down and started the process of finding a replacement, he'd gotten a call from a constituent in Wheaton who was concerned that her neighbor's tree was hanging too far into the street and needed to be trimmed.

She'd left three more messages while he drove back to town. After assuring her that someone would take care of the problem and soothing the tree-owning neighbor, he'd zipped over to the Wheaton dealership for a few hours. His payroll guy had botched the data entry and somehow deleted everyone's hours. Fortunately, Noah kept a backup since this wasn't the first time it had happened. He should probably let the man go, but he had a young family and he was trying hard. Maybe he could find a different role for him, one where Noah wouldn't have to put in extra hours of work every week.

And then he'd had to attend the weekly council meeting, where the mic had been hijacked by an overly confident Pete Peters wanting to resubmit a request for rezoning. Really, was it any wonder Noah wanted to shut his eyes and let the day end?

As he pulled down the side road that led to the house, he wondered if Sabrina would be around. He'd read her article on Pete before all hell had broken loose. Balanced and fair, it had made the man look a lot nicer than he was. Noah had waffled long enough. If Sabrina was around, he'd tell her tonight that he wanted to do the interview.

A smile tugged at the corner of his mouth when he thought of seeing her. She'd made herself at home the past week, setting out huge pots of flowers and a pair of Adirondack chairs on the porch. He often heard her singing along to the local country station at the top of her lungs. Her dad hadn't been lying about that, but neither had she. She was always on key.

When he turned into the driveway, he spotted her on the porch on her hands and knees scrubbing at something. He enjoyed the sight of her butt as he rolled by. He was tired, not dead.

He parked by the detached garage and left the windows open to cool the vehicle. It had been a hot day and the interior had retained a lot of the warmth. As he walked toward the house he felt a little more of the tiredness in his bones float away. There was something to be said for being greeted by a great pair of legs and a fine ass.

When Sabrina turned to greet him, Noah nearly stopped dead in his tracks. Clad in a thin white T-shirt, a pair of denim cut-offs and red cowboy boots, she was his high school fantasy come to life. Oh, hell.

"Look at this." She gestured sharply to the porch behind her.

He dragged his eyes away from those boots. The porch was a mess. All those heavy pots she'd dragged to the perfect positions last weekend now lay in shards around her. Piles of dirt were ground into the white planks and the blooms had been crushed, judging from the footprints, by someone wearing sneakers. "What happened?" He looked from the disaster area to her.

Sabrina put her hands on her hips. "That's what I'd like to know. I know Marissa wasn't happy to see me back, but what did these flowers do to anyone? They're innocent."

All the time she'd spent sprucing up the front

wasted by some kids who were bored. "You okay?" He'd heard the thread of tension in her voice, understood it. She was rattled and wound tight, as anyone would be who came home to find their home damaged.

"I'm fine." But her smile didn't reach her eyes. There was a dirt smudge near her hairline and another by her knee. The colorful scarf tying back her hair blew in the light breeze.

Noah surveyed the chaos as he walked up the steps to stand beside her. "Were you here when it happened?"

She shook her head. "No. I was getting paint from the hardware store." She knelt to start cleaning again and Noah felt the tension in his body ease.

He moved to help her, pressing a knee into the step for leverage and lifting what looked like half a pot into his arms. Dirt spilled down his blue golf shirt and gray pants as he carried the pottery to the plastic garbage can she'd dragged to the porch. "When did you find things like this?"

"Maybe fifteen minutes ago." Sabrina followed behind him and tossed a few pieces of clay pot into the bin. They made a dull thump against the thick plastic. "I'm surprised. I didn't realize things like this happened here."

"Teenagers." He tried to focus on what he was saying and not on the fact that he could see the lace outline of her bra through the soft material of her T-shirt. But when he looked away, his gaze landed on those little shorts instead. As if his imagination needed any help after all that talk about the shower last weekend. "Sometimes they get bored and do stupid things."

Sabrina smiled again and this time it reached her eyes. "These ones are plenty stupid. They left a note." She pointed to the porch railing.

Noah walked over and saw a message gouged into the wood. *Fuq*.

"Charming, isn't it?" She scooped up a bunch of blooms and dirt. Together, they dumped the last of the mess into the garbage can. Her spicy-sweet scent overpowered the aroma of fresh dirt when she stopped beside him. "You don't think they'll come back, do you?"

"No. I don't." He was surprised they'd dared to do it in the first place. Most times, any vandalism happened at a construction site left unguarded for the evening. Occasionally on the school or other public building where it would achieve maximum impact. "Are you worried?"

"Of course not." She scoffed as though the very idea was an insult. "In case you've forgotten, I've spent the past nine years living in the heart of Vancouver. A couple of punk vandals are nothing."

She was quiet for a minute. Noah watched while

she swept the piles of dirt off the porch and onto the flowerbeds below with her foot.

"But I'd be happier if it hadn't happened at all." She sighed and kicked some more dirt. "Thanks for helping me clean up. If this had happened at my old apartment, my neighbor would have called the landlord to complain."

"About vandalism?"

She shrugged. "He didn't like me."

Noah thought the man was clearly an idiot. He dusted his hands off. "No problem." Sabrina's smile could knock a man off his feet if her boots hadn't already done the job. He cleared his throat. "I'll get a broom for the rest of this." A clearer head would be nice, too.

He focused on what he'd need to repair the gouges in the wood—some sandpaper and a coat or two of white paint—and not on the way Sabrina looked in those shorts. And boots.

But his fingers tightened around the handle of the push broom he'd pulled from the shed when he saw Sabrina bent over again. So he said the first thing that popped into his head. "You know, this might have been a message for me."

"For you?" She glanced over her shoulder at him. "The town's golden son? I highly doubt that."

Noah wasn't the town's golden son, but this wasn't the time to correct her. He walked up the steps. "If you're worried about them coming back, you could get a dog."

"A dog?" She stood up, pushing her hair back.

"Yes." A big, slavering dog that would keep vandals and bored teenagers away. "For safety." So that any troublemaker who showed up would get a surprise. A toothy, barky surprise. Actually, it was a pretty good idea for spur-of-the-moment thinking.

But Sabrina shook her head. "I'll be fine. I've got city instincts. And you're probably right, these guys won't come back." Her eyes met his. "Besides, I can't get a dog—I'm not staying. What would I do with a dog when I left?"

Noah nodded. She was right. A dog was a foolish idea. It would be irresponsible for her to get a dog when she knew she wasn't staying and the dog couldn't go with her. Maybe *he* should get a dog. But then he wasn't home enough to make that a reasonable option, either.

He started sweeping.

"I can do that." She held her hand out for the broom. "Really, you've done more than enough."

But Noah just kept sweeping. He could easily go inside, break this little connection they were forging. Sabrina wasn't staying. She knew that. He knew that. The whole town knew that. And yet he didn't leave the porch.

His eyes tracked her hands as she rubbed them

on the seat of her denim shorts. He wondered if it were possible for him to institute a bylaw that banned those shorts. Or perhaps one that required Sabrina Ryan to wear them at all times. He swept harder.

She stood by the damaged railing, fingers tracing the ugly message. "Are you always like this?"

"Always like what?" Trying to pretend that his body wasn't screaming for him to stop thinking and start acting?

"Doing things that aren't your job."

"I'm the mayor."

"So?" The colorful scarf holding back her hair trailed over one shoulder and around the curve of her breast. Noah feared he might snap the broom's wooden handle. "That doesn't mean you're responsible for everything that happens within town limits."

Noah swallowed and told his body to get back to sweeping. His body told his brain that it needed a moment. Just one moment as his eyes drank in every curve of her body. "I don't act like I'm responsible for everything."

She cocked her head. "Oh, really?"

"Yes." He didn't; he just tried to help out. Not the same thing at all.

Sabrina nodded, but didn't look like she believed him. "I know it isn't the dinner I owe you, but how about some coffee to say thanks for helping with the dirty work?"

Noah glanced down at his pants which were streaked with dirt. He'd have to spray and presoak them before washing. He looked back at Sabrina. She shook something deep inside of him. A part of himself that he kept carefully caged. He glanced over at the sun, dipping below the horizon. A secretive time, when people acted out of character and blamed it on the night. "It's late."

"Right." But her face fell and dragged his stomach with it.

"It's late for coffee," he heard himself say. "I've got an early start tomorrow. If I drink coffee now, I'll be up all night."

Sabrina's face brightened and Noah felt his stomach do a slow somersault. "Something else, then?"

He should say no. He balanced the broom against the railing. They could part now and go to their respective homes feeling good about the interaction. Just a couple of neighbors. But he didn't want to say no. "Sounds great."

He tried not to watch her go, those boots flashing, hips wiggling, but failed. And when she came back with two water glasses and handed one to him, their fingers brushing, he felt a flash of heat that had nothing to do with the hot day crest through him.

Her throat bobbed as she took a long sip. Noah blinked and reminded himself that licking her neck would not be considered appropriate mayoral behavior. He thought about doing it anyway.

She sat down and leaned back, resting on her elbows. The movement outlined the lace bra she wore. There was a streak of dirt on her shoulder. He knew his own clothes hadn't fared any better. But he didn't care. His fingers pressed harder against the cold glass.

"How are Marissa and Kyle?"

Noah blinked. He was thinking about peeling her out of her clothes and she wanted to talk about his family? "They're fine."

She nodded. "I haven't seen them. I guess they're avoiding me."

Noah swallowed some more water and tried to bring his mind around to the conversation they were having, not the one he wanted to have, which involved climbing out of their clothes. "Does that bother you?"

Sabrina swiveled to look up at him. "Yes." Her eyes, normally so bright and cheerful, looked sad. "I'd hoped, well, it doesn't matter what I'd hoped." She played with the end of her scarf. "Did Marissa ever tell you that I tried to apologize?"

It took a second for the words to sink in to Noah's heat-soaked brain. "You did?" His dear sister-in-law had never mentioned that. But then, to be fair, the topic had been a sensitive one for Marissa, who had felt more judgment over the unplanned pregnancy than Kyle.

Sabrina nodded, her fingers twirling the scarf around and around. "I called right after she had the baby, but she wouldn't talk to me."

Noah considered that little nugget of information. Marissa had always given him the impression that, after the interview, she'd never heard from Sabrina again.

"I sent a gift and a letter." Sabrina smiled to herself. "I guess I thought it might prove to her that I was sorry. As if a fuzzy white stuffed animal could make up for what I wrote."

"A toy dog," Noah said. He knew that dog. It had been Paul's favorite as a baby, and though the doll was now gray with age, it still held a place of honor on his bed.

Sabrina's eyes widened. "Yes. So she did get it. I was never sure."

Noah nodded slowly. "It was a difficult time for them." New parents, newlyweds. A hard time for anyone.

Sabrina traced her finger along the rim of her glass. "I keep hoping I'll see her, so I can tell her I'm sorry." She put her glass down on the steps and turned toward him.

A tingle worked its way up his spine. The sun dropped farther, leaving them in a silent twilight.

His eyes followed the curve of her cheek, the dark shadow of her lashes as she peeked up at him. No one else would be making an appearance here tonight. No one could see them from the road or the yard.

For all intents and purposes, they were alone. Completely alone.

"I still miss her." Sabrina's voice was low, intimate. "We were best friends. I thought we'd be friends forever. And then I wrote that snotty article." She looked down at her lap. "There are times I wonder if I did the wrong thing. If I'm a bad person."

The tremor in her voice dove right into Noah's heart and stayed there. "You're not a bad person." He sank down on the step beside her, tangled his fingers with hers and squeezed.

"Your sister-in-law would disagree."

"She doesn't know everything."

"Don't tell her that."

He laughed and put his glass down. He didn't want to talk about Marissa anymore. He didn't want to talk at all. He tugged on Sabrina's hand, drawing her closer to him. First their shoulders touched, then their hips, then her legs pressed against the length of his. Her face tilted up, glowing in the soft evening light.

"Mr. Mayor." Her breath tickled his lips as he bent closer. "Are you going to kiss me?"

Noah stopped. Had he read the entire situation wrong? Was she just looking for a neighborly visit where they sat on the porch and talked about the day's problems? The tips of his ears burned and his chest tightened. "I was."

"Then what are you waiting for?"

CHAPTER SIX

OH, YES.

Sabrina's eyes slid shut as Noah's lips touched hers. It had been so long since she'd been touched by anyone and she reveled in it. A loose warmth curled through her. Satisfaction tickled the base of her neck. It was probably wrong to be kissing the man she hoped to interview soon and whose brother she'd dated in high school. But it felt so right.

He placed a hand on the side of her cheek and stroked once. A light butterfly touch that sent a shiver through her. So, so right. She melted toward him.

Noah wasn't the kind of man she usually kissed. He didn't drive a fast car or refuse to wear shoes that weren't made of real Italian leather. He didn't live in a penthouse suite with a view of the city lights below and attend parties every night to both see and be seen. He didn't do yoga on Tuesdays, Thursdays and Sundays or count every carb that got near his mouth. He was the kind of man who chose shoes for utility and performed manual labor to keep his physique. At least, she hoped so. Sabrina was really looking forward to seeing a shirtless Noah mowing the lawn outside her window.

Hot, sweaty yard work. She ran a hand down his arm, feeling the pull and bunch of his muscles. She'd go out and personally shake the leaves off the trees for him to rake if she had to. Followed by a lovely pasta dinner, which Noah would relish instead of looking at her with horror and ask if she was trying to make him fat.

That he sat on the porch in the bits of dirt that still clung to the wood slats wasn't lost on her, either. Sabrina was used to the urbanites who complained if dust gathered on their leather car seats. Not a single one of her friends in Vancouver would ever have jumped in to help clean up the mess of crushed blooms and broken pots. And they never would have sat down on the porch, not even if it had been freshly scrubbed.

She curled against him. His hand rested on the nape of her neck, his thumb drawing slow, easy circles. Although the night was warm, she shivered. She thought they should stay here for a while. A very long while.

Sabrina could forget while she was out here, wrapped up in his arms, in his taste and smell. Everything in her life that hadn't been so great seemed less important.

Noah trailed light kisses from one corner of her

mouth to the other. So sweet, so careful, so unlike what she was used to. But when she urged him for more, pressing her mouth more firmly against his, trying to take the wheel, he simply continued at the slow, sweet pace.

And to her surprise, she burned all the hotter for it. More than if he'd shoved his tongue in her mouth and tugged at her neckline.

His cheek was stubbly. So different from the smooth, baby softness of her last boyfriend. And the way he smelled. Just fresh air and pine tree. Sabrina inhaled deeply, feeling the heat pool in her body.

She turned her torso, trying to press against him, wanting to throw her legs around him, but unable to do so without breaking their lip lock. Oh, the tragedy of choice. Her fingers curled around his hard biceps, appreciating the strength hidden beneath the clean-cut shirts and tidy persona.

Noah's tongue darted out to touch hers, just a flick, a recon mission to determine if this was acceptable. Sabrina sighed. More than acceptable. Her body softened, molded itself to his while he stroked her face, her neck, her arms and shoulders, all while keeping up an uninterrupted appreciation of her mouth. He was barely touching her, nothing under the clothes, no intense grabs or grips and she'd practically melted into his lap.

But it was like a tickle, creating a delightful

itch beneath her skin, and this wasn't enough to soothe it.

A tingle skittered down her spine when he stroked down her neck and along her arm, stopping to play with the soft skin on the inside of her elbow. He caught her wrist and pressed a kiss to the same spot. Sabrina had never thought of the area as being particularly sensitive, but the shudders coursing through her said maybe she should pay a little more attention.

Her breath escaped and she shivered against him, but not because the air cooled as the evening slipped fully into night. She didn't notice.

For her, there was only Noah. His hands holding her close, large and strong enough to wield manly man tools but treating her like her mother's fine crystal; his voice whispering in her ears and across her skin; his lips brushing along her neck, the shoulder he'd bared and her lips.

Her worries about her job, her home, her city life slipped away as easily as the sun.

Sabrina rose, straddled him, then pressed a hot kiss to his neck. Noah's fingers tightened on her hips as he pulled her closer and he groaned when she ran her tongue from his collarbone to his ear. She knew how he felt.

But he didn't grab her, didn't thrust himself against her and grind their bodies together. Still so thoughtful, so controlled. Each movement a precise, choreographed scene created for maximum enjoyment. She wanted him to let go. She bit the tendon that connected his neck and shoulder. He inhaled sharply and stilled.

Sabrina's breath caught. Too far? Was he going to pull back, gather his thoughts and realize that they were outside and anyone might wander up the driveway?

But then Noah's fingers curved into her hips again, hard this time, and his body surged against hers. Definitely not too far. He gripped the back of her head, dragging her mouth to him.

And the soft, slow pace changed, becoming harder and faster. Sabrina could feel just how much he liked it. Their mouths connected, teeth clicked, tongues tangled. He yanked the hem of her T-shirt up, exposing her torso to the night and cupped her breast. Her entire body seemed to scream *yes* and she couldn't hold back a wild moan when he rubbed her nipple, pinching it between his thumb and forefinger. She arched her back, no longer thinking about some random neighbor walking over.

For all she cared, they could enjoy the show.

She raked her hands through Noah's hair, mussing up the precise part. The wood steps were digging into her knees, but she didn't mind. Not when Noah was sucking on the side of her neck, his stubble raking her sensitized skin.

So Mr. Mayor wasn't really this calm and perfect persona he displayed to the world. Behind that cool blue gaze he was all pent-up emotion and hunger. She smiled.

"Just so you know," he said between love bites, "I was going to agree to the interview anyway."

"Hmm?" Sabrina heard the pop of stitches when he pulled the neck of her T-shirt farther away from her body. Why was he talking? She had a neck that needed kissing.

"The interview." His teeth scraped her skin. "This week."

She shuddered, letting her head loll backward. His hands held her hips firmly in place so she had no fear of falling, even if she stretched back fully. Noah was a man who wouldn't let a woman fall.

His kisses weren't gentle any longer. They were bossy and demanding. She gripped the bottom of his golf shirt and tugged it off. Oh, he was just delightful under that preppy exterior. All hard muscles and cut abs. She let her fingers trace the ridges while she kept kissing him. His skin burned under her as though the outside temperature wasn't even a concern. Sabrina pressed closer, wanting nothing between them.

"Did you hear me?" he asked between hot, hard kisses.

"Yes. Interview. This week. You and me. More

kissing, please." She didn't care about the job right now. Just the man. This man.

His body was warm against hers. She wanted to melt into him. To forget about everything but them for just tonight. And then his phone rang.

He let out a curse and bent his head to look at his pants, which were vibrating. Unfortunately, it wasn't from her.

"Seriously?" Sabrina pulled back and looked down, too.

"No." Noah shook his head. "They can wait." He started kissing her again, beginning at her neck and trailing his tongue down to her collarbone.

Sabrina's desire revved up again. She pushed against him, tangled her fingers in his hair.

The phone rang again. Sabrina sighed and let her hands fall to her side. "Maybe you should answer."

She had the feeling that the mayor never let his phone go unanswered, and that the person on the other end of the phone might start to worry and send someone to find out if something was wrong. She wasn't against a little making out in the great outdoors, but the thought of the police or fire coming over to determine why the ever-responsible mayor was out of contact would be front-page news. And that was a story she didn't want to see written.

"No." Noah shook his head. His hands spanned

her waist, big and warm. "They can wait. I'll turn it off."

He kissed her again, and he tasted really good, so she kissed him back and she forgot about his phone and she could only assume he did, too, because when it started ringing again, he jerked and swore. "I cannot believe this." He lowered his forehead to hers.

His obvious distress eased some of hers and she laughed. "It's okay, Mr. Mayor. I'm not going anywhere. Answer your phone." The mood was shot anyway. She tugged her shirt back down and climbed off him so he could take the phone from his pocket.

"Mom? What's up?"

And any remaining lust that might have been lying in wait, just hoping for a chance to bloom, shriveled up for the night.

SABRINA DIDN'T BOTHER telling herself it was for the best that she and Noah had been interrupted because it wasn't. Just trying to tell herself otherwise only annoyed her.

Even more annoying? She'd barely seen him since that hot make-out session Tuesday night. Not that she thought he was still avoiding her. It had only been three days and he'd come into the coffee shop every morning, but it wasn't the same as sitting on his lap, letting him kiss the breath out of her.

She checked herself out in the mirror and adjusted the sleeves on her gray blazer. At least they'd have today. Not that there would be any kissing or touching or anything of that nature, but she was getting her interview, and spending Friday afternoon with the sexy mayor wasn't the worst way to end her week.

Her fitted jeans with a pretty pink top and turquoise scarf were attractive and appropriate. The business suit and skyscraper heels that she usually wore for her interviews would be out of place in Wheaton no matter the occasion and Noah had said to make sure she wore something she was comfortable moving around in. The boots had only a three-inch heel and were beginning to feel like flats after all her practice wearing them at the coffee shop.

Sabrina smoothed her hair back into a ponytail, added a pair of silver earrings and made sure the small digital camera she used for photos was in her bag. She double-checked her note cards and that she had plenty of pens.

Some reporters preferred to use a laptop to take notes or simply used a recorder, but Sabrina found that most people reacted better to a more relaxed environment. Often, she didn't even pull her note cards or pens out, committing everything to memory and scribbling everything down in one long session once the interview was complete. Over the years she'd honed her ability to recall most conversations word for word. She'd then follow up via email and make sure to verify any and all quotes.

Not that her attention to detail and covering her ass always worked. On occasion, people claimed she'd misquoted them, wanted the paper to print a retraction or demanded an apology. Sometimes all three. But Sabrina had always been able to prove the truth of what they'd said with her paper trail of emails.

Until Jackson James and Big Daddy. Oh, sure, she'd had the long list of emails, the back and forth between Jackson and her that showed he'd approved everything she'd written. But none of that had mattered to Big Daddy or apparently to her boss.

Sabrina pushed the memory out of her head. No point in dwelling on it. Nothing would change no matter how long or hard she thought about it. And she knew because she'd spent many, many hours thinking about the entire situation since receiving the phone call that fateful January day telling her she shouldn't come in to the office that morning or at all.

She had other things to keep her occupied today.

Sabrina headed out of the apartment into the cheerful June afternoon. It wasn't quite as warm as it had been so she was comfortable in her long sleeves. Her spirits lifted as she inhaled the clean air and locked the door behind her. Today was just another step toward getting her life back.

Noah had asked her to meet him at his dealership and she was looking forward to spending a few hours with him. When he was around, she didn't feel quite so lost or as though her return to her hometown meant she was an epic failure. A little fling appeared to be just what she needed and she could think of no man better suited for the job than Noah Barnes.

Okay, so he was her high school boyfriend's older brother and normally that was the kind of thing that would have made her feel a bit strange. She'd never been able to fully immerse herself in the casual dalliances and bed-hopping of her city circle, preferring a string of monogamous boyfriends, ones that didn't know each other. But she and Kyle had been out of touch for so long that he was a stranger now and, in truth, they'd never been all that serious anyway. Sabrina knew there were people who married their high school sweethearts, had heard of people who held torches for their first loves, but she wasn't one of them.

Plus, it wasn't like she was going to marry Noah. She just thought they could have some fun while she was in town. No harm in that.

The wind gusted through the open window of the SUV as she pulled out of the driveway.

According to her search online, Noah's dealership was number one in town. Of course, it was also the only dealership in town....

Sabrina sang along to the radio letting the wind blow away all her troubles. She had plenty of good things to think about. Her interview, a list of article ideas to pitch to Trish, dinner with her parents. Whether or not Noah would undertake some sweaty, shirtless yard work this weekend.

Her pulse fluttered when she pulled into the dealership's parking lot and saw him waiting for her at the entrance. The man could fill out a pair of pants. And a shirt. And a jacket. And shoes. She shook her head and smoothly parked the SUV as though she hadn't just been thinking about what he looked like under all those clothes.

"Good afternoon, Mr. Mayor." Keep it professional and businesslike.

Noah held the door for her as she climbed out, then closed it behind her. "Are you always going to call me that?"

She pretended to think about it. "Yes. I think it's got a nice ring. Or are you looking to give up your title?"

"Not even close. You look good." He leaned toward her. Her pulse sped up. Was he going to kiss her? Right here? In the parking lot, in front of everyone? "I miss the red boots, though."

Then he offered his arm and led her toward the back corner of the lot.

Sabrina exhaled coolly as though she hadn't just been about to let him jump her bones. "I didn't think they matched the pink top. So what's on the schedule for today?"

She hoped it wasn't a show and tell of the dealership followed by a recitation of his platform. She'd read his website multiple times last night—she'd finished painting and needed to do something besides watch TV or wait for her friends to return her texts—and she was well versed in what he planned to do as mayor. Or planned to continue doing. Increasing community services, lowering taxes, raising tourism. All excellent points, and far more useful than Pete's platform, which seemed to consist of changing zoning laws. But she was looking for a more personal angle. The kind of thing that would make readers take notice, call a friend and tell them to pick up the paper, too.

"Cedar Oaks." Noah's hand on her elbow was big and warm. She remembered how it felt pressed against her bare skin and a shiver rolled through her. She batted the feeling away.

"The retirement complex?" Sabrina knew Cedar Oaks well. Her grandfather had moved there after her grandmother died and spent the last five years of his life in comfort and luxury. But she hadn't been there since he passed away when she was fifteen. "Why?"

"I volunteer there on Friday afternoons."

Of course he did. Because Noah Barnes was practically perfect in every way. She grinned at him. "So exactly what do you do there? Play bridge? Lawn bowling? Shuffleboard?"

"Clichés," he told her with smile. A real one. None of that faux mayor in sight. "We dance."

Sabrina stopped walking, pleased when Noah stopped, too. His hand held her arm just a little tighter. Or was that her imagination? Either way, she liked it. "You dance?"

"Well, I don't dance, but the residents do."

She tilted her head to look at him. The sun was bright and warm on her face. That's what was making her cheeks feel heated. Well, that and the fact that her fevered imagination was picturing Noah's moves on the dance floor and elsewhere. But only for a second because this was an interview and she was a professional. "And what do you do while everyone else is out there bumping and grinding?" She feigned seriousness as though this were a question that was the crux of his election strategy.

"I make sure everyone else is having a good time." His thumb rubbed across her inner elbow. She definitely wasn't imagining that. Her breath caught. "But a small piece of advice—don't mention bumping and grinding to George Cuthbert."

"Why?" They started moving again. Sabrina knew George's granddaughter, Julie, who'd used to babysit her when she was little. Julie was awesome. She'd let Sabrina eat ice cream for dinner and stay up past her bedtime. "Will he get upset and yell at me about the dangers of premarital fornication?"

Noah snorted. "Not likely. And don't mention fornication, either. You'll give him a heart attack."

"You could handle it," she said as they reached his car and he opened the door for her. His hand lingered on her waist as he assisted her inside. She'd once gone on a date with someone who'd actually started the car before he'd even bothered to unlock the passenger door for her. This was much nicer. "I'm sure you know CPR." Probably had his lifeguard certification and ambulance training, too.

Noah's upper lip curled. "I have no interest in spending my Friday afternoon giving mouth-to-mouth to George Cuthbert."

"Aw, the poor man probably needs a kiss. Really, it's your duty as mayor to ensure his needs are met."

"No."

"It would only be a kiss," Sabrina continued, enjoying the horror Noah was trying valiantly not to show. "I'd hardly call it making out. Or have you been married to the town too long to know the difference?"

He leaned down, looking at her so hard that she shivered. His voice was so quiet she had to lean forward to hear it. "Are you asking for another demonstration?"

Sabrina's breath caught. She hadn't been, but now that the idea was out there, floating through the air and her head, she wanted one. A long, hot demonstration.

But before she could take him up on his generous offer, Noah stepped back, shut the door with a click and made his way around to the driver's side. Tracking him, noting the effortless way he moved, probably wasn't her brightest idea. She did it anyway and felt a flicker of longing when he slid behind the wheel.

"You're a bit of a bad boy under that polished exterior, Mr. Mayor." He blinked as though this information was new to him. Had he been playing the town's golden son for so long that he'd lost touch with who he was? "Do your constituents know?"

His hands were loose on the steering wheel as he headed out of the parking lot and pulled onto the street, handling the powerful car easily. A man like that could handle a lot of things easily. "Only if you plan to tell them."

"Don't tempt me." She watched him change gears smoothly. She wasn't much of a car person, but there was something insanely sexy watching him control the car. She stuffed the thought away for later when there was no interview or car or anything else to get in their way.

Like everything else in town, Cedar Oaks was only a ten-minute drive away. The complex was more like a luxury apartment building with small private suites for the residents and a lower level filled with spacious rooms used for everything from entertaining to eating.

There was a small wing off the main level for those residents who required more hands-on care for physical or mental reasons. There the coded locks prevented anyone from wandering off and helped the employees keep an eye on all residents as some didn't like signing in and out of the log the way they were supposed to.

Sabrina's grandfather had been one of them, insisting that putting the information down in the logbook was inviting thieves to break into his suite and rob him of all his belongings. The fact that there were no recorded break-ins at Cedar Oaks did nothing to soothe him. He could not be convinced that his decades-old plaid shirts and khakis were of little interest to these hypothetical thieves.

Finally, in a burst of inspiration, Sabrina's mother had suggested he sign "Captain Midnight" instead of his own name to fool anyone who might be looking. And for the rest of his time at Cedar

Oaks, Robert Ryan had been more than happy to participate in movie outings, shopping trips and any other activity that took him away from the complex. But only as the anonymous Captain.

Sabrina smiled and wrote down "Captain Midnight's granddaughter" as she used to do when she visited him. Her grandpa had laughed long and hard every time he saw her signature in the book. She smiled at the memory.

"Noah, Sabrina. Welcome."

Sabrina looked up from the book, smiling when she saw Kyle and Noah's mother, Ellen Barnes, coming toward them. She hadn't changed a bit. Still tall and slender, with her blond hair cut short and a pair of jeweled earrings hanging from her earlobes.

She enveloped Sabrina in a strong hug now. "It's good to have you back." Her smile was all warmth and affability. "You look like life's treated you well."

"It has." And the tension she'd felt about seeing Ellen again melted away. She wondered if that was because Noah was here or because Ellen wasn't the type to hold a grudge.

"I'm so glad you could come with Noah today." Ellen linked an arm through Sabrina's. Ellen was the director of Cedar Oaks and her upkeep and care of both the building and residents was evident. "Everyone is going to love seeing you. Many of them still remember your grandfather. He was a popular fellow."

Sabrina smiled through the sudden prickling behind her eyes. Although Captain Midnight had been gone for years, she still missed him. How he'd pretend that his old car (nickname: Betsy) was low on gas and they might not make it into town. The jokes he told over and over. How when she used to stay with him as a little girl he always made her soup and let her choose the flavor, which was a pretty big deal to a six-year-old. Being here brought back those memories and even though they made her heart ache, it was a good ache.

"I'm looking forward to seeing them." Sabrina wasn't even lying. As she recalled, the residents were always happy to see visitors and treated most of them like long-lost family. She looked forward to visiting with them. Had it really been more than a decade? She wondered how many had slipped away while she'd been gallivanting in the city, focused on her own life. She glanced at Noah. Though there was no way he could have anticipated her reaction to Cedar Oaks, she was grateful he'd chosen it for their interview.

Ellen led her away from the front desk through the cheerful lounge area, leaving Noah to follow a few steps behind. There was a TV on with the sound muted and a small table where a couple were involved in a rather serious chess match.

Sabrina noted the changes. The carpet that looked brand-new, the fireplace that was currently unlit but would add a homey feel during the cold winter months, the patio off the back so residents and visitors could enjoy the garden in the summer. "Tell me about the complex. Things look different from the last time I was here."

Ellen was only too happy to fill her in. Not only was there a new patio out back, but a new gym and a small movie theater where they showed second-run movies or important hockey games—which in Wheaton was all of them.

"Noah paid for most of it."

"Did he?" She glanced over her shoulder at Noah who was trailing along behind them. "Very generous."

He looked a little embarrassed. "Mom, stop. I didn't pay for it. I helped fundraise. And you promised you weren't going to tell people about that anymore."

"I never promised," Ellen said, "and why wouldn't I tell people? You did a wonderful thing. And, as your mother, I've earned the right to brag."

Sabrina had expected Noah to look pleased about his mother's revelation. Not smug because that wouldn't fit his generous image, but pleased that someone who wasn't him had managed to slide in a piece of info that was sure to appeal to voters.

Instead, he sighed and pinned her with a look. "This isn't part of the article."

She blinked. His generosity was exactly the kind of thing she'd hoped to focus on. A complex like Cedar Oaks didn't come cheap. Although she was sure Ellen did her best to keep costs down, the day-to-day overhead would eat up most of the money residents and families paid. The complex relied on government grants or donations from the community for the extra perks. And judging from the size and scope of the changes, Noah's donation must have been generous indeed. "Why not? It's a great story."

"It was a few years ago." He caught up to them, walked on the other side of the Sabrina. "It isn't part of this election."

And yet, she knew it would appeal to voters. "I'll think about it." She grinned when he frowned at her.

They reached the end of a long hallway with a pair of double doors. Noah opened one, holding it while his mother entered, and turned his attention to Sabrina. "I mean it. I'd really prefer you not write about that."

Sabrina studied him, noted his concern in the crunch of his brows and the frown on his lips. Exactly what was so bad about sharing his donation with the world? It wasn't like the information would come as a surprise to anyone in Wheaton. "But why?"

"Because I asked you not to."

She considered it. Considered him. Then nodded slowly. She didn't understand it, but she could accept it. If he wanted to keep his good works private that was his business. "Okay. I won't write about it."

Relief spilled across his face, made him look younger as if, for once, the weight of the town wasn't on his shoulders. "Thank you."

She wondered about that relief, too. But didn't have a chance to ruminate long as Noah escorted her through the doors and into a large, square room.

It was set up as a ballroom with wood floors, tables and chairs lining the edges and a chandelier hanging from the middle of the ceiling. Most seats were filled with chattering residents who turned en masse as they entered.

"Noah."

"Mayor Barnes."

"It's about time you got here. I don't have long left, boy. You think I want to spend it waiting on you?" An elderly gentleman with eyebrows that looked like they could qualify for their own address wheeled his way toward them.

Sabrina didn't recognize him, but Noah clearly did. "You know how to work the stereo, George."

Noah excused himself and walked across the room to where groups of women were calling out to him. Sabrina almost expected to see a trail of handkerchiefs fluttering. He stopped, spending a moment or two with each one, making sure no one was left out. She felt a flicker in her heart.

Then she turned back to the infamous George and gave him the once-over. He did the same to her.

"I like Elvis." He wiggled his eyebrows at her. Large bushy eyebrows that could probably be used to knit a sweater. Then he leaned back in his wheelchair. "Who are you, girlie?"

"Sabrina Ryan." She stuck her hand out. "I'm a reporter writing a piece on Noah for the paper."

George ignored the hand and looked up at her. She could see gray hair sprouting from his ears. "Didn't ask what you did, asked who you are. You got potatoes growing in those pretty ears?"

"No," Sabrina said, knowing the best way to deal with trouble was head on. "Do you?"

He threw back his head, the top of which was free of any sprouts of hair at all, and roared with laughter. "According to the staff, I do." He grabbed her hand before she could retract it to safety and motioned for her to bend down. He had a surprisingly strong grip for a man of his age. "You said you're a reporter? You should write something about this place. Always trying to make a man wash when he's perfectly clean. Go to bed when he's wide awake. And they feed me baby food."

"It was a special diet for your ulcer and was only temporary," Ellen said from across the room. "Don't think I didn't spot that empty potato chip bag in your room last week. You know they're bad for your stomach." No doubt she was used to George's difficult behavior.

His eyes zeroed in on Sabrina again. "What'd you say your name was?"

"Sabrina Ryan."

George crinkled an eye at her. She wasn't sure if he was winking or trying to see her more clearly. "You famous?"

"Not particularly."

"Good. Don't like famous people." He shot a sly look at Noah and raised his voice to be heard over the buzz of conversation. "They get too big for their britches, if you know what I mean."

"No, George," Noah said. This was clearly a practiced routine between the two of them. He opened a panel in the wall. "No one knows what you mean."

"Well, when a man…" but the rest of George's response was drowned out by a big-band tune that filled the room. Sabrina noted the pleased smile on Noah's face as he shut the panel door. She bit her lip and tried not to laugh. She failed.

"You think he's funny, girlie?" George shouted

over the music. The other residents moved toward the middle of the room, already paired off as they danced to the swinging beats.

Sabrina nodded. "Yes."

George humphed. "Thought you might have some taste." He narrowed one eye at her again. Too vain to wear glasses, Sabrina decided. "You said Ryan. You related to Robert?"

"His granddaughter."

George nodded. "I knew him, you know. He was a good man. He'd have wanted you to be nice to me."

"And I know your granddaughter. Julie used to babysit me. She'd expect you to behave yourself."

George snorted. "Don't have time for niceties." He peered at her again. "You the mayor's girlfriend?"

"No." But following the surprise was a curl of pleasure. Ridiculous. She was only thinking about a fling. No point in getting tangled up with someone when she couldn't stay. "I'm his reporter." Which didn't have quite the same ring.

"What the hell does that mean?" Sabrina didn't get a chance to explain because George was grabbing her hand again. "I don't care. Let's dance. Make an old man happy."

Sabrina glanced at Noah, felt a zing when she found his eyes on her. Just his reporter, she reminded herself as George tugged her to the middle of the dance floor. And maybe, if she had her way, his fling. That was all.

"I like you," George said, then shouted the same pronouncement across the room to Noah. "I think I might keep her." George wheezed out a laugh.

"Do I have a say in this?" Sabrina asked, keeping a sharp eye out as George continued to reverse into the crowd, fearful that he was going to run over a foot or worse. But the residents were clearly used to George and shifted to make way.

"Why? You got a problem with it?"

"I might."

"I'll convince you." His eyes twinkled from beneath his bushy eyebrows. "Put on something with a little swing," he called to Noah. "I've got some moves to show your girl."

"My name is Sabrina." George lifted one brow and drove around her in a circle, then patted her on the bum. "Hey, now." She frowned at him as she whirled to face him. "None of that."

"What is this, prison?" He snickered and patted her again before zipping out of swatting distance. As if she would hit an old man. Even if he deserved it.

She shook her finger at him. "Behave yourself."

"I'll try, but you make it tricky." The music changed to a swing tune that reminded Sabrina of Michael Bublé. George wheeled closer and grabbed her hands, pulling her down to his level. "So what do you think of our boy?"

"Noah?"

"You see any other boy in here?"

Sabrina glanced over to where Noah had retreated to the corner with a gaggle of ladies surrounding him. He looked up, smiled. She swallowed. He could only be a fling. Nothing more. And now wasn't the time to be thinking about that anyway. She was here to do a job. She turned back to George. "I don't see any boys here at all. Now, what can you tell me about our esteemed mayor?"

CHAPTER SEVEN

NOAH WATCHED GEORGE CUTHBERT wheel around Sabrina on the dance floor. He looked every inch the eighty-year-old coot with a new lease on life thanks to the beautiful woman on his arm. *Lucky bugger.*

"Noah, dear." He turned and smiled at Mrs. Mann who had carefully made her way over to him. "Would you play some Duke Ellington? My Howard and I loved Duke. We used to dance all night." Her eyes sparkled as she tapped an orthopedic shoe in anticipation.

"I'd be happy to." He did not offer his arm to take her out for a turn around the dance floor. As he'd told Sabrina earlier, he didn't dance. Ever. And Mrs. Mann's feet, protected by that thick orthopedic leather or not, would thank him.

He cued up Duke Ellington, watching as George continued to grip Sabrina's hands, keeping her at his mercy. She laughed at something he said, her head tipping back and causing her dark hair to flow down. Noah remembered how it had felt brushing against his neck, sliding through his fingers.

He exhaled slowly. Recalling how close he'd come to scooping her off the porch, carrying her inside and having his way with her. Not very mayoral at all.

He should probably be glad for his mother's timing and her clogged sink. But he wasn't. Even knowing that he wasn't the kind of man who slept with a woman before he knew her—before he'd so much as taken her out on a date—didn't help. Nor did the cold showers he'd been subjecting himself to every morning.

Because he still wanted Sabrina. And even though he knew the town expected more of him— to meet a nice girl, one who loved the town as much as he did, who would want to settle down and be the perfect mayor's wife, hosting teas and other community-type events—Noah couldn't deny the attraction to this woman who'd left Wheaton as soon as she could and had made it clear that settling down here wasn't an option.

"Why don't you go rescue her?" His mother slipped through the ranks of adoring ladies to stand beside him.

"I don't dance," he reminded her, happy for the interruption and to think about something other than his caveman urge to throw Sabrina over his shoulder and take her somewhere private.

"Why don't you start?"

Noah dragged his gaze away from Sabrina who

was now admonishing George for patting her on the ass and focused on his mother. Although Ellen hadn't given birth to him, she was the only parent he'd known. In some ways, he thought he loved her more because of it. They hadn't been thrown together by genetics. They'd chosen each other.

When his father died in a car accident not long after he and Ellen were married, no one in town had thought she'd keep Noah. She had a one-year-old and a husband to bury. Taking on the full-time care of a five-year-old was something no one thought she'd want to cope with.

Noah could still remember people talking in hushed whispers that they didn't think he heard or understood. But he had. *Can't be expected to keep him. Placed in a nice foster home somewhere. Not even hers.* He still remembered sitting on the bed in his new "older brother" room the day after his father's funeral. The room Ellen had helped him paint a sky blue, the pillowcases that had pictures of fire engines on them.

She'd knocked and asked if they could talk. Noah could only nod, a lump the size of his fist clogging his throat. She was going to tell Noah that he had to go away. That he wasn't going to be part of the family. He'd resolved not to cry. But when she'd put her arm around him and rocked him a little, he'd started to blubber into her shoulder.

Everything had come pouring out of him then.

How he knew she was going to send him away, but he didn't want to go. He loved her and his baby brother and he'd be the best boy ever if she'd only let him stay. She'd looked at him with those kind eyes and told him that of course he wasn't going anywhere. They were a family and families stayed together.

By the end of the year, she'd officially adopted Noah and the town had adopted all of them. They were simply The Barnes Family. No explanations needed.

But he'd never stopped trying to be the best boy ever.

"I don't dance," he repeated.

Ellen glanced back to the dance floor. Noah's eyes went there, too. Sabrina was wagging her finger at George again, but they were both smiling. "Maybe it's time you tried something new."

He wasn't averse to the concept. But dancing was not that something. Something about the thought of getting out on the dance floor made him highly uncomfortable, as though he'd be demanding attention for the wrong reasons. Running for mayor and standing in front of a crowd were different. Then, he was the mayor, acting out a position, working on behalf of the town's residents, taking care of their needs. But dancing, well, no. It just wasn't him.

"I'm happy with the way things are." He answered his mother's pointed look.

She tilted her head. Her earrings caught the light. "Are you?"

"Of course." But he worried he'd answered too quickly. He looked away from his mother's assessing stare and found Sabrina again. Her tight jeans showed off her curves, curves he remembered touching and stroking. His fingers curled into his palms.

She'd hurt his brother and Marissa. She was only here for the interview. She wasn't staying.

He didn't hear his mother leave, just noticed that she'd stepped away when he cued up the next song. There was no reason he shouldn't be happy with his life. He had his health and his family. A great job that not only provided for him personally but others in the community, as well.

Noah rubbed the back of his neck. He'd made certain choices in his life. Returning to Wheaton after university. Running for mayor. Helping Kyle. But those had been the right things to do and he was content with his decisions.

His eyes tracked Sabrina. Women like her weren't part of his life. City dwellers with big dreams and ambitious careers. People who couldn't wait to leave the town he loved so dearly. Her laughter sparkled through the room causing those around her to join in. She'd been gone for close to a decade and yet it seemed as though she'd slid right back in, as though the town had just been waiting for her to appear.

Sabrina caught his eye, said something to George and walked over. Noah felt his lips twitch and warmth spread through his body. She might not be staying, but she was here now.

"Nice try, pal, but I'm onto you."

Noah forced the image of her straddling him on the porch away and tried to remember that they were in a public place with lots of eyes and a surprising number of cell phones. He had a mayoral rep to protect. "What's that?"

She stopped in front of him. "Don't pretend you didn't plan to foist George on me. He copped a feel. Three times."

"I saw." Noah thought George was a lucky man. "I did try to warn you about him."

"And yet you didn't come over to cut in and protect me. Really, I feel it's your civic duty as mayor to ensure residents are able to shake their booty without having it patted."

He couldn't help looking at the body part in question. And a fine booty it was. "I'll be sure to bring it up at the next council meeting."

"Please do. But for now, you can make it up to me by dancing with me."

Noah balked. Like a stubborn mule, he just dug in his heels. "I don't dance."

She put a hand on his arm. "You do now."

"No." He shook his head. "I really don't."

"Come on, Mr. Mayor." Sabrina's fingers slipped into his. "For me. It'll be fun."

Noah knew fun. And dancing? Was not fun. "I'll crush your toes."

"I'll live." She managed to drag him a step forward.

The music changed to a cheerful dance tune that reminded him of one of those old black-and-white movies the residents liked to watch. The dancers spun before him, all certain of time and place, of rhythm and flow, things that eluded Noah.

"Come on." She pulled him forward another step.

He wasn't sure how he felt about this, this sudden shifting of his carefully plotted-out life. Kissing on the porch, in the relative privacy of his own home, was one thing. But getting up in front of everyone and being vulnerable in a whole new way was not part of the deal. "I'd prefer to watch."

"Yes, you've made that obvious. I prefer that you dance. Consider it part of your 'getting involved in the community' strategy."

"I'm involved." Sometimes he felt like getting involved was the only thing he did. But he let Sabrina tug him forward another few steps, felt his resolve weakening. She smelled so good, and like a siren she lured him toward his death on the rocks.

Or death on the dance floor, which was practically the same thing.

"There you go." She kept her hands wrapped around his once she finally got him out onto the floor. Probably thought he was a high flight risk. She was right.

Noah felt as if a spotlight was trained on him, as if everyone was watching. This wasn't the same as giving a stump speech or addressing the crowd at a grand opening. He couldn't hide behind the mantle of mayor now. His mouth felt dry and he wanted to hurry back to the security of sidelines, but Sabrina's firm grip kept him in place. He could shake her loose easily, but that would cause a scene. He didn't do scenes. He swallowed, but it didn't help his dry mouth.

"You're going to be fine." Sabrina ran a soothing hand up his arm and around the back of his neck. "Now, step side to side. You know how it's done. You were in grade seven once."

He shuffled awkwardly. He could feel the room staring at him. He didn't dance. Heat prickled up his spine.

"You." George zipped up. Noah had never been so grateful to see the old man. "First you got to have two working legs and then you got to steal my woman?"

Some of the tension in his shoulders eased.

George, he could handle. Dancing, not so much. "Your woman?"

George nodded. "I asked her to dance first and now I'm cutting in."

Noah gripped Sabrina's waist more tightly, then realized what he was doing. Acting like she was with him, as if they were a couple. Overprotective and jealous. Not the kinds of attributes he wanted to be known for. He started to step back, to allow George to replace him. And then he saw George's hand, his palm extended, heading straight toward Sabrina's ass. Again.

And something primal woke inside him.

Not on his watch. No one would be patting any part of Sabrina's anatomy but him. He deftly spun her to the side and felt George Cuthbert's hand connect with a different ass.

His own.

"Hey!" George jerked back and shook his hand as though to rid it of something. "Not funny, boy."

Sabrina started to laugh.

"That stays off the record," Noah told her. There was nothing right about George Cuthbert's hand on his ass in any universe. Ever. "But you remember that I took one for you when you're writing your article."

Her eyes twinkled with humor. Sure, it wasn't her ass in the line of fire. "You're quite the white knight, Mr. Mayor."

"Quite something," George said and wheeled off in search of easier prey.

Sabrina smiled at him and he felt his heart stutter. "Quite something, indeed."

He tried to remember all the other people in the room watching. But the music shifted to something slow. She moved closer and looped her arms behind his neck. His skin tingled where she touched him. He reminded himself that she was here to do a story. That he was perfectly content with his life. That this wasn't a great idea.

But he suddenly wasn't sure about anything.

NOAH TRIED TO KEEP his distance from Sabrina the following week. He needed to know how he felt about her without the question of the article hanging over his head. Was she being honest when she said she wasn't planning to write anything that might harm his campaign? Or was it all a ploy?

But he couldn't ignore her. The sound of her music floating through her open windows and her pleasant voice when she sang along. The scent of her perfume that occasionally lingered near the front door or the porch. The way he was drawn to her.

Her article had come out this morning. A charming and thorough treatise that made him seem a hell of a lot nicer than he felt. There was no mention of his donation to Cedar Oaks. Noah couldn't articulate why it was so important that she omit the information. It just felt wrong to include it, as though he'd done it to buy the town's love instead of for his real reason, which was that it was the right thing to do. Not just for the town, but for himself. He was glad she hadn't pushed him to explain.

He'd hoped to see her today to thank her, but she hadn't answered his knock this morning and he'd been at his out-of-town dealership all day, before driving straight to Kyle and Marissa's for dinner.

Kyle opened the door before Noah even unfolded himself from the car. "Nice article, Mayor Barnes."

Noah shot his brother a look but didn't correct him. "Thank you." Like he'd had anything to do with it. But a flicker of pride settled over him. It was a nice article.

He and Kyle managed about three seconds of quiet in the living room before Daisy screeched in, hair flying, eyes wild. "Uncle Noah." She jumped into his lowered arms and promptly squealed in his ear. Ah, yes. It was good to be around family.

In twenty seconds, Noah was inundated by kids all scrambling for attention and airplane rides. He laughed as he played with them. This was what he wanted, what he lived for. Family and love. Children and home. Things he already had in Wheaton.

He tossed Scotty in the air and caught him, wrestled with Paul and after putting Daisy in a gentle headlock was forced to admire her latest drawings, which featured a girl in a tiara with a sword. The kid was no Monet, but he had one of the masterpieces tucked in his pocket for placement on his fridge anyway.

She informed him that the picture needed to be displayed "right in the middle so everyone could see it" and was so enthusiastic in her description that when the doorbell rang he wasn't sure if he was hearing things or it was simply a reverberation from her shouting.

But when she scrambled off his lap and ran for the door, he knew he hadn't imagined it.

He looked at his brother. It wasn't uncommon for Noah to come over for dinner on Saturday night, which now that he thought about it was a sad statement on his bachelorhood, and it wasn't uncommon for Kyle and Marissa to invite other friends, but neither of them had mentioned other guests. Not that they needed to run the dinner guests past him, but the omission struck him as odd.

He caught Kyle's eye. "Who—"

"Yeah, I should have mentioned it. Sorry, man," Kyle said, lowering his gaze and hurrying to the door before Daisy could greet the new arrivals with a chorus of shrieks.

Noah frowned at his brother's back. Why was he apologizing? He followed Kyle out of the living room and saw who was at the door. Oh, hell. He was going to kill Marissa.

Noah ducked into the kitchen rather than greeting the new guests. Not his usual M.O., but desperate times… "Marissa, tell me you aren't matchmaking."

She smiled. "Good to see you, Noah."

He realized he'd been rude, hadn't even stopped in to say hello or give her the wine he'd brought. Actually, he hadn't even carried the wine in from the car, so wrapped up he'd been in thinking about Sabrina and the article. Well, the wine could wait. He came around the counter, gave her a quick kiss on her upturned cheek and repeated his statement.

This time she answered, a tiny smirk on her lips. "Okay, I'm not matchmaking."

He frowned at her. This was no time to play cute. "Then why do I see Linnea—" he lowered his voice on her name "—out there?" He'd told Marissa before that he wasn't interested in a setup and certainly not with Linnea Grimes. She wasn't his type, despite the fact that Marissa had tried to push them together on more than one occasion.

She claimed it was because she thought they'd make a cute couple. Noah suspected it was because she was friends with Linnea. Their oldest boys were the same age and they already spent hours of hockey practice huddling together while the boys skated. So the relationship would be easy for her.

Noah loved his sister-in-law, but he was only willing to go so far for family.

"Linnea and I are friends," Marissa said. "I invited Faith and Stephen, too, so we'd have a nice even number."

He glared at Marissa. She didn't fool him with her rationale. But he didn't get a chance to respond before Linnea breezed into the kitchen on a cloud of heavy perfume that made Noah's nose itch.

He pasted on a gracious smile and bent to kiss her on the cheek. "Nice to see you, Linnea."

"Noah, I'm so glad you're here." She rested her hands on his chest. Her nails were polished a dark red. She seemed to be admiring the way they looked against his shirt.

He stepped back breaking the contact. "What can I get you to drink?"

Dinner was a tortured affair. Even before they'd finished the first course, Noah was wishing that he was somewhere else. Anywhere else. Even the dance floor at Cedar Oaks.

But Noah kept his smile in place and tried to make polite conversation. He managed well enough, surreptitiously stealing looks at his watch, counting the minutes until he could depart. Until the subject of Sabrina arose.

"I read the article she wrote on you today," Linnea said and leaned closer to him as she'd been doing all evening. "Are you okay?"

"Of course." Why wouldn't he be okay? It had been a good article. A great article. But even so, he felt a sudden anxiety. Had other people seen something he hadn't?

"What do you mean, Linnea?" Kyle asked. His voice gave nothing away.

"I just thought it seemed obvious that she was using you." Linnea patted his arm, her red fingernails standing out against his skin. "Trying to get in good with the town. Why did she even come back? I thought she was some big-shot reporter in Vancouver?"

The table was silent. Not even the clink of glassware or cutlery to break the stillness. When Noah spoke it was carefully, slowly. Each word distinct and separate. "Do you know Sabrina, Linnea?"

"Well, I haven't seen her since high school." Linnea seemed to relish being the center of attention. "But I seriously doubt she's changed. We're just concerned about you, Noah."

"I'm not concerned," Kyle piped up. "Just wanted to point that out."

Noah might have laughed had the moment not been so fraught with tension. He shot his brother a grateful look and then faced Marissa and raised an eyebrow. "Did you read the article?"

She nodded.

"And?" His tone was quiet even though he felt as if he might snap the stem of the wineglass with his grip.

She exhaled. "It was a good article."

Some of the tightness in his chest eased, until Linnea opened her big mouth again. "I still say she should never have come back." Linnea sniffed, her lip curling as she sipped her wine. "But I guess she doesn't realize that she isn't one of us."

Noah's shoulders stiffened. *One of us?* "I'm not sure I understand your meaning." His voice was composed even though the hairs on the back of his neck were standing up.

Linnea leaned forward as though imparting an important bit of advice. "She doesn't belong."

Didn't belong. The way he didn't belong. He hadn't been born into one of the founding families. Residents didn't have memories of him as a squalling baby. They didn't tell stories about Noah learning to walk or reminisce how he looked so much like his parents at the same age. He wasn't the only person to ever move to town, but there were days when it felt like it.

His ears pounded and all those old emotions swarmed through him. The lonely orphan sitting on his bed. Afraid he was going to be sent away. Keeping his head down at school so the teacher wouldn't call on him. So no one would notice him. Because if they didn't know he was there, they couldn't send him away.

To hell with that.

The annoyance Noah had been damping down through the entire night roared up, like banked coals finally given enough oxygen to blaze. "You know, I just remembered something else I have to do this evening."

"Noah." Marissa rose when he did.

"I'll see myself out. Thank you for dinner." He didn't bother to tell her the night had been lovely. They'd all see that for the lie it was. Marissa, at least, had the grace to look pained, but the wine that lingered on his tongue tasted sour.

She followed him to the front door. "I don't know why Linnea said that. It was a good article."

His nod was brusque. He didn't want to stand here chatting. He wanted out into the night, wanted the freedom to just breathe.

Noah had nowhere to go and nothing to see, but anything would be better than returning to the dining room, to Linnea's snide commentary and superiority complex.

Actually, he did have somewhere to go and someone to see. Assuming she was home.

CHAPTER EIGHT

SABRINA STARED AT her computer screen and sipped her tea. She was rereading her notes from her interview with Noah. She'd used barely a quarter of what she'd gathered. She could do a whole series on him. If he'd let her.

Of course, she'd have to catch him to ask him. The mayor seemed to always be on his way to or from something important whenever they crossed paths. She might have taken it personally had she not seen the spark of interest in his gaze when he thought she wasn't looking. Unless she'd been imagining things. She hadn't been above giving her butt a little extra wiggle each and every time anyway. Just in case.

But the unused information sitting in front of her was fantastic. In particular, George's story about the time Noah had driven him down to the lake and taken him fishing last summer. How Noah had carried him from the car to the dock since George couldn't walk the distance and the ground was too bumpy for his wheelchair and set him up with a lawn chair, a rod and a fully stocked cooler.

Then the two of them had sat there the rest of the day, eating sandwiches, drinking bottled water and shooting the breeze. George's only complaint had been that Noah refused to let him have beer. George didn't think that Noah's reasoning—he didn't want to cart George to the woods to do his business all day—stood up since beer is "ninety percent water anyway." But that hadn't stopped him from telling Sabrina to inform Noah that George expected another trip this year.

Sabrina considered starting the second article anyway. Noah would probably agree and Trish would love it. She'd even typed the opening sentence. But the words didn't flow, so she brainstormed some other potential ideas instead. The Northern Lights festival was happening in a few weeks to kick off the summer season and the July holiday weekend. Trish probably already had a plan to cover it, but maybe Sabrina could find a new and exciting angle. She wrote down a few other ideas, as well, and then fizzled out.

Working on a Saturday night. How sad was that? The last time she'd lived in Wheaton she'd been a teenager with a curfew and other parental restrictions and yet she'd managed to have a full and busy social life. And tonight? She'd been forced to drop in on her parents for dinner so that she didn't have to eat alone.

Not that her parents had minded. On the contrary, they'd been thrilled and used the opportunity to push their move-back-permanently initiative. She smiled. Even if they were her parents and expected to love her no matter what, it was still nice to feel wanted. It certainly helped to dispel the disappointment that her Vancouver friends seemed to have forgotten about her. Not one of them had returned her calls or emails.

Sabrina took another sip of tea to ease the sting. She didn't expect them to spend hours texting with her or even offer to visit, but a timely response would have been nice. Oh, well. All her free time had at least provided her with the opportunity to finish decorating the apartment.

The walls looked great—a huge improvement over the ugly stripes—and with all her furniture and other decor, the place was starting to look like a real home. Too bad she wouldn't be around to appreciate it for long.

Sabrina checked her email, but her in-box remained empty. Nothing from her editor. Nothing from her friends. Not even a piece of junk mail promising millions from a foreign prince if only she'd share all her banking information.

She fired off a few of the better article ideas to Trish and then powered down the computer. She'd already fulfilled her patheticness quota for the day; no need to add to it by doing more work. Although sitting in front of the TV with her tea might be even sadder. Seriously, how was it that the busiest her social life had been since she arrived was going to a dance with the residents of Cedar Oaks?

Still, Sabrina had enjoyed herself and not just because of Noah. Though he'd certainly been part of the appeal. She wondered where he was tonight. She'd looked for him when she got home from her shift at the coffee shop, but his car was gone and was still missing when she returned from dinner with her parents.

So when she heard the crunch of wheels turning into the driveway, it was only reasonable that she get up to check and see who it was. She turned off the lights so he wouldn't notice her peering through the window at him. Yes, this was what passed for excitement in her life these days.

Noah walked up the front steps, a tired cast to his features. Sabrina leaned closer. Judging from the green polo shirt and pressed khakis—his usual daily uniform—he'd been on the go since this morning. Did he ever take time for himself? Ever say no or do something he wanted to do instead of busting his butt to do things for everyone else?

She didn't think so. Mayor, brother, son, neighbor. He was always being someone for somebody. Even for her. And now he was providing her with some eye candy, albeit unknowingly. Guilt prickled at her and Sabrina stepped away from the French doors, letting the curtains she'd hung earlier in the week fall closed. A man should be able to enter his own home without being ogled.

She'd only just flicked on the light when he knocked on the door. For a moment, excitement flooded through her. Then reality hit. Most likely, he'd noticed her spying and wanted to know why.

Great. Just great. She inhaled slowly. She'd been busted like a teenager with a crush, which wasn't too far from the truth.

"Mr. Mayor. What a pleasant surprise." Her pulse sped up when she looked at him. He looked tired, but good. Really good. All tall and strong and perfectly pressed, but he frowned at her.

"Were you just peeping at me through the windows?"

"No." Sabrina swallowed. Maybe if she acted innocent, he'd think he'd been mistaken. She reached up and brushed a thumb along the grim lines carved around the side of his mouth. "You'll get wrinkles."

"I don't care."

"You should." She heard the rise in her voice, hoped he didn't notice. "Good skin maintenance starts now." He had seen her and he wasn't happy about it. She let her hand fall back to her side.

Really, there was no reason for him to be bothered by a little peek. Maybe she'd just been checking to make sure the flower destroyers weren't back. Yes, that's what she go with if he pushed.

"It looked like you. Right there." Noah pointed to the exact spot she had indeed been standing.

Sabrina flipped her hair, going for airy disinterest. "I don't know what you saw, but I was just hanging out watching TV."

"The TV's not on."

"I was about to *start* watching, I meant." Damn. "Do you want to come in?" She hadn't expected him to agree so quickly, but he was in her apartment in a matter of seconds. He smelled like pine and the outdoors. Her breath was shaky. Even so, she managed to find her manners. Her mother would be so proud. "Can I get you something? Tea? Coffee? Water?"

"Water, please." His eyes tracked the room. "You took down the wallpaper."

She pulled a jug of water from the fridge, letting the cool air wash over her warm skin. "Do you blame me? It took a whole day, but I think it was worth it." Thought so every time she looked at the clean, fresh walls.

He ran a finger along the mantel, looked at the pieces she'd placed there, then sat on the couch. "It looks great in here. Very homey."

"Thanks." A flush of pleasure swept through her as she handed him the glass. "So what brings you here tonight?" It obviously wasn't just about the peeking. Noah had asked, she'd answered and if that were all, he'd have taken himself across the hall to his own apartment, not settled himself on her couch.

"I read the article."

She studied his face, but it showed nothing. Simply that cool, composed mayoral look he was so good at. She hoped that wasn't bad. "I'm guessing since you aren't ignoring me, you liked it."

He stared at her. "I lied. I didn't come because of the article."

"Oh?" Sabrina's breath was caught in her throat and that flush was back, now heating her cheeks. "Then why did you come?"

He didn't answer, just sat forward to put his glass on the coffee table, then slid across the couch and cupped the back of her head. His lips were firm and warm when he pressed them to hers.

So she hadn't been imagining that spark of interest in his eyes and he'd definitely noticed her wiggling. Good.

His hand slid around to the small of her back. She should probably pull away, ask what was going on here. She wasn't looking for a lifelong commitment, but she also wasn't going to be a booty call. A good fling should last at least a month. But it was a slippery thought and one that was impossible to hang on to when he kept kissing her like this.

When they broke apart, Sabrina's lips felt swollen, but her shirt was still on. She wasn't sure how she felt about that.

"Thank you." Noah's hand remained at the back of her head, his fingers twirling through her hair. "I needed that."

"Why?" It was a natural question. "Not that I'm complaining, but I was pretty sure you'd been avoiding me all week." She saw the guilt flash across his face and suddenly the answer was obvious. "You were waiting to see the article."

His throat bobbed as he swallowed. "I'm not proud of it, but yes."

Sabrina swallowed the chilly nausea that was trying to overtake her warmth. "Right. Of course. Because you don't really know me, and I've certainly never given you or your family any reason to trust me when it comes to my articles."

Did she sound bitter? She thought she sounded bitter. She hadn't meant to. She picked up her tea and washed the taste out of her mouth with a small sip.

Noah put a hand on her leg when she tried to shift away. "I was wrong."

"No." She shook her head. "You weren't." It was a hard thing to admit, but she could see it from his perspective. Hadn't she made a career of writing not-very-nice things about people? "You were protecting yourself. I don't blame you."

His gaze was steady, as steady as the hand that remained on her leg. "I was wrong. I should have trusted you." Sabrina felt a flutter in her chest.

"Nothing you'd done or said gave me any reason to think you were lying."

"I don't exactly have a stellar history with your family, though."

He studied her. "Still, I should have given you the benefit of the doubt. I should make it up to you."

She was surprised and touched. "You don't have to make it up to me. You're allowed to have feelings."

He shifted his hand to cup her cheek. "I want to. How about dinner?"

"I already owe you that." She pinned him with a look. "Or are you going to keep putting me off?"

"No." Noah's smile turned rueful. "You pick the time and I'll be there. But this would be something else."

His thumb stroked across her cheek. Sabrina swallowed. "Are you serious or is this just banter?" Casual jokes and conversation that never went anywhere because they weren't meant to. She felt hope begin to percolate, make her all tingly. Or maybe that was his hand.

"I'm serious." And he certainly looked serious. There was no teasing twist to his lips, no sardonic smirk or cheesy wink that undermined his words and told a different truth. His body language was as open and honest as she hoped his words were.

"Would you be interested in letting me write

another article about you?" One that used some of the information currently sitting on her computer.

To Noah's credit, he blinked but didn't jerk back though she saw the shudder pass through him and felt the brief tightening of his hands that were still on her. "What kind of article?"

She tilted her head, so her cheek rested in his palm and suppressed a shiver. "A more personal piece. Something that would showcase you as a person as opposed to the mayor."

He winced. "I don't know if I'm comfortable with that."

Sabrina put her hand on his knee. "It'll be great, Noah. Better than today's article."

He didn't look convinced. He pursed his lips and he lifted his hand from her cheek.

"Or not." She exhaled. Apparently, he didn't really trust her. She wasn't sure why that stung as much as it did. Maybe because he was the only person in town besides her parents who'd spent any time with her since she'd been back. Maybe because she didn't understand how he could kiss her like that if he didn't trust her. She moved her hand away, too.

He caught it, wrapped his fingers around hers. "Okay." His voice was soft, almost a whisper.

"Okay what?"

"You can write another article." His eyes caught hers.

She stared back. "You sure?" Because she didn't want to pitch the idea to Trish only to have him back out at the last minute. Trish had been more than generous in agreeing to allow Sabrina a part-time position at the paper, but family friendships only went so far. Sabrina needed to provide solid and interesting articles, too.

He nodded.

This time, she was the one who slid forward and kissed him. Hard.

"Is this because I said yes?" Noah asked when they came up for air.

"No." Their noses were practically touching, their eyes mere inches apart. "This is because I wanted to." She kissed him again and felt some of the angst guarding her heart begin to lessen.

CHAPTER NINE

THE MORNING OF THE festival dawned bright and hot. Sabrina slipped her red cowboy boots on and then twirled in front of the mirror. The pretty white eyelet dress wasn't Alaïa and the shoes weren't Manolo Blahnik, but she was happy. The realization surprised her. She hadn't expected to be happy. Not here. Not in Wheaton.

But her reporting job was going well. Trish had been wholeheartedly in favor of her article ideas over the past few weeks, which ranged from a feature on porch gardening, showcasing her very own porch, to a piece on a homegrown artist who was gaining recognition across the country. And that was her humming along to the music playing from her iPod speakers and smiling as she put on lipstick. How long had it been since she'd felt this way? Since she was fired? No, longer than that. She just hadn't realized it. What else had she not realized?

But Sabrina didn't like thinking about that, so she pushed the thought away.

She had plenty of other things to fill her mind

today. Not the least of which was spending more time with Noah. She spritzed on her favorite lavender scent, rubbing her wrists together.

Although she and Noah had been seeing each other a few times a week, she was still looking forward to today. Rather than using her leftover information from the original interview session, she and Trish had decided a behind-the-scenes feature on Noah at the festival was likely to interest more readers. And Noah had agreed.

Sabrina wondered if the town knew just how much he did for them. Probably not and she wasn't certain that following him at the festival would get the point across. This was a special event and of course he would be busy. But it was a start.

As well, she'd be busy covering other festival highlights and taking photos. A standard report on the whos, whats and wheres. People were interested in learning who took home the blue ribbon for the best pie and who was going to represent the town as their pageant princess, and Sabrina liked knowing that she'd be able to preserve their moments of glory for them.

Supporting each other and celebrating accomplishments was part of the glue that held small communities together. She'd forgotten about that. Though she was reminded every week when people made a point of complimenting her articles in the paper's latest edition.

The circulation might be a fraction of that in the city and she might not be interviewing any bold-faced names, but there was something satisfying about knowing that her work was being read, being recognized.

Sabrina had always loved the Northern Lights festival. In her mind, it was the true kick-off to summer, always happening on the first weekend in July. Even the year she'd been uncrowned for underage drinking behind the tents while still wearing her tiara and sash hadn't dampened her enthusiasm. She grabbed her purse and jacket and was waiting by the front door when Noah knocked.

"Oh, my God." She looked at him, lounging in her door frame like a cowboy from one of those hot romances she liked to read in the bath. She clapped her hands, unable to contain her delight. "You're wearing a hat." A white Stetson. Like a real cowboy.

He touched the brim uncertainly. "The crowd likes it."

"I do, too." She rose onto her toes to give him a kiss on the cheek. She couldn't resist. His hesitation and sheer hotness was a potent blend. "It's perfect."

"No." But a shy smile crossed his lips. She kissed them, too. "You look amazing."

She noted the flick of his eyes to the boots. Which was exactly why she'd worn them. Underneath his calm and proper exterior, Noah had a thing for her bright cowboy boots. Oh, he'd never say so, but she could tell.

She locked the door behind her and they headed outside. Noah's fingers caught hers and held. The birds were busy tweeting and singing to the world. Everyone looked forward to the town's annual festival, even those of the avian persuasion. Noah led her past his dark sedan and down to the detached garage, which fit only one car.

The doors made a loud rumble when he raised them. It was the first time she'd see what was inside. Sabrina blinked, her eyes adjusting to the dark interior. A dark green truck sat inside, all glossy paint and shiny chrome. An old truck. One that had clearly been lovingly restored. She looked at Noah. "Special event?"

He nodded and ran a hand along the edge of the flatbed, then patted it lovingly. "I don't take her out too often."

"It's gorgeous." Sabrina trailed a finger along the bumper. Captain Midnight would have loved it. And named it.

Noah's eyes lit up and he started talking about original paint colors and a V-8 engine and something about a flathead. The information was beyond her limited car knowledge, but the excitement in his face made her smile.

He caught himself and stopped. "I'm boring you,

aren't I? Sorry. I know most people don't get this excited about cars."

"No, I'm happy to listen." It was clear why he'd decided to go into the business he had. His love of automobiles was evident. She placed a hand on his sleeve, and the cool material of his blazer felt lovely beneath her fingers. "I can't swear I'll understand everything, but I'm happy to listen."

For a second, he just stared at her. Then he hugged her. Hard. "Thank you." She wondered how often other people let him share his true loves.

They got premium parking. One of the perks of being the town's leader. Of course, that also meant they were accosted before they even climbed out of the truck. Still, Noah came around to close the door behind her, politely listening as a crowd of people called for his attention.

But they weren't all calling for Noah. A few people stopped to tell Sabrina that they'd enjoyed her latest article in the paper. She'd decided to use some of the information gathered during her interview with Noah to write an article about Cedar Oaks, which had run in this morning's edition. She thanked them, pleased they'd taken the time to search her out.

So different than Vancouver. She shrugged off the thought. Different city, different residents, different experience. One wasn't better than the other, just different. Okay, twenty-four-hour coffee places were better...so long as she didn't have to work in them.

And the possibility of her return to Vancouver was looking up. Although nothing had changed on the paper front, she'd finally realized she needed to take a two-pronged approach to the matter. If she couldn't convince the paper to ignore Big Daddy's demands, then maybe she could convince Big Daddy to rescind them.

On Thursday, she'd received an email from the man himself. Granted, it was a terse note stating that he hadn't changed his mind, but it opened the possibility to further communication. Something she intended to take full advantage of. If he could be convinced to remove his ban on her employment, she saw no reason why the paper wouldn't take her back. She'd already sent back a friendly missive asking if they could get together via phone or in person for a chat.

Couldn't hurt.

Sabrina stayed with Noah while he made his way to the grand stage for the official opening speech. The festival had launched Friday night, but everyone knew that the real event didn't begin until Saturday. She snapped a few behind-the-scenes photos from the sidelines, knowing it was the kind of insight Trish and the readers would enjoy.

The smell of popcorn and cotton candy filled the air, the squeals of kids on the rides and the laughter of everyone enjoying themselves. She'd missed this. Not just the festival. All of it.

Well, she wouldn't stay away so long next time. She'd come back, even if she could only make it once or twice a year. She looked at Noah who finished his speech to loud applause and saw the light in his eyes when he caught sight of her. And she would come back to see him.

They didn't separate until later that afternoon. He had to award another ribbon in the baking category and she needed to get some photos that didn't include Noah. Maybe some kids on the rides, with sunny smiles and that glee in their eyes that indicated either bliss or trouble. Sometimes both.

Sabrina staked out a spot by the kiddie carousel and pulled her camera out. There was a little blonde girl screaming with laughter, her head thrown back as she went around and around. Sabrina snapped a couple of shots then looked for the parents.

She caught a glimpse of a hand waving to the girl and a flash of blond hair. Blond hair that looked familiar. She looked back at the little girl. And a smile that she recognized, too.

Crap. Marissa. She didn't need the crowd to clear and show her face to know it was her.

Sabrina rubbed her suddenly chilled hands together. She wasn't afraid to talk to Marissa. Not exactly. But it had been a long time. She'd been in town for two months and they hadn't even crossed paths.

Obviously, that had been intentional on Marissa's part, but Sabrina realized she needed to take some responsibility for their continued separation, too. She could have approached Marissa, called, dropped by her house. But she'd allowed it to slide because that was easier. Easier to just go along rather than face what would likely be a difficult reunion.

But she didn't want to be timid anymore. She was taking charge of her professional life, contacting Big Daddy and doing what she could to make things better. It was time she did the same in her personal life.

She gathered up her courage, pasted on a smile and moved toward the person who'd once been her best friend in the entire world.

"Marissa."

Marissa turned, a cheerful smile on her lips. It disappeared when she spotted Sabrina, replaced by a wary gaze. "Sabrina."

Well, at least she hadn't spun away on one heel or shouted at her. So that was a win. "How are you?"

"Fine." Marissa's tone was cautious and careful. She studied Sabrina, but said nothing more.

"Good, good." Sabrina swallowed. Such enchanting and delightful repartee. "You look great."

Marissa did look great. Her hair was the same

pale shade of blond it had been all through high school. And though she'd had four children, her slender figure was the same, too. Sabrina bet she could still fit into her prom dress. Sabrina could not. She knew because she'd tried when she'd found it in the back of her old bedroom closet. She could wiggle it over her hips, but the material was stretched tight and the zipper wouldn't move anywhere past the middle of her back.

"Thanks. You look good, too."

They eyed each other again. Awkward, uncertain. Sabrina glanced at the carousel, which was still moving in slow circles. The tiny blonde girl waved at them as she went by. "Is that your daughter?"

"Yes." Marissa's eyes softened when she looked at her daughter. "Daisy."

"She looks like you." In fact, now that she looked again, Sabrina wondered if she hadn't subconsciously recognized her. She could have been a double for Marissa at the same age, a fact Sabrina knew very well.

"That's what everyone says."

Sabrina felt a pinch in her heart. She should have been around more. She'd missed so much. Marissa's marriage, her children. The knowledge made her sad. Maybe she should have done things differently. But she couldn't go back, she could only move forward. "Do you think she'd want to be in the paper?"

"Daisy?" Marissa's eyebrows shot up.

"The feature photo for my article." She turned the view screen of her camera to Marissa to show her the shots she'd already snapped.

Marissa smiled as she flicked through the pictures. "She'd love that." She handed the camera back. "But I don't think so."

Sabrina smiled through the sinking feeling in her stomach. "I understand." She did. "Marissa, I'm really—"

"Stop." Marissa held up a hand. "I'm not ready to hear this."

"I just want to—"

"You've been gone a long time. A long time." Marissa's eyes were bright, too bright. "Just give me some space, okay?"

Sabrina felt her own eyes prickle, probably becoming dangerously bright themselves. "Of course. Whatever you need, Riss." The old nickname slipped out.

Marissa nodded. "Thank you." She blinked and then painted on a smile Sabrina knew very well as she bent to hug a blond-haired bullet that flew into her legs.

"Did you see me? I was flying!" Daisy chattered away explaining the joyous experience of riding the kiddie carousel. She wore a checked pink button-down shirt, an orange skirt and blue cowboy boots with lopsided pigtails to complete the look.

Sabrina grinned and felt the prickling slip away. How could she not in the face of Daisy's exuberant retelling? She'd be perfect on the front page of the paper. Messy pigtails and all. But Sabrina wouldn't go against Marissa's wishes. Even if she didn't need signed release forms, she wouldn't have done it.

Daisy finished telling her story and took a breath. Then she noticed Sabrina. She turned. Her smile was wide and guileless. A child who was well loved and loved in return. "Hi. I'm Daisy."

She held out her hand, gently shaking the little girl's hand. "I'm Sabrina."

Daisy nodded as though this information pleased her. "I like your boots." She looked up at her mother. "Can I have red boots?"

"You have blue boots."

Daisy looked down at the toes of her boots. "But they're not red."

"Blue boots are nice, too," Sabrina said. "I was thinking of buying some." She wasn't, but the cheery smile from Daisy and grateful blink from Marissa told her it had been the right thing to say.

"Then we could be sisters," Daisy said. "I don't have sisters. Only brothers." She wrinkled her nose. "I'm five and three-quarters. How old are you?"

"Twenty-seven."

Her mouth dropped open. "That's old."

"I know." Sabrina nodded. "I'm practically a relic."

"What's a relic?"

"Someone or something that's very old."

Daisy nodded in sympathetic understanding. "My mom's a relic, too."

Sabrina snorted, her eyes catching Marissa's. They shared a smile. It wasn't much, but it was a start.

SABRINA FOUND NOAH twenty minutes later looking like he'd rather be anywhere else but here. Oh, it wouldn't be obvious to most people. He had that faux mayor look down to a fine art, all grand gestures and warm welcomes, but the pinched look in his eyes screamed for rescue. And who was she to refuse?

She waded through the crowd toward a long table covered with a checked blue-and-white tablecloth and practically groaning under the weight of pies. The smell was heavenly. Peach and blueberry, strawberry, raspberry, traditional apple, ginger and cloves, lemon and lime. All covered in homemade pastry because no baker would dare to use store-bought. Not when there was a blue ribbon on the line.

"Well, Mayor Barnes?" A tiny white-haired woman was staring up at him, a zealous look in her eye. "Who wins?"

Clearly naming anyone other than her would be tantamount to a declaration of war. Sabrina recognized her. Miss Phillips. Her high school French teacher. She used to enforce the "only French in my classroom" rule even outside of class hours. On the plus side, Sabrina doubted there was a single person in town who didn't still remember how to ask to go to the washroom *en français*. Anything to get out of Miss Phillips's class.

Sabrina slipped through the throng until she stood as close to Noah as possible without actually bumping into him. The entire crowd quieted as he opened the envelope. And read out a name that wasn't Miss Phillips's. "Congratulations, Marie Pepper."

"Excusez-moi?"

Sabrina internally rolled her eyes as Miss Phillips turned to glare at Noah. As if he were responsible for selecting the winner rather than just announcing the names.

"So sorry to interrupt." She touched Noah's arm and felt a rush of pleasure when he turned to look at her. "Can I get a photo of the winner and the mayor? For the paper."

Miss Phillips sniffed, but didn't argue. Sabrina noted the grateful look in Noah's eye. She took her time setting up the photo, too, ensuring that everyone else began to wander away in search of something more exciting than the photo they'd see in the next edition of the paper anyway.

"Thank you," Noah said when Sabrina finally decreed they were done and Miss Phillips was no longer in the vicinity.

"Don't you mean *merci?*" She snickered and put her digital camera away.

"That, too." He rested a warm hand on her back. She shivered and sank into it. "Got a minute?"

He sighed. "Not really." But his hand didn't move.

She nodded. She'd expected the answer. In the time she'd been tailing him he hadn't had a second to rest. The poor man hadn't even had a chance to eat because every time he might have, someone else was dragging him away or wanting to talk. And he graciously acceded without complaint. Sabrina didn't know how he managed. She was tired just watching and this was only one day for her. She suspected this was pretty much his normal routine. "Let's make one then. Come on. We'll hide."

She knew she was right about his exhaustion when he didn't disagree and allowed her to lead him off the main paths. She spotted a roped-off area and ducked under the barrier.

"There now." She tugged until they were tucked out of sight, behind one of the tents, away from the pressing needs of everyone in town. "Better?"

"Definitely." Noah lifted a hand to brush her hair off her shoulder.

"You know, you can tell them no." A spark of pleasure arced through her when his hand came to rest on the side of her neck.

"It isn't that easy." Actually, it was. But clearly he got something out of the behavior, too. "How did your photo taking go?"

"Good. I snapped some pics of your niece for the paper."

Noah smiled and some of the tiredness disappeared from his face. "She must have loved that."

"She didn't know. Marissa asked that I not use them."

"Ah." Noah nodded. "So you talked."

"A little." Sabrina thought of Daisy, of all the years of Marissa's life that she'd missed. The tingling pressure behind her eyes started up again. "Do you think I'm a bad person?"

"What?" She felt the jolt go through him, but she didn't check his face. She'd prefer to keep her eyes focused on the center of his pristine white shirt, thank you very much.

"I think I might be." Why hadn't she called Marissa the minute she arrived in town? So what if it would have been hard? Marissa deserved an apology in person. Not some stuffed toy and a letter. Her heart throbbed. But maybe it was too late for any of that.

Sure, they could become polite acquaintances, exchanging friendly hellos as they passed through each other's lives, but no more than that. If you'd asked her a few months ago, Sabrina would have said that was enough. But being back, being here with Noah, it didn't seem like enough.

"Sabrina." Noah's voice was soft. Gentle and kind. Like the type of man he was. "You're a good person. You're thoughtful and smart and beautiful. Do you think I'd be with you if you weren't?"

Her chest cracked. Just cracked wide open. She looked up. "Are we together, Noah?"

The brim of his hat protected both of them from the sun and anyone who might be watching. Of course, the tall, sexy man in the white, good-guy cowboy hat, wearing jeans and a blazer was pretty recognizable even from behind.

But he didn't lean forward or bend down to kiss her. He stared at her. The breeze blew her skirt around her thighs and she shivered. But she'd be lying if she said it was solely due to the wind.

Noah kept staring. As if he was looking deep into her soul, into those dark places she had done her best to ignore for the past nine years, and seeing everything. Her throat tightened. She didn't want him to see. Didn't want anyone to see the ugliness inside her. Those bits she'd buried and tried not to think about. The bits that stayed buried when she was in the city where her friends didn't care about much beyond the next round of parties and whether or not they could get reservations at the hottest restaurants.

Not like Wheaton.

"Do you know how long it's been since I kissed a woman?" Noah asked. As though this were casual conversation, something brought up at a dinner party for everyone to join in.

Sabrina blinked. Not what she'd been expecting. She raised her chin. "In fact, I do." She recalled the feel of his mouth against hers very well. "Just this morning at my front door."

The edge of his mouth curved. "Before you."

Heat tickled up the curve of her spine. The memory of their kiss. The way his voice whispered across her skin. The way he looked at her now. Actually, the way he looked at her all the time. "No."

"Six months." He lifted his hand, ran a knuckle down the side of her cheek. It was all she could do not to turn into it and purr like a kitten.

"That doesn't sound so long. For me, it was..." She paused to think. She'd kissed some random guy at a club the night she'd lost her job. Hard to forget that night, though she'd done her best to drown it under a flood of vodka. Six months ago. And then the cute assistant from her yoga class before she'd had to drop that small luxury in order to make her rent payment. Four months ago. The barista who gave her free lattes on Tuesday mornings. Three months ago. And the trustafarian her friend had set her up with just before she'd left Vancouver. Two months ago. And now she had Noah to meet all her kissing needs. She smiled. Marissa used to call her The Kissing Bandit in high school. Seemed like little had changed. The smile fell away.

Except for everything else.

Sabrina sighed. "I've made a mess of my life."

"It can't be all bad." He lifted her hand and kissed it.

Delicate tingles raced down her arm. It would be so easy to let him tease her into a better mood. To pretend that nothing serious was going on in her life. That it was okay. That she was okay. But she couldn't do that. It was time to face certain things head-on. "I haven't been entirely honest with you. I didn't really come back to write a book about my experiences interviewing celebrities. I was fired."

Instead of the shocked outrage, the pulling back and overreaction that she'd expected, Noah simply nodded. "I figured."

A ball of panic formed in Sabrina's stomach, attempted to draw her down to her knees. She held strong and clutched Noah's hand more tightly. "Oh?" She wasn't sure she managed the light tone she was going for, but at least she hadn't collapsed into a mewling puddle. So, yay. "Does everyone know?"

If he said yes, she might collapse into that mewling puddle yet.

"No." He captured her chin when she would have turned her head. "No, they don't."

"Are you sure?"

"Positive." He slid his hand around to cup the back of her head. "I'd have heard."

His eyes were clear, like the lake her parents used to take her to when she'd been a kid and too young to complain that she didn't like camping or dirt. She knew he was telling the truth. And he was right. Her firing was the kind of secret that would have spread like wildfire.

Sabrina exhaled. "I wish I'd never written that stupid article." And she wasn't thinking of the one that got her fired. Instead, she was thinking back to the one that started it all. For all these years, she'd told herself that the end justified the means. That the loss had been worth the reward, but she should have found another way to make it. And she wouldn't have had to write snarky articles for the last nine years of her life. Articles that made readers feel superior to her subjects. Articles that pointed out a person's shortcomings and laughed at them. Articles that had slowly eaten away at her soul.

Noah's thumb massaged her neck. "I'm glad you did."

She gaped at him. "Pardon?"

"I'm glad." His gaze was clear, sure. "Because it brought you here. To me."

She looked up at him, really looked at him. He looked back. And Sabrina had the sudden sensation that he was looking at those dark little places but wasn't finding her lacking.

"Thank you for telling me why you came back."

Heat flushed her cheeks, but this time she didn't try look away. "You're welcome."

"That means something." He slid a hand down her bare arm, turning her into a pile of melty delightfulness. "That you trust me."

Sabrina could only nod. It was true. She did trust him. Good ol' stand-up, dependable Noah. How entirely different from the men she'd dated in the past.

Her body migrated toward his as he brushed a kiss across her lips, as light and feathery as a butterfly's wing. Her battered heart rose up, tried to beat its way out of her chest as she leaned closer, needing more of him. But she breathed it back into place. She looped her hands behind his neck.

Oh, she could stay here all afternoon. All night. Forever, as long as Noah was with her. She gripped his shoulders. She wouldn't let go. She didn't care what anyone else said, what they thought. This was between them.

Noah slipped his hands behind her head, anchored her and deepened the kiss. His tongue flicked out to tease the inside of her mouth. She felt the answering shudders roll through her body. Her grasp on him tightened. He was going to be an amazing lover. The care he took with her, following the silent signals of her body to intensify every feeling, every emotion.

She could fall for him. So, so easily.

Sabrina's legs grew weak and she pressed herself against him, ignoring the flutter of panic in her stomach. She couldn't stay in Wheaton. She was simply enjoying Noah's company while she was here. That was all.

But in one of those dark little places inside her, a tiny voice asked who she was trying to convince. Good thing she wasn't listening.

CHAPTER TEN

NOAH GROANED. HE FELT like a randy teenager. Was acting like one, too. But he didn't break the kiss or ease back. He couldn't. Not if there was an earthquake. Not if a fire broke out under his pristine cowboy boots. Not even if someone whipped around the corner and asked what they were doing. What they were doing was obvious; Sabrina was plastered against him, her body pliant, mouth warm and wet, the way Noah knew she would be everywhere.

His entire body stiffened at the thought, demanded attention and satisfaction.

The fact that they were making out in the backstage area of the festival wasn't lost on him. Although it was private, far more so than the main area where resident voters milled around nibbling on corn dogs and sipping soda, there were still plenty of people around. Plus, it wasn't as though security guards were stationed at the ropes to prevent unauthorized people from ducking under. No one had looked twice at him and Sabrina.

She sighed into his mouth and Noah felt a little

piece of his armor snap off and fall away. When he was with her, all his duties and responsibilities took a backseat and he could be himself. It was freeing, not thinking of himself as a brother or a son or the mayor.

He pulled Sabrina more tightly against him until their bodies were mashed together and he could feel every curve through that thin white dress she wore. A dress like that could cause a man to act out his most secret fantasies. All prim and pristine with those little decorative holes all over, teasing, making him think that if he looked close enough he might spot paradise.

Coupled with her red boots, Noah thought he should be honored for lasting as long as he had.

"Um...excuse me. Sorry to interrupt. Mayor Barnes?"

Noah could have cheerfully body checked the speaker. Driven him hard into the boards with a strong right shoulder, leaving him dazed and wondering who his own mother was. But he didn't. He kissed Sabrina once more—how could he resist when her pretty red lips were right there?—then turned his attention to the intruder behind him.

A young man—one of the volunteers, Noah knew, from the green vest he was wearing—smiled, but there was a twitch around the edges. Noah schooled his features into a more serene expression even though the primitive part of him was screaming to chase the kid off and return all his attentions to Sabrina.

The volunteer swallowed. "The singer is here. I was told you wanted to greet her personally?" He looked to his left as though praying for salvation or for someone else to come along and handle the situation.

Noah exhaled. One more responsibility to check off his list. "Be right with you."

The kid took the hint and beat it out of sight. Noah turned to face Sabrina again. She smiled up at him, and he was glad to see the pain in her eyes was gone. He reached out to touch her again, sliding his hand up her bare arm and along her exposed collarbone.

"Duty calls, Mr. Mayor."

It did. But for the first time in his life, Noah wanted to tell duty to take a hike. Just tell it to piss off, that he was his own man and he had his own life. That he didn't have to bend to everyone else's wishes for a change. That maybe he wanted a little time for himself to kiss a beautiful woman.

He didn't.

"Right." He forced his hands to his sides. If they'd had a voice they would have yowled in disappointment. Probably told him he was ruining their life and they hated him, too. "Meet you later?"

Sabrina nodded then lifted her hands to cup his

face, pulling him down until her mouth touched his. "Something to think about while you're fulfilling your mayoral responsibilities." She turned with a swish of her skirt. "Come find me when you're done."

Noah could only watch as she sauntered away, her white skirt swirling around those shapely legs, red boots taunting him. He swallowed, uncurled his fingers and reminded himself that there were duties he needed to fulfill. The unwritten contract he'd signed with the town so many years ago.

He turned to go do what was required.

After greeting the singer and her mother/manager, he had to announce the winner of the jam-and-jelly competition and stand for photos that were taken by the paper's actual photographer and not Sabrina. Then one of the lambs got loose from the petting zoo and Noah was co-opted into helping capture it. The fact that he'd never been a rancher nor lassoed an animal in his life seemed moot.

By the time the lamb was back in its pen and Noah had calmed the disturbance, the temperature was beginning to drop. The sun wouldn't set for a few hours, but it was a long, slow descent to the horizon and full darkness. Residents continued to make a point of saying hello, talk about something they'd read in the paper or ask his opinion on any number of things.

The festival lights, strings of bulbs laced through

the posts set up along the paths, were on before he managed to extricate himself long enough to grab an ear of corn. Fresh, locally grown ears that came with little cups of butter. He was practically wobbling on his feet from lack of fuel.

He hadn't even managed his first bite, one eye out for those bright red boots, when he heard someone else call his name. Or more accurately, his title. "Mayor."

He glanced to his left and spotted George Cuthbert waving at him, an imperious gesture that demanded Noah come to him now. Hell.

George was settled at the edge of the dance floor in his wheelchair with a lap blanket tucked around his legs. Noah hoped he was wearing pants. Wouldn't be the first time George had found them "too constricting."

Noah swallowed a sigh and navigated his way over. But if George announced that he was going commando, Noah was leaving and insisting his mother cut the Cedar Oaks cable package to basic.

The other residents of Cedar Oaks sat with George and were thrilled to receive personal attention from the mayor in front of the town. He resigned himself to spending a few minutes with them.

"Boy." George waved imperiously once Noah had shaken the last hand and bussed the last powdered cheek. "Come here."

Noah sighed out loud this time. His corn was definitely cold now and the butter was beginning to solidify. "What can I help you with, George?"

George crooked his finger, requesting Noah to come closer. Noah did, knowing it would be easier than refusing. "Can you sneak me a beer? Your mother says I'm not allowed."

Noah shook his head. "I am not taking the heat for that. She'd kill me."

"You afraid of your mother, boy?"

"Yes." Noah bit into the corn. It was sweet and juicy. And cold.

George snorted a laugh and fixed his blanket which had fallen slightly forward. Noah was grateful to see he was wearing a pair of khakis. "Then maybe you could pick me up one of them adult movies?"

"George, I'm not picking you up an adult movie."

"And why not?" George managed to look offended even through his leer. "A man my age has got to get his kicks where he can. This is cruel and unusual punishment."

"I won't be responsible for giving you a heart attack," Noah said. "I'd have to deal with my mother."

George grinned. "Your mother's quite a woman. She like older men? I know one who's available." He waggled his crazy eyebrows.

Noah shook his head. "You go ahead, George.

But don't come crying to me when she shuts you down."

"I don't cry. Never have. Not even when I was a baby." He shrugged. "Where's that pretty little girlie you brought around? Maybe she likes mature men."

"She doesn't." And Noah would flatten George with a single hip check if he tried anything. Wheelchair or not.

"Have you asked her?" George wanted to know. "Maybe she just didn't want to tell you, afraid it might hurt your feelings."

Noah bit back a laugh. It was best not to encourage George. "We about done here?"

"Yeah, yeah. You go on." George shooed him away. "You're cramping my style anyway." He attempted to sling his arm around Mrs. Mann who frowned and removed his arm. "You give that girlie a big kiss and tell her it's from me."

Noah would do nothing of the sort. Well, he'd give her a big kiss but he wasn't bringing George's name into the mix. Not unless he wanted to kill the mood.

Unfortunately, his stop with George and the other Cedar Oaks crew indicated to everyone else that now was a good time to chat with him. Since he still hadn't spotted Sabrina's red boots and he'd managed to finish his corn, he accommodated them.

It wasn't until the lights surrounding the stage finally went down and the young singer was introduced that Noah was finally able to escape. He headed down to the hay bales that surrounded the dance floor. Normally, he would have looked for Kyle and Marissa and shared their blanket with the kids, but not tonight.

The hay bales were packed, people teetering on the edges. Noah knew that people would have squished together, found a spot for him, but he didn't want to intrude. So he stood in the corner, sticking to the shadows and searching for Sabrina.

The honesty she'd shown him, the trust, made him wonder about her real reasons for coming back. She wasn't as distanced from the town and its residents as she liked to say. She could have worked at a coffee shop in the city, tried to get her job back at the newspaper there, but she hadn't. She'd come home to the place where she knew she'd be accepted. Maybe she knew she belonged here.

Though there were lights strung up on poles all over the festival grounds, a person had to be right under one to be recognizable. He didn't see Sabrina until she slipped her hand around his waist.

"Hello, Mr. Mayor. It's about time you showed up."

Noah smiled even though no one could see him in the dark. "I've been looking for you."

"You found me."

He hauled her up against him, lifting her onto her tiptoes and kissed her until they were both breathing hard. He didn't stop to think that although it was dark, there was a string of light above them and anyone looking would know it was him. The bright white cowboy hat gave him away.

"Well," she said when he stopped, "remind me to let you look for me more often."

He held her face in his hands. "No. I like you right here. Beside me." She smiled and it was the sweetest smile Noah thought he'd ever seen. "You know, we could sneak out of here."

"What? And keep the constituents from seeing your dance moves? I don't think so."

He laughed and caught her hands, putting them behind his back so she would mold her body to his. "I told you before, I don't dance."

"And yet, I've see you with my own two eyes. As has everyone at Cedar Oaks."

"They'll never tell."

"You're right. You've got them wrapped around your finger."

Was that what she thought? The notion surprised him, but he didn't delve further into it. "Where have you been?"

"I was around. Getting hit on by George. He wanted to know if I'd bring him a porno." Sabrina laughed. "He never stops, does he? I chatted to your mom for a while. Ran into some old high school friends. Just around."

Just around. Despite being gone for almost a decade, she'd found a way to fit right in, to slide into the fabric of the community like she'd always been there. While he ran around trying to do things for everyone else, trying to fulfill his duties as mayor so perfectly that no one would ever think he didn't belong. "I'm glad."

"Glad enough to dance?"

"Don't push your luck." But when the band played the opening notes to a popular radio hit, one Noah had heard Sabrina singing in her apartment, she started tugging him forward. Really, he had no choice but to follow. It was walk with her or be left alone in the corner. Walk or no longer feel her sweet body pressed tightly to his.

"I'm not dancing," he said as they moved closer to the stage. There were more lights over there. Extra strings hung so dancers wouldn't trip and break an ankle or worse. They illuminated her face and he recognized the sparkle of challenge in her eye.

"Okay," was all she said.

"I mean it." He tried to look firm, but didn't

think he pulled it off. Hard to look serious when he felt like laughing.

"Got it." She continued walking backward.

The dance floor, which had been packed pretty much since the set started, was getting closer. Noah could make out some familiar faces, their Stetsons and boots and Wranglers. Everyone was kicking up their heels, enjoying the music, not caring if their moves weren't perfect. If only it could be so easy.

"Mayor Barnes."

Noah turned at the call, for the first time all day grateful for his demanding constituents. Sabrina couldn't expect him to ignore a voter now, could she? Not when the election was only a couple of months away.

Sabrina slowed her steps, but didn't stop. "Noah's off duty, Mrs. Thompson," she called over Noah's shoulder.

"I can talk to her," he said.

"No." Sabrina shook her head. "You can't. You're already busy." She dragged him the last few feet so they were at the edge of the dance area and stopped. "You don't have to be on call 24/7, you know."

"I'm not." He wasn't. But he believed in making himself available for the town. Why else did one go into public office in a small town? It wasn't for the money.

Sabrina cocked her head and looked at him. Her long, dark hair spilled over her shoulder and along his arm, tickling the exposed skin at his wrist. All he wanted was to kiss her. To take her home, away from all this and just be together.

And then reality made itself known.

"Mayor Barnes. Might I have a word?"

Noah swore internally, but made sure his features were schooled into a friendly expression when he turned to see who needed him now.

"Seriously?" Sabrina asked. "Can they not see we were sharing a moment? Ridiculous."

But Mrs. Long didn't care. And she wasn't alone. There was a group barreling toward him. He recognized the intent looks on their faces. They had something to say and wouldn't leave him alone until he'd heard.

Sometimes he really wished his mother hadn't instilled such good manners into him. That he could turn away, pretend he hadn't heard or seen them and just leave. Take Sabrina's hand and escape for the rest of the night.

She shifted to stand beside him, laced her fingers through his and squeezed. "I'm pretty sure we can outrun them."

It was a testament to how long the day had been that he considered it. But then his phone would start ringing and if he didn't answer someone would come to his house to find out why. And that would be worse than just dealing with the situation now. "It's fine. I'll handle them." But he didn't let go of her hand.

He listened while Mrs. Long complained about the theft from her vegetable garden. Noah thought the birds and other small animals that lived in the forest behind her yard were the most likely culprits. But sometimes it was as much about being heard as finding a solution. Mrs. Long was a widow and lived alone on the edge of town. She probably just needed someone to drop by and have a visit. He promised to come by next week and take a look at the garden in person. And maybe talk to his mom to see if there weren't some services that Mrs. Long could take advantage of.

He felt less inclined to be patient with Jack Burns who wanted to complain about the tourists on Trout Lake, a popular fishing spot twenty minutes out of town. As though Noah could personally patrol and prevent anyone with a valid fishing license from using the spot. But he listened until Jack ran out of steam and stood, huffing and puffing, like a bear drunk on honey, though in this case it was honey lager. Noah could smell the hoppy fumes drifting off him and made a mental note to make sure Jack had a ride home.

The pair finally left, satisfied with Noah's handling of their cases, but he could see the eyes of others watching. All of them wanting or needing something.

Sabrina tugged his hand, this time leading him away from the dance floor and lights. "Let's go. You've been on duty long enough."

"I'm always on duty." A truth he didn't always see. But today had made it so painfully, blatantly obvious that anyone would notice. Even him.

"Not tonight. I'm taking you home."

But she'd been enjoying herself. The festival, the music, the almost dancing. He didn't want to take that away from her. "Did you want to stay? I'm fine."

He faced her and the concerned look in her eyes almost undid him. She wasn't thinking about herself. She was only thinking of him. It had been a long time since someone had looked at him like that. "No. I want to go home. With you." Sabrina cupped his face and rose on her toes. Her kiss was hard, strong. The meaning clear. "Take me home, Noah."

Take her home and forget all about the things constantly tugging and pulling at him. He practically carried her out of there in his haste.

CHAPTER ELEVEN

SABRINA COULDN'T KEEP her hands to herself. She found herself running her hand over Noah's knee, up his thigh, along his biceps. Brushing her fingers along his hairline, around his ear. Finally. Touching him completely. As if she'd been waiting for this moment for weeks. Which maybe she had.

Noah shot her a heated look. One that made her sizzle from the inside out. She put her hand back on his thigh, slid it a little higher. She'd have been happy to continue her upward trajectory, have a little fun on the ten-minute drive, but Noah quelled her with a hand, capturing her fingers in his.

"Wait." He raised her fingers to her lips, kissed lightly. "I want to touch you, too."

And the sizzle turned to a flame that made her wonder if she was going to melt right here on his seat. Just a puddle of white dress, red boots and burning hormones. If her city friends could see her now. Decked out like a small-town girl, no heels or smoky eye makeup in sight. Hair loose and tumbling, in dire need of a trim and shaping.

Ready to make out with the mayor in full view of anyone who might look.

Even once he let go of her hand, navigating the truck around a series of corners that led to the center of town and their shared house, his touch lingered. A memory of what had been and what was to come.

Sabrina put her hand back on his leg, allowing her fingers to dance over his knee, never going any higher than mid-thigh. Simply wanting to create the same kind of hunger in him, instill an equal desire until he let go of his perfect Mr. Mayor persona and took her.

It worked. Because by the time he pulled into the garage, he was breathing hard and he didn't even let her get out of the truck before he dragged her against him and kissed her until her breath was gone.

Oh, yes. Her stomach muscles tightened, sucked in as she pressed into him. Thank God for bench seats and gear shifts on steering wheels. She slipped one leg over him, straddling him. He stroked the side of her neck, lighting up the nerve endings before he ran his tongue along the same spot. Her body practically sang.

He flipped open the door, letting the cool night air in. It did nothing to stem the fire burning through her blood or slow the beating of her heart. She was pretty sure Noah felt the same since his hands tightened on her, touching her everywhere, fingers slipping under the neckline of her pretty white dress and stroking the skin beneath while his tongue traced a trail down her neck.

So worth coming home for.

Sabrina wriggled her hips closer, plucked the hat off his head and placed it on the seat she'd vacated so she could drag her fingers through his golden hair as his concerted and determined touch made her head fall back to catch her breath. He played her quietly, carefully and so beautifully. As though he knew just where to place his finger, his mouth, his leg to draw the greatest pleasure out of her. The edge of the steering wheel jammed into her back. She didn't care. It could fuse to her skin as long as Noah kept touching her.

A finger curving over the slope of her breast, toying with the lacy edge of her bra. A tongue pressing to her collarbone, teasing its way across to the dip at the heart of her throat. Her fingers gripped his head more tightly.

"Mmm. Nice." His breath left a hot trail across her skin. Better than nice.

She lifted her head and looked at him. He smiled. A soft, secret smile. One that spoke of the many delightful ideas he had planned for her.

"Inside?"

Sabrina hesitated. Going inside would lead to more of what they'd started, this thoughtful, careful touching. He'd slowly tug the sleeves of her dress over her shoulders, unhook her bra, slide the garments from her body and lower her onto the bed so gently that she'd barely feel the landing. Pleasurable as that would be—more than pleasurable— she wanted something else. Like what they'd had that night on the porch when Noah's eyes had darkened and flared, his tight rein on control bending and then breaking.

"No." She rubbed against him. She wanted him unleashed, wanted him to let go of that strict restraint and just feel. She tugged the sleeves of her dress down until they slid off her shoulders. She was rewarded with the sight of his eyes darkening, his fingers gripping her waist to settle her more firmly on his lap. A shaft of pleasure ricocheted through her. Yes. Right here.

She leaned forward, sucked on his bottom lip, nibbling and tasting, pushing his boundaries. Slowly at first, then more aggressively. The shoulders of her dress slipped a little farther down her arms. She felt his fingers hook into the sleeves and tug, dragging them the rest of the way and exposing the cups of her lacy bra. She pulled her arms free of the constraints, watching the way his eyes flicked lower.

Sabrina arched her back, offering herself, encouraging with her body. His breathing increased, his chest rising and falling faster with every inhale as he palmed a breast in each hand. Her nipples hardened, begged for more when he stroked a thumb across one then the other. When he lowered his mouth to follow the same path, she almost ripped the bra off herself.

Her own composure, the desire to tease him until he couldn't think, began to slide. She sucked in some cool night air, hoping it might clear her head. Allow her to regain some semblance of control. It didn't work.

Sabrina arched further, giving more of herself. Heard the growl in his throat, felt the rumble of it go through her as he took more, sucking harder and causing a strong pulse that tugged through her body.

She wanted to mark him, mess up that proper and tidy facade. Wanted him to think about nothing but here and now. He shifted his attention to her other breast. So fair, Mr. Mayor. Always making sure no one was left out.

She dug her fingers into his scalp as lust made her body quake. She shut her eyes, trying to maintain a hold on her thoughts. It was a losing battle. Even when she squeezed her lids tight, thought about her lost job, the lack of contact from the city, she just couldn't find it within herself to care. Not with Noah's relentless battering of her defense. Steadily, like a general on a battlefield, he wore down her guard, broke through the citadel she'd installed, until she clung to him, begging him with more than her body to finish her. "Please."

Just please. Finish what he'd started, ease the ache deep inside her and then she would take care of him the way he deserved.

"Please, Noah." It was more of a strangled gasp this time, the steering wheel and Noah's hands the only things keeping her semi-upright.

"Not here." He swept her out of the truck, kicking the door shut with his boot. Sabrina barely noticed how they made it up the driveway and inside the house. Didn't care. Not when Noah was slamming the door shut behind them, pushing her against it. The quiet darkness of the entry, serene and cool juxtaposed with the rasp of their breath, heightened her senses.

The hardness of his strong shoulders. The flex of muscle under her fingers. The hot wetness of his mouth on hers.

She slipped her hand inside the collar of his shirt and yanked, hearing the sound of shredded thread followed by the bounce and clink of buttons bouncing against the hardwood floor.

"You ripped my shirt." There was a hint of awe in his voice. As if no one had ever before dared to invite him out of his self-created containment. Maybe no one had.

Sabrina lifted her head to look at him. "Does that matter?"

Noah met her gaze, still and quiet. She smiled when she saw the heat of desire in his eyes. No, it didn't matter. Not even a little.

She pushed the shirt off his shoulders, running her fingers across his chest and the smattering of hair there, then followed the same path with her tongue. His fingers tangled in her hair, holding on to her. A sense of power flowed through her. Power and trust. He could easily stop her at any moment, but he allowed her to continue, let her nudge and cajole him over to the dark side.

"Sabrina." Her name was a growl on his lips. His breathing sharpened and Sabrina could hear the pounding of his heart as she worked her way down his chest. She grew warm at the thought that she was the one pushing him to the edge, couldn't wait to push him over.

He gripped her upper arms, tugged her back to standing and pushed her against the door. Even the cool wood couldn't stem the tide of heat flooding her system when he curved his fingers in the tops of her bra.

Oh, my. Oh, yes. She kept her feet under her by holding on to Noah. His shoulders so wide and strong that she could imagine them carrying the weight of the world without bending. She wanted to feel them, to feel him. She fumbled with the shoulders of his shirt, again, shoving it down his arms. Her nipples budded against the brush of his knuckles as with one sharp pull he ripped her bra down, unveiling her breasts to his gaze. The air around them heated.

Sabrina flattened her palms against the door, bracing herself for whatever Noah might do next. What she prayed he would do. The door could hold them, right? Well, only one way to find out. She flicked a glance at him, beckoning him with her eyes. *Right here, right now.*

Noah lowered his head and sucked a nipple into his mouth. His hot tongue swept across it once, twice, then slowed to roll. Oh, God. Pure pleasure shot to her core. She nearly passed out from bliss. She was so ready. So, so ready.

She lifted a leg, wrapped it around him, inviting him to see for himself. He didn't need a second invitation. He shoved her skirt up, his fingers smoothing up the inside of her thigh, cupping her heat. "Oh," Sabrina said again.

Then she didn't say anything, just let her head thunk against the door as he delved under the edge of her underwear, removing the barrier of lace and silk until there was nothing between his hand and her. Noah's hands were magic. So was his tongue. She'd insist it be gilded for posterity if that didn't mean he could never lick her again.

He brought her right to the edge, stripping off her dress and undergarments until she wore nothing but her red boots and a smile. Who knew Mr. Mayor had it in him?

"Please," Sabrina managed, her fingers digging into his shoulders. The door had been useless, letting her slide halfway to the floor while Noah worshipped her body. She'd grabbed him and held on for dear life. "Just. Now."

He slowed, looking up at her. His shirt was gone, lying in a crumpled heap somewhere on the floor, his hair mussed from its usually smooth style. He looked good enough to eat and Sabrina planned to. "No."

"Yes." If she had to throw him on the floor and ride him cowgirl style? Well, she was totally up for that. And so was he, she knew.

"No." He shook his head and stood up. So controlled, he was practically shaking with it. What must it be like to curb all impulse, to place the needs of others before your own and to deny those emotions that cried to be released? Exhausting. Good thing she wasn't like that.

A drip of sweat ran down his chest, along the ridged muscles of his abdomen. Sabrina dipped her head and licked it off him. *Yum.*

"Sabrina." Noah's voice was scratchy.

She licked him again, liking the feel of his body flexing and clenching beneath her mouth. She opened the top button of his jeans and slid the zipper down. He groaned but didn't stop her.

There now. Wasn't this better? She certainly thought so. She smiled when he sucked in a deep breath as she worked his jeans and underwear over his hips.

"Seriously," he said. His hands ran over her back, smoothing and stroking. Sabrina didn't pause. There was no way he could possibly want to stop. His body language said otherwise. "Not like this."

"Like what?" She stroked a finger up the length of him once and then back down, gratified by the wheeze in his lungs. Wasn't so sure now, was he? Then she took him in her mouth using her tongue to feel every inch.

"Holy mother of—" Noah's hands stopped stroking, gripped her head, his fingers tangling and pulling the long strands. Sabrina didn't care. She *so* didn't care.

She sucked and rolled her tongue around him. He moaned above her. Her entire body flamed at the sound. This was much better than her fantasy. And why had they waited all these weeks?

And then he stopped her, using what she assumed must be superhuman willpower to back away and pull her to her feet. "Not here. Bedroom."

"Noah—" But whatever complaint she might have mustered was lost in the whirl of being picked up, lifted as if she weighed nothing and carried to her front door. For that alone the man deserved the ride of his life.

He'd managed to find her keys somehow and opened her door. They tumbled inside, a tangle of naked need and arms and legs until they reached her bedroom and the call of the mattress awaiting them.

Sabrina had been trying to drive him mad, to make him lose some of that much vaunted control, but somewhere along the way she'd lost her own, as well. All she wanted was Noah. Now. Everything and everyone else could wait.

"I wanted to take this slow," Noah said, looming over her on the bed. "Take my time."

"I like this," she told him, grabbing for the box of condoms she'd placed in her nightstand after their porch encounter. She stroked him with her hand, enjoying the feel of the velvety skin beneath her hand and the hiss of breath from Noah. She didn't want the controlled, never-rattled Mr. Mayor. She wanted him mussed and messy and not mayorly at all. "Let go, Noah."

Another drop of sweat trickled down his chest. She stretched up to follow the trail, her hand still stroking.

"Sabrina."

"Let go," she told him again. She rolled the condom on for him, then stretched out on the bed and spread her legs. He stood before her so tall and proud and hard. His eyes flicked down her body, up to her face, what he wanted warring with what he thought he should do. She made the decision for him.

There would be plenty of time to take it slow later. Plenty of time for him to worship her body however he wanted. But she needed him to take her now. She reached out and guided him inside her. He exhaled, low and slow, lowering himself on top of her. His forehead pressed to hers and she could feel the sheen of sweat there. But he was still so careful, bracing his arms around her so he didn't put any of his weight on her, letting her adjust to him.

Sabrina was tired of waiting. She grabbed his shoulders to anchor herself, then rounded her hips so he was fully sheathed. A small sigh escaped her lips. *Yes.*

He hissed her name through his teeth. His jaw clenched, muscles rigid. He hung on by a thread. One thin thread that Sabrina relished snapping. She tilted her hips upward, cradling him more firmly while her body opened around him. She wanted him. All of him. Now.

But Noah remained above her, holding himself just slightly apart. His arms propping his weight off her, that control still firmly in place. She wriggled against him, rubbing her nipples against his chest. He shuddered at her touch, but didn't break as he began to move. Slow and sweet. His body rocking gently into hers.

The friction created a lovely little buzz that Sabrina knew she could get off on. It would be gentle lovemaking full of polite orgasms and gasps that would never be heard outside this room. He'd make sure she came at least twice before letting himself do the same. She'd be sated afterward and they'd cuddle, murmuring soft words of gratitude. But this wasn't about her. It was about them.

Delicate shivers began to radiate through her as Noah continued his slow, thoughtful strokes designed to give her maximum pleasure. Lovely as it was, she was looking for something else. And there would be nothing thoughtful or slow about it.

She wrapped her arms around him, grabbed his world-class butt and forced him to increase the tempo. He jerked and tried to bring things back to a careful, gradual pace. She bit his shoulder.

"Sabrina." He sounded like he was being smothered. "I can't hold on if you keep this up."

"Good." She raked her nails up his back and grabbed his face. "Let go."

Noah's eyes centered on hers, the pupils dilating until they obliterated the bright blue iris. Checking, even now when they were locked together, to make sure this was okay, this was what she wanted. Did the man never put himself and his own needs first?

Well, he would now. He'd gifted her with acceptance, giving her the interview she needed, taking her to the festival and allowing her to feel that she still had a home in Wheaton. She might not plan to stay, she might not visit often, but he'd shown her that it was possible.

Sabrina's heart squeezed. She would give him the gift of freedom. The ability to be himself with her, the safety to know that she wanted to see him. All of him. Not just the naked parts. But the messy hurts and childhood scars that marked everyone in some way or another. She wanted to see those parts.

She placed her hands around the back of his neck, tugged him toward her so their lips could touch. A hot but gentle kiss. The kind he'd been pushing for all night. She felt the droop of disappointment in his shoulders before they returned to their stolid, stoic position. If this was what she offered, he would take it.

But she could tell it wasn't what Noah wanted. Not deep down in the parts he kept hidden from everyone. Probably even from himself.

And Sabrina knew she had him. One tiny nudge and he would let go, free the bad boy that lived behind those protective walls.

It almost killed her to do it, but she placed her hands on his shoulders and pushed. He frowned as their mouths separated, followed by their bodies. The ache of loneliness surrounded her as he slipped half out of her. But she was wagering that it wouldn't be for long.

Sabrina stopped him when only his tip remained within her. "Noah?"

His lips were pressed tight together. Yet another display on his well-developed control. He didn't say anything, a growl the only thing that came from his throat. Right on the edge. Right where she wanted him.

"Do you want me?"

His scowl was her only answer. He nodded.

"Then you're going to have to take me." She nudged lightly at his shoulders again, making her meaning clear. If he wouldn't take, then he'd get nothing.

Noah sucked in a strangled breath.

She lowered her hands to her breasts, pushed them together, offering him the juicy red tips. His eyes flared, so dark that the blue was almost invisible. "Take me, Noah. Now."

He hesitated a moment. Long enough for her to worry that she'd guessed wrong, that his training to be the golden boy would override his innate desires and he'd slide out of her and apologize. And then contentment settled over his features, followed by a slow, wicked smile.

It was a secret bad-boy smile that announced he relished the idea of letting go, he'd just been afraid to do so before. Sabrina's temperature rose and then spiked as he captured her wrists, brace-leted them in his fingers and jerked her arms above her head.

Noah's gaze was no longer appraising and thoughtful. It was predatory. A man who knew what he wanted and was going to take it.

Her nipples hardened under his hungry gaze and her entire body throbbed. When he sucked one hard bead into his mouth, tonguing the tip until it was a knot of pleasure that slammed waves through her body, she thought she might pass out. Now it was Sabrina who hissed his name.

He shifted, using one hand to hold her wrists captive, using the other to push her knees up, open-ing her more fully. He teased her, not going any deeper, leaving her with just the hint of what would come. When he was ready, when he wanted, and not a minute before. Her back bowed, offering ev-erything and more to him.

Her mind flooded with desire when Noah drove home, all the way inside, leaving no question as to what he wanted. Her.

The bed thumped against the wall as his hips bucked into hers. An endless, delicious pounding. She ached to grab him, to feel those hard muscles as he worked in and out of her. To score him with her nails, so that everyone would see he was hers. But his hold on her wrists was firm and noth-ing she did loosened his grip. She was caught, bound completely, bared for him to do whatever he wanted.

She was drowning in him, in them. He pounded harder. The bed hitting the wall at a faster pace. Good thing there were no neighbors to complain. Sabrina raised her knees higher, welcoming him inside, needing more of this, more of him. She wanted whatever he had to give.

Bolts of pleasure began to shoot out from her core, making her gasp. She tried to tell him more. Or harder. Deeper. But the connection between her brain and mouth seemed to have been severed and all that came out was a throaty moan as he slid into her again and again until she was delirious with need and with the desire to come. She was so close, hovering on the verge between pleasure and pain. Her body tensed but didn't release.

He moved faster, pumped harder, reading her body's signals. Thank God. Release shimmered, so close yet so far. She could have cried. But even as she craved the liberation, she hungered for more. For Noah to stay with her until they were lost together.

Her fingers curled and flexed. She wanted to hold him. She wanted him to keep her just as she was. She felt feverish and cold. Starved and sated. She'd started out intent on forcing him to lose his infamous control and instead she was the one on her knees. Well, on her back.

Another moan eased from her throat. A secret call from a place hidden deep within her. Noah slipped a hand between their bodies, rubbed his thumb across her. He heard what she needed, what she didn't even know.

Sabrina looked at him, stared deep into his dark eyes, and silently begged him to come with her as the edges of her vision began to flicker. Her body tightened around his, drawing him down to her. He reached up, lacing his fingers through hers. Together. United as one, they broke in a long, pulsing release.

And for a moment, there was nowhere else she wanted to be.

CHAPTER TWELVE

NOAH SUCKED IN A BREATH, then another. Because when a man had just done what he had, a breath or two was in order.

"Hey."

He looked down and saw Sabrina smiling up at him, her legs still hooked around his back. They fit just right. Like they'd been made for each other. Here, in her arms—and legs—he felt at home.

She stretched and her pretty rosebud nipples rubbed against him. He hardened again even though he was no longer sixteen. He wanted to suck on those nipples, tease them until they were hard and at attention, demanding he never stop. Given the chance, he might not.

But that couldn't happen. Someone or something would intrude, calling on him and his time. As common sense returned, shattering the carnal bliss, he realized he was probably crushing her. He moved to shift off, but she wrapped her legs tighter.

"No, just stay."

"I'm too heavy," he pointed out, lowering himself onto his elbows.

She sighed and closed her eyes, wrapping her arms around him. "Don't care." Her voice was sleepy, slow. As though she'd be happy to stay like this, too.

Hope banged against his ribs. He ignored it. "Sabrina."

She opened one eye and peered at him. "Seriously? You're going to fight me on this?"

He blinked. She was right. What was he thinking? The choice between staying surrounded by Sabrina's warmth and softness or rolling off and flying solo was not a difficult one. But Noah adjusted his weight so that he wouldn't turn her into a pancake. Her curves matched the hard lines of his own body, soft where he was hard, forgiving where he was not. He lowered his face into the slope between her chin and shoulder and shut his eyes.

Just for a couple of minutes. Two, three at the most, and then he would roll off her. It was the last thought he had before the morning sun woke him up.

For a fraction of a second, Noah wasn't sure where he was. The sun didn't come into his bedroom at this angle. His sheets were navy blue, not white. And there was very rarely a woman in his arms these days.

They'd shifted in the night, turning so they were on their sides. Sabrina had one leg thrown over his hips, her arm resting on his waist. His arms were wrapped securely around her as though he'd been trying to prevent her from going anywhere in the night. Not a bad plan.

But his back was stiff and his knee, the one he'd wrecked in college, burned. He needed to get up and stretch them out. Warm up so that he didn't spend the day hobbling around like an old man. Although Sabrina did seem to get a kick out of George Cuthbert.

He studied her while she slept, her lips pursed as she exhaled. They looked sweet and innocent now, but he knew just what kinds of naughty things they were capable of. Very naughty, very wonderful things.

Suddenly, his stiff back and bad knee didn't feel quite so pressing. Not when she was wrapped around him, all soft and warm. He brushed the hair off her face, but she didn't wake up. Just rolled more firmly against him.

Her scent surrounded him, that spicy sweetness. He reveled in it, nuzzling the side of her neck, but she merely sighed and snuggled more securely in his arms. He was content for the moment.

Noah had been in women's beds before, and had them in his, too. He was thirty-one and liked sex, so it was expected. He'd never kicked anyone out of his bed or rushed home once the sex was over. No, that would be rude. He'd stay, cuddle if that's what she wanted, call the next day and set up another date. Even when he already knew it wasn't going anywhere, he was a perfect gentleman.

Long, lingering kisses that were meant to calm and soothe. Careful caresses and polite sex.

He trailed a lazy finger up and down Sabrina's back. There'd been nothing polite about what they'd done last night. A smug satisfaction joined the contentment running through him. This town had been good to him over the years. But Sabrina was better.

He flipped onto his back, carrying her with him. She mumbled something, then curled around him. He laid there for a while, letting the sun bathe his face and Sabrina bathe his hidden hurts. Hurts he would never admit to.

She wasn't going anywhere for the time being, which was exactly what he needed.

WHEN NOAH WOKE UP for the second time that morning, the sun was no longer in his eyes but his knee was on fire.

He extricated himself from Sabrina's warm curves even as he longed to crawl right back under the covers. However, it wasn't just about his sore knee, but obligations for the day. He had more duties at the festival, including the closing ceremonies.

Their clothing lay scattered throughout the entry, causing Noah to smile as he strode through, slowly allowing his knee to loosen with the careful movement. The hot shower in his own bathroom eased the aches in his knee and lack of sleep from the night before. Not that he was complaining.

He tossed on a pair of blue jeans and started up his coffee machine. The coffee perked to readiness while he cleaned up the entryway then padded into Sabrina's apartment.

She remained blissfully unaware of his presence while he folded her clothing and put her red boots in her closet. So much for those city instincts she'd claimed on the night of the porch vandalism. A thief could enter, clean the place out, and she'd probably just hug her pillow more tightly.

It wasn't until he waved one of the freshly poured cups of coffee under her nose and kissed her on the neck that she finally surfaced to wakefulness.

"Hrmm?" Or semi-wakefulness. She stretched, the sheet outlining her body and then opened her eyes to look at him. She smiled and Noah felt his heart swell.

"Good morning."

"Rugfen." Sabrina sat up, the sheet slipping off her shoulders and revealing her body in all its glory. Noah stared, struck silent. His fingers aching to touch. She took the coffee from his hand and hitched the sheet up to her armpits.

Disappointment washed through him. There should be a law against covering up that kind of magnificence. As mayor, he should look into that. His plan lasted about two seconds, the amount of time it took for her to sip the coffee, place the cup on the nightstand and then reach out to wrap herself around him.

The sheet slipped to her waist again and her bare chest brushed against his as she pulled him back down onto the soft mattress. "Too early. Sleep now."

Noah balanced himself on an arm above her, ran a finger down her velvety cheek. Oh, he loved that soft skin. Wanted to show his devotion to it again this morning. Was painfully tempted if the status of his straining jeans was any indication.

"I can't," he said. His festival duties were looking more and more like a bother. "I have to go and be mayor." He wasn't due at the site for a few hours, but he had other obligations to see to before then.

Sabrina pouted, those pretty lips looking eminently suckable as she turned them toward him. "I should have made you sound incompetent in my article." Her arms twined around his back, stroking up and down. "Then you wouldn't get re-elected and I wouldn't have to share you."

The idea wove through him, scary and exhilarating. He brushed it away. It would never happen. He would win the election and remain mayor. There was no other option. Not for him and this town.

"Of course, then I couldn't call you Mr. Mayor." Her lips grazed his ear. "And there's something terribly sexy about that." She stretched against him, all warm, supple womanliness, and he thought he might pop the button on his jeans.

"You're doing that on purpose."

"Guilty." She rubbed again like a contented kitty.

Noah wondered what would happen if he didn't turn up at the festival. If he stayed in bed all day with Sabrina and let someone else handle things for a change. His phone would start ringing off the hook, someone would come by looking for him and word would eventually get around about exactly what he was doing. He sighed and pushed himself off her though his body wept at the loss of contact.

Sabrina didn't pull the sheet up to cover herself this time. His mouth went dry and he picked up her coffee.

"If you stay," she said, drawing a hand up and over the curve of her hip, "we can share more than coffee."

He'd love that, was more than halfway to saying yes when his sense of duty kicked in. "How about we do something later tonight?"

"Like what?" Sabrina plucked the coffee back out of his hand and sipped.

Noah tried not think about how that mouth had sipped on him last night. He ignored the bountiful feast for his eyes, kept his gaze on her face and the little smirk there. She knew exactly the effect she was having on him, the little minx. He'd pay her back later. "You'll have to wait and see."

Then he removed the cup from her hands and placed it carefully on the bedside table. The bed shifted under his weight as he lowered himself over her, only his blue jeans separating him from her heat. And then only until she helpfully peeled them off for him.

He was only a little behind schedule when he finally tore himself free.

"NOAH." KYLE BLINKED when he opened his front door. "I didn't expect you until later."

Although Noah was on duty at the festival today, the family still intended to meet for their weekly Sunday dinner. He hadn't planned to make a pit stop at his brother's this morning, but after last night he felt he needed to. He couldn't just go off to the festival and then show up at dinner as though everything was the same as it had always been.

"You have a minute?" The sun beat down on the back of his neck and the starched collar of his shirt.

"Sure." Kyle pushed the door wider. "You want to come in?"

Noah glanced around for the family. Being interrupted by the kids or Marissa was not part of the plan.

Kyle read his wariness and grinned. "They're out. Marissa took them to the festival about an hour ago. They won't be back for a while."

Noah's shoulders relaxed. "How did you get out of going with them?"

"I promised I'd be on morning kid duty for the next two weekends." His grin widened. "Want to help?"

"Uh, no." Noah stepped into the house and followed his brother to the kitchen. There was no warm coffee in the pot or any coffee at all. As he'd done many other times in this house, Noah opened the cupboard and dug out the grounds, setting up the machine and turning it on before facing his brother.

"So what's up?" Kyle lounged in one of the kitchen chairs, completely at ease with himself and his life. Noah envied him. Kyle never worried about his place or how he fit. He just was.

Noah shook the feeling off. He'd made his place and it might not feel as comfortable as Kyle's or have come as easily, but he'd worked hard for it. "It's about Sabrina."

Kyle's eyebrows rose, but he didn't say anything. One of the many things Noah loved about his baby brother was that Kyle always waited to hear the full story before speaking and rarely passed judgment.

Noah took a calming breath and dove into the deep end. "Were you two serious?"

The question had been eating at him since he stood under the spray of the shower and realized it was something they'd never discussed. Something he should have asked weeks ago, right after he kissed Sabrina on the porch. Noah might have told himself that he could keep his distance from her, but it was obvious now he'd just been fooling himself. Actually, it was obvious that he'd held back, afraid of what Kyle might say. Because if Kyle had felt uncomfortable about Noah seeing Sabrina, then Noah would have felt duty-bound to stay away.

He swallowed. Kyle might still ask him to stop seeing her, but Noah was no longer sure that he could. Nothing Kyle had ever said or done gave him the impression that he had any lingering feelings or that he thought of Sabrina as anything more than an old friend. But that was before Noah had slept with her.

His fingers tingled and his stomach rolled. If this was a problem, he wasn't sure what he would do. He'd never do anything to hurt his family, but the idea of walking away from Sabrina hurt, too.

"Me and Sabrina?" Kyle's eyebrows assumed their standard position. He shook his head. "No. We were never serious."

Noah hadn't realized how much tension he'd been holding until it was released. "Good."

A smile appeared on his brother's face. "You like her?"

"I do." Simple and straightforward, the way they always were with each other.

Kyle nodded and clapped his hand against the table as he pushed himself to a standing position. "Good. She's a great girl. Is the coffee ready?"

"I think so." As if there was nothing unusual about Noah walking into the house to talk about a relationship.

"You going to bring her to dinner tonight?" Despite his laid-back attitude and ability to go with the flow of those around him, Kyle had an unerring sense of discerning other people's motives and wants.

"I was considering it." Noah poured two cups then added a splash of cream to both. The thought had popped into his head about the same moment he realized Kyle wasn't bothered by him dating Sabrina.

"You should." Kyle nodded and took a hearty gulp of the coffee Noah handed him.

Noah took a gulp of his own coffee, then broached the next topic. "You think Marissa will be okay with it?"

Kyle put his coffee down. "If you're serious about Sabrina, she will be. We were all close in high school. No reason we can't be again."

Like it was nothing, no big deal. Noah studied

his brother. There was no guile in his eyes. Kyle wasn't covering anything up or saying what he thought Noah wanted to hear. He just was.

Noah smiled. "Then we'll see you tonight."

CHAPTER THIRTEEN

"WHEN YOU ASKED if we could do something to-night, this was not what I had in mind," Sabrina said as Noah piloted the car toward Kyle and Marissa's house. She'd been thinking more along the lines of dinner out or having a relaxing evening at home. The thought of heading over to her former best friend and ex's house for a family dinner had never crossed her mind. But here she was, show-ered, scrubbed and lotioned to within an inch of her life.

Her stomach gurgled, but it was from nerves rather than hunger although the pie on her lap did smell delicious. She was grateful that her mother had happened to have all the ingredients to make her town-famous blueberry-and-lime pie. One that Marissa had always loved.

Sabrina didn't know why that had been the first call she'd made after she'd agreed to Noah's out-rageous suggestion. Why hadn't she called him back to explain that this idea was a bad one? She and Noah had only slept together once. Well, okay, more than once, but one night. It was too soon to start introducing each other to the family. The fact that they already knew each other's families was moot. The step of joining a family dinner was a big one, a sign that this was the start of something permanent.

She clutched the pie plate tighter. And yet, she hadn't said any of that, hadn't made a peep about it. No, she'd taken her time getting ready, treating this as if it was her first time meeting the family and wanting to make a good impression. Then she and Noah had driven to her parents' together to pick up the pie, which meant being invited inside and staying for a drink since, according to her mom, the pie wasn't finished baking.

Sabrina wasn't naive enough to think that had been an accident. She could practically see the hope circling her parents' heads, cartoony white doves and stars, filled with the optimism that perhaps Sabrina might stay in town. Forever. And she'd done nothing to quell the idea.

"Would you rather not go?"

Sabrina realized she was frowning and schooled her features into a more neutral expression. Wrinkles were no one's friend. Plus, she'd been invited. It wasn't as if she was crashing a party, as likely to get an escort out the door as a welcoming smile. But the lump in her throat didn't appear to get the message. And as they pulled up outside a pretty blue-and-white house, she suddenly had a wild desire to ask Noah to turn the car around. She could feed him the pie in bed, so it wasn't as if it would go to waste.

He turned the car off and faced her, placed a warm hand on her knee. Sabrina felt some of her anxiety ease or at least loosen the chokehold it had on her. "If you really don't want to do this, we won't."

But she could see the look in his eye. The one that told her this was important to him, that he wanted to go to dinner with her by his side. And she couldn't deny him that.

She exhaled. So what if she was nervous? She'd been nervous before and survived. She had no reason to think the dinner would be anything but lovely. Ellen would be kind and gracious as always, Kyle had given no indication that he had any problems with her and even Marissa had been courteous when turning down her request to use Daisy's picture.

She put her hand on Noah's, drew strength from his stability, his solidness. "I want to." And when his face lit up, she realized she meant it.

Daisy came down the porch steps before Sabrina even managed to get out of the car. "Hi, Uncle Noah!" She waved madly like there was a chance they might miss her when she was wearing a pair of black-and-white striped tights, her blue cowboy boots, a gauzy purple skirt and a lime-green T-shirt. She turned her cheerful smile on Sabrina. "Hi." But when she looked at Sabrina's feet a frown swept over her tiny features. "Where are your boots?"

Sabrina looked down at her feet, too. She'd selected a pair of gold wedges that added a little city fabulousness to her baby-blue vintage dress. "I didn't wear them today."

"I like your boots."

"I do, too. But these shoes are pretty."

Daisy put her hands on her hips and studied them, giving them a good once-over before nodding. "They are pretty. Can I try them on?"

"No, Daisy." Noah came around the car and took the pie from Sabrina's hands. "You have your own shoes."

She looked down at her blue cowboy boots. "But they aren't red." Her mournful tone spoke of the trials and labors she suffered on a daily basis.

"You'll live," Noah told her and placed a light hand on Sabrina's back as the rest of the family poured out the front door.

Both Ellen and Kyle greeted her warmly with acknowledgments of how good it was to see her again and how happy they were she'd decided to join them. She was introduced to Paul, the recipient of that long-ago-sent stuffed dog, who watched her quietly and looked away when she smiled at him. Scotty, the toddler, was more effusive in his greeting and ran to her legs, lifting his arms in the universal toddler language for "pick me up." So she did, surprised at how comforting she found his easy acceptance and warm hug.

Marissa remained at the top of the steps holding the baby. Timmy, Sabrina recalled from stories Noah had told. But she wasn't frowning or giving any other sign that she was unhappy and she welcomed Sabrina graciously enough as she herded the family back into the house.

Sabrina navigated the steps carefully, still carrying Scotty and making sure she listened as Daisy chattered on about her day. "And then we went on the smashing cars."

"Bumper cars," Paul clarified and then ducked his head when Sabrina looked at him.

"Bumper cars," Daisy repeated and then continued her story of the best day ever. Apparently, Marissa had taken all the kids back to the festival this morning to go on more rides.

By the time Sabrina got through the front door, she felt like she'd been part of the crowd her whole life instead of less than five minutes and her cheeks were beginning to hurt from smiling. It was a good hurt.

Conversation was easy, moving from the upcoming election to the festival's closing ceremonies—which Noah had seen to just before he picked Sabrina up—from the local junior hockey team's chances to Daisy's excitement about starting first grade in the fall. And Sabrina fell into the amiable nature of her once-closest friends as though she'd never left.

But there was a cool side to Marissa's words and behavior. Nothing that could be deemed rude or even unfriendly—more cautious. Sabrina couldn't blame her; she'd do the same in Marissa's position.

She followed her into the kitchen after dinner, the first time Marissa had been alone since she'd arrived. "Marissa?"

Her former best friend glanced over her shoulder and nodded politely at the plates and cutlery Sabrina had carried from the table. "You can put the dishes by the sink. I'll do them."

"I'll help." Sabrina put everything down on the counter and returned to the dining room to get the rest.

Marissa had already filled the sink when Sabrina came back and was up to her elbows in sudsy water. "You're a guest," she told Sabrina. "You don't clean. Go enjoy yourself."

"I am enjoying myself." Sabrina didn't want to be a guest. She took the dish towel from the oven-door handle and began drying the plates Marissa had set in the rack. She held her breath, but Marissa didn't say anything else, simply returned to washing and Sabrina let the breath ease from her lungs.

She wanted her friendship with Marissa back. She hadn't known how much she'd missed it until now.

"I'm sorry." She blurted out the words before Marissa had a chance to stop her. "Really sorry."

But Marissa merely turned to look at her with no change of expression. "I appreciate your apology."

Wait. That's it? Sabrina hadn't expected the cool and dismissive acceptance. Not that she'd dreamed Marissa would jump up and down or throw her arms around her, either, but something more than a civil tone and courteous smile. Her chest tightened and some of the good cheer from the evening skittered away. "I should have said that a long time ago, should have come back a long time ago."

Marissa nodded and continued cleaning.

Sabrina barreled on. "So, I just wanted to tell you. That I'm sorry. And I hope we can be friends again."

Marissa sighed. "I don't know if I'm ready for that, Sabrina. The friends part." She stopped washing and turned so there was nothing between them but the dish towel Sabrina still held. "You've been back for a while."

"I have." Sabrina folded and then unfolded the cloth.

"So why did it take you this long to say anything to me? If you really want to be friends?"

Sabrina exhaled. It was a fair question and one

she wasn't sure how to answer. She hadn't purposely set out to avoid Marissa, though that's how it looked from the outside. There had been myriad reasons for not getting in touch with Marissa earlier, but only one truth.

"I was afraid. I didn't know how you'd react." And Sabrina hadn't been sure she could stand the thought of being snubbed by someone she'd once been so close to. Not when everything else in her life had been lying in shambles around her.

The hard line bracketing Marissa's mouth softened for a moment. "So what's changed?"

She had. But Sabrina didn't say that. She put the dish towel on the counter. Her tongue felt dry, as if she'd downed a jar of peanut butter instead of a delicious roast with all the fixings.

Marissa's face got tight again. "Because to me, it feels like you're only being nice to get in good with Noah."

"No." Sabrina's tongue came unstuck from the roof of her mouth, shocked that Marissa had so badly misinterpreted her olive branch. "That's not it."

Marissa raised an eyebrow and a wave of guilt swept through Sabrina. Of course Marissa would think that. Had she been given any reason not to? Sabrina cursed her earlier fears. If she'd tried with Marissa when she'd first come back, they wouldn't be having this conversation now.

"I thought it would be easier if I stayed away," she said. "Let you set the tone since I didn't think I'd be here long." It still surprised her to look at the date and realize she'd been in town since April and it was now the beginning of July. Almost two months. It surprised her more to realize that she wasn't desperate to leave. "But obviously, that didn't happen."

"Why are you still here then?"

Sabrina ignored the question. An old reporter's trick. Don't answer the question asked, answer the one you want to. "I don't know how long I'll be here, but I'd like it if we could spend some time together while I am. And not because of Noah. Because I miss you."

Marissa blinked and her fingers flexed. "Do you really? You haven't contacted me in nine years."

"You haven't contacted me, either," Sabrina pointed out. "But maybe we could start fresh."

"I'm still not sure I can trust you." Marissa spoke slowly as though she was weighing each word carefully before saying it aloud. "You hurt me before. How do I know this isn't some trick to get me to open up to you so you can use it in another article?"

"I won't." Sabrina didn't know how she could prove her sincerity, so she just tried to put as much sincerity into her tone as possible. "I have no reason to do that, but I wouldn't anyway. I just want some of what I lost back."

There was soreness in the back of her throat. She didn't deserve absolution from Marissa and her family, but she wanted it anyway.

"I won't push you," she told Marissa. "But I really would like to be friends again. Maybe a coffee one day?"

"Maybe." But Marissa's lack of enthusiasm made her think it was unlikely to happen.

Sabrina had known it was a long shot, didn't even know what had made her follow Marissa into the kitchen and start the conversation, but she still felt disappointed. She offered Marissa a weak smile, the best she could do under the circumstances, and returned to drying the dishes.

SABRINA DIDN'T SAY MUCH on the drive home, Marissa's words still swimming through her head. Was any chance at a friendship truly over between them? And what did that mean for her relationship with Noah? She'd seen how important his family was to him. Would he want to continue seeing her, knowing that his sister-in-law didn't like her?

Good thing she had no plans for permanent relocation or she would have found herself in a real conundrum. As it was she just felt resigned. She exhaled long and low.

"You're quiet." Noah reached over and put his

warm hand on her leg again. She really shouldn't get so much comfort from it. "Everything okay?"

"Fine," she said. Sabrina wouldn't tell Noah what she and Marissa had discussed in the kitchen. She didn't know how he'd react, but it didn't matter. She wouldn't force him to choose between her and his family, not even accidentally. "Just tired, I guess."

Mr. Lawrence was out watering his grass, his belly hanging over his plaid shorts. He waved as they drove by. Sabrina waved back, trying to remember the last time anyone in Vancouver had contacted her of their own accord. The day had cooled and Sabrina shivered, wrapping her arms around her torso. Maybe they were all busy, living their fabulous city lives, but that shouldn't mean they forgot about her entirely.

She let her head fall back against the headrest. Clearly, she hadn't gotten enough sleep last night. It was the only explanation for why she had a sudden acidic taste in her mouth when she thought about returning to her life in the city.

Sabrina reminded herself that everything would look better and brighter in the morning. Maybe her editor would have some good news or Big Daddy would come around. Maybe, not likely, since as of today the last missive she'd received from her editor had been terse, informing her that he was well aware of her situation and would let her know if anything changed. And Big Daddy hadn't bothered to contact her at all. But it was all still possible.

She chewed her lip. Things were good here for now. She had a job with the local paper, a beautiful apartment and an extremely handsome man in her life. She should really focus on everything that was right with her life, not everything that was wrong.

She put her hand on top of Noah's and breathed in and out. By the time they arrived at the house, she didn't feel so tired. Not when Noah's hand slipped up her leg with each passing mile.

And by the time they walked into her apartment and he locked the door behind them, Sabrina wasn't thinking about anything but the sexy man in front of her and the heated look in his eye.

CHAPTER FOURTEEN

SABRINA WAS WIPING DOWN the counter at the coffee shop when the front door jangled open. She glanced up. It was close to eleven on Saturday morning and the end of her shift. The early-bird customers had long since cleared out and the second rush wouldn't start until midafternoon.

She blinked when she saw who walked through the open door and up to the counter with a half smile on her pretty face.

"Marissa." Sabrina hadn't seen her since that conversation after dinner more than a week ago. She curled her fingers in the rag then realized what she was doing and tossed it before turning to run her hands under the sink. "What can I get you?"

But Marissa didn't look up at the attractive menu board that hung at the top of the wall and she didn't place an order. "I read your article on Noah."

Sabrina felt a hiccup of nerves followed by a tentative trickle of hope. The article she'd written about Noah's day at the festival had run in this morning's weekend edition of the *Wheaton Digest*. Sabrina was pleased with her work, not just the insight she'd been able to share, but how she'd been able to show him as he really was. A leader who cared deeply about the town and the residents in it. Truly, the work was something she was proud to have her byline attached to. "What did you think?"

While a part of her knew she shouldn't ask a question she wasn't sure she wanted to hear the answer to, she did anyway. Noah had liked it. She'd gotten up early to make sure she got to the coffee shop on time for her six o'clock start, and when she'd returned to the bedroom after her shower, he'd been propped up against the headboard with the paper beside him and a smile on his face.

Then, because he'd insisted on showing her just how much he liked the piece, he'd almost made her late. A small smile twitched on her lips. Being late would have been totally worth it.

But then Noah was predisposed to like her work. Marissa was not.

"It was good." The half smile on Marissa's face bloomed into a full one. "Really good."

Sabrina's breath caught in her chest and her smile matched Marissa's. She might have pinched herself if she didn't know how small-town and hokey it would make her look. "Thank you. That means a lot."

Marissa nodded and twisted her hands together.

"I thought maybe we could have that coffee you mentioned?"

"Really?" And there she went again asking a question that had only one good answer. But then Marissa wouldn't have asked as a joke, right? There had been no snide tone, no hidden meaning in the words. And Marissa had never been one for cruel pranks. Sabrina doubted that had changed in the preceding nine years. "What can I make you?"

Marissa ordered a plain latte, nonfat with no flavoring, and Sabrina set to work making a pair of them. She watched Marissa select the small enclave of cushioned chairs in the corner of the shop, the same ones she would have chosen. Anticipation knotted in her stomach and she wondered if she should have bothered with the second drink since her nerves might make all fluid intake an impossibility. Oh, well, it would give her hands something to do.

She accidentally splashed hot coffee on her hand when she added the milk too quickly, but on the plus side, she remembered to remove her apron and she was wearing her best jeans today. The ones that lifted her butt to heights it hadn't known even when she'd been a teenager and drew a whistle from Noah when she put them on after he was finishing thanking her.

Her stomach got all soft and squishy when she thought of him. Actually, her entire body filled with that soft, squishy feeling. So she was almost relaxed when she carried the steaming cups over to Marissa and carefully set them on the low table.

Marissa picked her cup up and sipped, watching with the blue eyes Sabrina knew so well. But Marissa didn't seem inclined to start the conversational ball rolling, so Sabrina did.

"I'm glad you came by." She was. Though she still believed her time in town was temporary, she'd begun to feel isolated and alone. It wasn't fair to turn to Noah for everything, and being so near Marissa, faced with all the wonderful memories they'd created in their youth, made her realize how much she'd missed their bond.

Marissa nodded again and put her cup down. She stared at the steaming contents for a moment before she spoke. "I feel like I might have been a bit hard on you." She raised her gaze to meet Sabrina's. "I was wrong to tell Noah not to give you the interview."

"He never mentioned that to me." It made sense, of course. Marissa had been hurt by what Sabrina had written once long ago; obviously she would advise anyone else to avoid putting themselves in the same situation. She swallowed against the nerves that clawed at her throat. Marissa had said she was wrong. She hadn't come here to lay down threats, idle or otherwise.

"No, he wouldn't." Marissa swept her hair back.

"But it was unfair of me. It's just...your being here brings up a lot of old feelings."

Sabrina knew that. She felt them, too. She put her cup down and her fingers curled into the seat cushion. "But they're not all bad feelings. We were best friends once."

Marissa sighed and leaned back against the chair. Her lashes fluttered down, stayed down as though it was easier to speak if she didn't have to look at Sabrina. "Best friends," Marissa repeated. "I haven't thought about it in a long time, but when you came back and then wanted to interview Noah, it scared me."

"I understand." She did. In Marissa's position, she'd have been a lot more vocal about it.

"And I'd be lying if I said I didn't want to punish you."

Sabrina understood that urge, too. If only Marissa knew just how Sabrina had already brought down swift and severe retribution on herself. Big Daddy still refused all contact and her editor had sent her an even more terse email last week stating that unless Sabrina had something newsworthy to share with him, he'd appreciate if she stopped filling up his in-box and voice mail.

But Marissa didn't know. No one except Noah knew. She paused. Maybe her reason for coming back didn't matter any longer. "You know why I'm back? I got fired."

Marissa's mouth fell open. "No."

"Yes. For an article I wrote." When Marissa's eyebrows shot up, Sabrina nodded. "Fitting, right? Guess I didn't learn anything."

"What happened?" Marissa looked more curious than gleeful and the tight grip of fear holding Sabrina's heart eased.

She proceeded to spill all the details of her life since her January dismissal right down to the fact that her return was starting to look less and less likely. "Not quite the fabulous city life I wanted you all to believe I led."

"Why are you telling me all this?" Marissa asked. "Aren't you afraid I'll tell people?"

The thought of everyone staring at her, knowing she was back with her tail between her legs as opposed to just having a summer visit, made Sabrina feel hot and cold all over. But she wouldn't ask Marissa to keep it to herself. "I think you deserve to know."

Marissa sighed. "I won't say anything."

"Riss…" She could remember sitting across from Marissa and Kyle, hearing that they were getting married and having a baby. Her best friend and her ex. The betrayal had felt absolute. And her friendly article turned ugly. "I'm so sorry. If I could go back, I'd never write that stupid article. I don't blame you for hating me."

"I don't hate you. I'm here now, aren't I?" Marissa had a point.

"I'm still sorry."

"Me, too." Marissa tilted her head. Her blond hair fell across her shoulder, as pale as it had been when they were kids. Then she smiled and Sabrina had the sense that everything was going to be okay.

Even if she was still without her job and stuck in this little town.

SABRINA ALMOST CHOKED on the tea the salon receptionist had made for her when Marissa dropped her little bomb. "Are you in love with Noah?"

She'd thought they were just going out for a girls' afternoon. Getting their nails done, chatting about their lives, sipping tea. She hadn't realized there was something else to Marissa's invitation.

They'd been spending more and more time together since their conversation at the coffee shop three weeks ago. Sabrina had become a regular guest at the family's Sunday dinner and had even hosted a dinner party at her own apartment. Some of that old closeness was back and now that she had it, Sabrina knew she'd never let it go. Not even if it meant discussing something she was doing her best not to think about at all.

"Marissa." Sabrina tried to laugh but the sound choked her more than the tea had and she ended up coughing instead. "I barely know him." Though that felt like a lie. While it was true they'd had lit-tle contact when they were younger and she'd only been back in town a few months, the connection felt deeper, stronger than the length of time would indicate. But how did she say that to Marissa when she could barely think it to herself?

"You are." Marissa nodded. "Good. I didn't want Noah to be alone out there."

"Alone out where?" What was Marissa talking about? Sabrina shoved the obvious response out of her mind. Ridiculous. She didn't love Noah and he didn't love her. But her legs tingled and her breath bottled up in her chest.

"Out in Loveland." Marissa spun the rack of nail polish colors before selecting a hot pink. "It's good that you're in it together."

"We're not—" Sabrina broke off before she finished her sentence. *Together.* Because they were together. Just not the way Marissa thought.

Marissa's eyes zeroed in on her, pinned her in place. "Don't try to deny it. I know it's true."

But was it? Sabrina cared for Noah, but love? That was so huge, monumental. The kind of thing a person changed her life for. Moved for. Fear tangled in Sabrina's stomach. She wasn't sure she was ready to give up that flashy, big-city life. "I'm still working to get my old job back. When I do, I'll be leaving."

Marissa didn't stiffen in defense of her brother-in-law. She didn't straighten up or point her finger or do anything that might showcase the disappointment Sabrina feared her statement would create. She simply smiled. "That's what you think."

Sabrina didn't say anything. Wasn't sure what she could say. Because that active, anxious part of her that kept her on the move in the city, always on the chase, hunting the next interview, the next new nightclub, the next tropical vacation had quieted in the past few weeks. As though she no longer needed to find that elusive something.

But that was simply complacency. It wasn't because she was actually considering what living here permanently might be like. It was because there was nothing to find in Wheaton. What were the town's breaking news items? That the high school was buying new athletic uniforms for the start of September? *Woo*.

"Riss, I'm happy to be back now. But I'm not staying. I can't." Sabrina pretended to look at the nail polish bottles lined up in front of her, but it was a just a blur of colors. A rainbow of indecision. Her insides felt more snarled than her hair after prom when she'd used a can of hairspray and Marissa had backcombed it for at least twenty minutes to get enough height.

She felt Marissa's eyes on her, and not a casual, just-checking-things-out look. No, this was a hard-core stare, one intended to see down deep into the heart of things. "How does Noah feel about that?"

Sabrina wanted to draw back from the thought. They'd talked about her leaving. Just because they were now dating didn't mean anything would change. He knew that, right? But her fingers holding the tea cup went numb. Sabrina could see the handle in her hand, knew the ceramic was hard and cool, but she felt nothing. She faced her oldest friend. "I don't know."

Sabrina almost couldn't breathe as the possibility washed through her. Stay here? Remain in the small town she'd been so eager to leave and in no hurry to return to? Never go back to the city lights? Give up on all those dreams she'd had?

Even if there were things she liked about small-town living like knowing everyone who came into the coffee shop and greeting them by name. Not just the regulars, either, but the ones who only came in occasionally who asked how she was and truly wanted to know the answer. Not caring if her shoes were the latest style and cost hundreds of dollars. Not worrying that if she ate an extra carb, her skinny jeans would be too tight. Knowing that she had a place here. Even if it wasn't the one she'd expected.

Marissa plucked another bottle out of the nail polish lineup and handed it to her. "This. It matches your boots."

Since it did and Sabrina was just happy for the change of topic, she accepted the bottle and curled her fingers around the cool glass.

"I'm happy you're back," Marissa told her, and some of the feeling returned to Sabrina's extremities. "I mean, it is a little weird to think about you and Kyle, but that was a long time ago."

"A very long time ago." Sabrina refrained from making a face or saying *ew* since she didn't think Marissa would be particularly pleased to hear that the idea of being with Kyle made her cringe. "We were never that serious."

Marissa lifted an eyebrow. "You were each other's firsts. People don't forget their firsts."

"You think that Kyle and I—" Sabrina stopped talking before she *ew*-ed aloud this time. The idea that she would have done everything she had with Noah after having done the same with his brother was enough to make the single sip of tea she'd had come back up. Not that Kyle was a hideous beast— far from it. But the idea of sharing something so intimate with him was just wrong. "No, we never did that. Or it. Whatever."

"Really?" Marissa's eyebrows came together. "But what about that night you came back from the lake?"

Sabrina was confused. "What night at the lake?"

"You know—" Marissa waved a hand as though this was information Sabrina should have sitting at the front of her memory just ready to be accessed "—the one when you were supposed to be staying at my place. And you snuck out the window to meet Kyle so that you two could do it. When you came back your hair was all messed up and you wouldn't tell me what happened, just that you'd had a good time."

Sabrina started to laugh. She'd forgotten all about that night and with good reason. She and Kyle had gone up to the lake with the full intention of having sex. She'd been horribly nervous and not in a good, butterflies-in-the-stomach way. More in an afraid-she-was-going-to-regret-this kind of way.

But a mouse had run across the floor as soon as they walked in the cabin and Sabrina had used it as justification to head back outside and tell Kyle, who hated rodents as much as she did, that she wasn't going back in until he found the mouse and got rid of it. He'd told her there was no way he was touching that thing and that it wouldn't climb into bed with them, but he hadn't pushed very hard. At a stand-off, they'd decided they were no longer in the mood and come home.

Personally, Sabrina thought he'd been looking for a way out as much as she had.

"So why didn't you tell me?" Marissa wanted to know when Sabrina explained.

"I don't know. I probably wanted you to think we had done it. I was embarrassed. I'd been bragging about how adult I was and then I chickened out. The mouse was just an excuse. I didn't want to have sex with Kyle."

"You really didn't sleep together?"

Sabrina shook her head. "No. I lost my virginity on a single bed in my dorm room second year of university with a party going on in the lounge downstairs. There were vanilla candles and cheap wine. Very romantic."

"I lost mine in Kyle's bedroom. With his poster of Jaromir Jagr looking down at us."

Sabrina snickered. "Okay, you win."

Marissa laughed, too. "You can never tell anyone that. It's so cliché."

"I won't say anything," Sabrina assured her. "Whatever you tell me doesn't leave this salon. It'll be like Vegas." Since the nail techs were busy with other customers on the opposite side of the store and there was no one else waiting—even the receptionist was away from her desk—Sabrina felt safe is thinking that whatever happened in the salon would stay in the salon.

"You know, I've never even been to Vegas?"

"Oh. Well, it's not as great as people say." Sabrina knew that had to be true for some people. Had to be just based on the laws of averages. Someone, somewhere hated Vegas. And they likely had a bunch of compatriots. But her? She loved it. And Marissa would, too. "It's not like you can't go. We'll plan a girls' trip. It's more fun without men anyway."

The idea caused a fluttery sensation in her stomach. She'd love to go with Marissa to Vegas. The fun and trouble they could find...

"I have the kids."

"So leave them with their dad and uncle." Sabrina thought of how happy Noah would be to learn that she'd volunteered him for the job so that she and Marissa could go on vacation. And then she smiled, thinking of all the ways she'd find to make it up to him.

A lightness Sabrina hadn't known she was missing began to fill her. It was different than the way she felt with Noah. With him it was strong and steady, a slow-burning heat that would keep her safe. This was thinner, a loosening of old emotions and regrets that floated away into the summer day.

"But you're not staying," Marissa pointed out.

The lightness flashed out, like a shooting star at the end of its arc. Sabrina brushed the dribble of uncertainty away, determined not to let anything spoil the day. "We can still go. You can fly into Vancouver first and we'll have some fun in the city. Or we can just meet in Vegas."

"Or you could just stay here and we could go together."

Sabrina pressed her lips together and was grateful when the receptionist returned and took them to a pair of unoccupied stations just far enough apart that they'd have to share their entire conversation with the room if they wanted to continue.

She crushed the flutter of possibility rising within her. That secret part that sighed about how wonderful it would be to come home to Noah every night. As she'd told Marissa, they barely knew each other so any fantasy about a future was ridiculous.

Sabrina ignored the niggling reminder that every relationship had to start somewhere, relied on two people making concessions because it was more important to be together. This was different.

Now, if Noah came back with her, moved to Vancouver, she could see them staying together. But he wouldn't. He was tied to this town as firmly as the signage that welcomed tourists and residents alike.

Just like she was tied to the city. Right?

CHAPTER FIFTEEN

NOAH WAS IN HIS dealership office, number crunching the business's budget when Sabrina breezed in looking as fresh as the summer day outside. Warmth filled him the way it always did when she appeared.

"Hello, Mr. Mayor." She placed the picnic basket she was carrying on his desk and proceeded to settle herself on his lap for a kiss.

And a damn fine kiss it was. Not that he could fully enjoy it with his door ajar and anyone capable of walking by and seeing everything. "Sabrina. The door."

She shrugged, pinning him with a teasing glance. "It's nothing people haven't seen before."

He couldn't even deny her claim, seeing as her sudden appearance at his office followed by a thorough kiss was starting to become a regular thing. He sighed. "I'd still prefer my staff not think this is appropriate behavior during working hours."

He might have loosened up a little over the past couple of months, but this wasn't a free-for-all.

"You're the boss." She toyed with the edges of

his hair. He'd just had it cut last week, so she was basically stroking his neck. He enjoyed the sensation of her fingers on him. "That means you get special perks."

Noah struggled for composure when everything inside him said to give her the kiss he wanted to. The staff loved Sabrina and would turn a blind eye to the games they played in his office, but he didn't want to be on full display. What went on behind closed doors could be explained away. But providing a direct view could not. "The door," he repeated.

"Fine." She climbed off his lap long enough to shut the door with a snap and then snuggled back into position, pressing her soft curves against him. "Better?"

"Yes." Then he gave her a proper kiss. One that started with tongues and ended with him breathing hard.

"Much better," she said, her chest heaving, too.

The strength of his feelings continued to surprise Noah. He tightened his arms around her waist, making sure she stayed in place. Though they spent every evening together and often parts of their day, he wanted more.

They hadn't discussed their future, but he knew she remained out of contact with the man who'd had her fired from the paper. As the days slipped by, the night now carrying a nip that spoke of the coming fall, he'd begun to wonder if she still wanted to return to the city.

Sabrina rarely mentioned getting her job back anymore and talked about the city and her life there even less. She and Marissa were friends again. They were both tight-lipped about what had passed between them, how they'd eased their way into finding friendship again, but every time Sabrina mentioned Jaromir Jagr with a naughty gleam in her eyes, Marissa blushed and laughed.

Noah didn't mind not knowing the details. Marissa was happier than he ever recalled seeing her and the kids were fully in love with Sabrina.

She was good for them, good for the town, good for him.

"To what do I owe the pleasure today?"

"Picnic," she said pointing at the wicker basket. But when he leaned forward to flip the lid, she slapped his hand away. "A surprise picnic." She pushed herself up. "Let's go."

"Now?" It was a warm September day, the kind they wouldn't have for much longer, but it was the middle of the week and Noah had been guilty of letting things slide the past little while. He should have had this budget completed at the start of the month and he'd only done the basics to prepare for the upcoming election. Election day wasn't until the third week in November, but he needed to have his materials printed and ready to be posted the month prior. He hadn't even had new pictures taken or decided on a slogan.

"Yes, now." Sabrina pushed herself off his lap, her hair wafting around them, tickling his cheek. He ran a hand over the length of it, loving that he could. The silky strands slipped through his fingers, made him think of how the ends brushed against his chest when they were in bed together, draping across his chest, his arms, his thighs. "You've been working too hard."

Noah had been working hard, but he still had a lot to do. "I can't." He glanced back at the computer screen, at the cursor blinking at him, waiting for him to finish the job, and scrubbed a hand over his face. "Can we do it another day?"

"No." She grinned and took hold of his hand, trying to tug him to his feet. "It's gorgeous outside. We might not get another afternoon like this."

She tugged harder, but since he was bigger and stronger she ended up back in his lap. She took her loss like a champ and circled her finger around his ear. "I have work," he said, trying not to be swayed by the sensitive touch of her fingers.

Sabrina peered over her shoulder at the computer. "Don't you have a bookkeeper?"

"Yes."

"So why are you doing the payroll?"

He didn't have a good answer for that. He still hadn't dealt with that problem, and with the introduction of Sabrina into his life, he had less time for all the little jobs he used to handle. Maybe the man would be interested in taking some night courses, or since he didn't seem to have a natural head for numbers, maybe there was another job at the dealership that would be a better fit. But making a decision about the situation could wait. Everything could wait when Sabrina was in his lap, wriggling against him.

"Come with me." She bent down and brushed a kiss across his lips. "It'll be fun. I promise."

Noah had no doubt about that. No promise required. But the payroll wasn't going to complete itself. "I would if I didn't have so much to do."

"Then tell me how I can help." She leaned forward until her body was plastered to his. Noah felt everything stir inside him. He loved it when she did that, and she knew it. "A few hours this afternoon won't hurt and I'll help with the workload tonight."

"You can do payroll?"

She tossed her hair at him. "I took a basic accounting course in university."

He wanted to say yes. An afternoon by the lake with Sabrina and whatever was in her basket sounded ideal. He glanced at the wicker longingly. But his night was already booked and, much to his eternal sadness, not to have some one-on-one time with Sabrina. "I have the kids tonight, remember?"

And as much as Noah might like to think he could work once the kids were in bed, they tended to eat into that time, too. There was always someone who needed something. Most often Daisy, who just needed one more story or a sip of water before she could be expected to go to sleep.

"So I'll babysit." Sabrina shrugged like it was no big deal. "I've done it before."

Noah snorted. "You babysat them on your own for one afternoon and you called me in when they got out of hand. I warned you not to give them sugar."

She laughed, her breath dancing across his neck. "No, sweetheart. That was all part of my evil plan to make you do the babysitting, and it worked." Her eyes zeroed in on his. "But I can handle the kids."

He was tempted, so tempted. The payroll would only take a couple of hours and didn't have to be finished until tomorrow afternoon. He could do it tomorrow morning in a pinch. As for the campaign he needed to start working on, he'd hoped to ask Sabrina for help on that anyway. She had a good sense of what appealed to people.

"It's good for you to take time for yourself. Makes you a better boss." Sabrina traced a line from around his ear, down his neck and inside the collar of his shirt. "Say yes."

Noah looked at the computer screen again, just as it went to sleep. Then he looked back to the woman in his arms. She smiled at him, all lush and warm and everything he wanted. How could he turn her down?

"Yes."

THE LAKE WAS SMOOTH and cool and, best of all in Noah's opinion, empty. Since school had started, the kids were in class and most people were at work in the middle of the week. The tall firs that surrounded the water gave a further sense of privacy, as though they were in their own little secret retreat.

He unfurled a blue checked blanket and laid it on the ground while Sabrina set down the picnic basket and unpacked grapes and cheese, a loaf of bread, sliced meats and a bottle of sparkling water from the picnic basket. They ate and drank, laughed and kissed. Noah felt the little bits of niggling worry about skipping out on work slip away.

They disappeared completely when she whipped off her dress, revealing a bright red bikini that matched her boots, and handed over a bathing suit that she'd taken from his dresser. He drained the water left in his cup to return his tongue to its normal size and, after a quick glance to make sure the lake was still deserted, slipped into the trunks and followed her into the water.

Really, there'd been no choice. Seeing her laughing and splashing, that tiny bikini providing a tantalizing glimpse of her body, he'd been powerless to resist.

He swam up behind her, slipped his arms around her waist and pulled her back against him.

The difference in body and water temperature was drastic and created a tingling feeling where they touched. Which was everywhere.

"It's cold," he whispered against her neck. "We should conserve body heat."

She laughed and let her head fall back against him.

Satisfaction and contentment swept through him. Surely, he must have experienced similar levels of pleasure at various times in his life, but right now he couldn't think of a single instance. Not when he was elected mayor for the first time, not when he opened his dealership in town and definitely not with any of the other women he'd dated. He kept one arm around Sabrina while he treaded water with the other.

She tilted her head to look at him. "I talked to Trish about that series for the paper." Sabrina had become a regular attendee of the Friday dances at Cedar Oaks, joining him there and convincing him to go out on the dance floor a few more times. Noah still didn't feel entirely comfortable doing it, but he did it for her.

A couple of weeks ago, Sabrina mentioned the idea of writing a series of feature articles interviewing one resident at a time as a way to share some of their experiences and encourage the strong bond between members of the community. Noah had encouraged her to move forward with the plan, knowing how important it was to keep the lines of communication open between active members of the community and those who'd slowed down. "And?"

She swiveled to face him. "She loved the idea and gave me the go-ahead this morning."

He grinned, knowing the satisfaction on her face was mirrored on his own. "That's great." He kissed her. Then kissed her again. "When will you start?"

"This week. I'd thought to begin with George, but I think he'd become insufferable."

"Don't you mean more insufferable?"

Sabrina laughed and splashed him. "Don't pretend with me. I know you love George. Insufferable behavior and all."

She was right. Despite George's proclivity for outrageousness—or maybe because of it—Noah cared about the old man. Even after he'd again asked Noah to find him a couple of dirty movies because the ladies in the retirement complex didn't appreciate what he could offer and a man had to take care of himself.

Noah had refused. He might take him fishing, might even sneak him a beer or two, but he was not going to smuggle porn into his mother's workplace.

But there was another reason for the good feelings winding through his body. If Sabrina was starting a series, a long-term project for the paper, then she had to be thinking about sticking around for a while. The words tripped over themselves when he spoke. "Does this mean you're staying?"

He concentrated on keeping his body loose and relaxed when every part of him wanted to hold her tight to him and demand that she agree. Demand that since she'd already inserted herself into his heart and a permanent place in his life, she should make the move official.

But Sabrina sighed and leaned back into the water, letting the sun beat down on her face. Noah tried not to frown. She hadn't said yes, but she hadn't said no, either.

They stayed like that for a moment, her looking at the sun, him looking at her, before she lifted her head. "What about you? Ever thought of leaving?"

There was a small ripple as he straightened in the water. "No." His answer was quick. His voice deep.

She smiled, but it was tight around the edges and didn't fully reach her eyes. "How did I know you were going to say that?" She rose up, wrapped her legs around him. "Why not?"

Plenty of reasons, none of which Noah wanted to chat about. He cupped her face, brushed a thumb across her lips. "You haven't answered my question."

"Noticed that, did you?" Sabrina traced a finger along the line of his neck and down his shoulder. "I don't know. I didn't have a horrible childhood or some scarring high school experience that sent me running away from here as soon as could. I just always felt like there was more out there for me than this." She ran her hand down his arm and into the water, spreading her fingers as she raked them through the water. "It's hard to explain when I'm not sure I know myself. I guess there was just nothing to keep me here."

"Family? Friends?" All those people who even now made themselves at home in her life and by extension his.

"I still have my family," she pointed out.

"And the friends?" He linked his fingers with hers and tugged her forward so their chests touched.

That sad smile was back. "I didn't really know what I was letting go. I wanted that big, flashy career. To be the one who left town and made it big."

"Why?" It was nothing Noah had ever thought of, ever wondered about. He'd known from the time he was a teenager that he was a good enough hockey player to get a college scholarship, but that's where his dreams would end. There would be no draft-day excitement, no training camps and no call up to the majors. Instead, he focused on getting a solid education that he could use to help his hometown, make their lives as well as his own better.

"Sometimes I wonder about that myself."

Her eyes turned down to look at their hands and his gaze followed the same path, noting how their fingers tangled together so effortlessly. The way her life could shift and merge back to Wheaton in the same way. Fear and yearning coiled in his stomach. "Then maybe you could stay?"

Sabrina didn't look up when she answered and her voice was so low he wouldn't have heard if they hadn't been so close together. "Maybe." She lifted her eyes to his. "That doesn't mean I'm still not going to try and get my job back. You know that."

Noah nodded, tamping down on the grand sweep of optimism that lifted his entire body. She hadn't said she was staying. Not yet. But he saw the confusion in her eyes, recognized it for what it was. She did see a place for herself in Wheaton, with him. He lowered his mouth to her ear, his lips tickling the softness of her skin. "I don't want you to go."

A shiver went through her like the wake left by a sailboat. She twisted her head to look at him, a new light in her eyes. "Maybe you could come with me."

His smile slid away. "I can't." He couldn't leave the town, the residents. Just couldn't.

The light dimmed and winked out. "Right. No. Of course not. I wouldn't ask you to."

They both ignored the fact that she just had.

THEY GOT HOME LATE that afternoon, well-fed, a little sunburned and ridiculously happy. The heavy discussion about leaving and staying had evaporated under the hot sun, leaving them with a sense of peace that things were going to work out just fine.

Noah kissed her on the lips, then on the strap line where her dress had been. "You need lotion," he told her and kissed the spot again.

Sabrina tossed a look over her shoulder as she opened the door to the entry. "You offering to smooth some on for me, Mr. Mayor?"

"I think I could find some time in my busy schedule for that."

She laughed and closed the door behind them. The entry was dim and cool. He followed her to her place since he'd already migrated clothing and some of his toiletries there. Even though it was only a small trek across the hall, it seemed silly first thing in the morning to climb out of her warm bed, tromp through the entry and get ready in his own place. Not when he could use those extra minutes in bed with Sabrina. And there was more than that, too; it was combining their belongings and their lives into the same space.

"What time do we have to get the kids?" she asked, taking the now empty picnic basket from him and carrying it into the kitchen.

"Not until seven." He stepped up behind her while she unloaded the used plates and plastic cups and slipped his arms around her waist. "We still have a couple of hours."

"Oh? Did you have something in mind?" She acted coy, but Noah saw her body react to his words. He slid his hands up her torso and cupped her breasts.

"I might."

She leaned back against him. "Well, then lead the way."

By the time they finished up everything Noah had in mind, which was quite a lot—she'd unleashed a creative side of him that he hadn't known existed—it was close to seven. Damn. He'd hoped for at least another hour stretched out beside her, feeling her body move against him.

He was particularly unhappy when she rolled away from him and levered herself to a sitting position at the side of the bed, so he took hold of her waist and dragged her across the sheets.

"Noah." She shook a mock reprimanding finger at him. "We have to go."

"Just a few more minutes." He tugged her back

down against him, running a hand along her side and over her hips. Her skin was satiny smooth. He loved the way it felt beneath his fingers and did a little more exploring.

"Not that I don't enjoy this." Her words came in short gasps that informed him just how much she did like it when his fingers dived lower, searching and exploring. "But if you start this, I'll expect you to finish and then we'll be late and Marissa will kill us."

True, but Noah wasn't sure he minded. Marissa would understand. She'd told him she wanted him to be happy and this made him very happy.

Sabrina exhaled, her breath fluttering across his neck, making Noah's entire body tighten with desire. Just a few more minutes. After another couple of well-placed strokes that had her arching toward him, begging him with her body, she agreed.

He was feeling rather smug about being on time when they drove over. Sabrina's hand was on his thigh, just resting possessively, letting anyone who might look know that they were together, while she talked. She explained more about her upcoming series for the paper. "Did you know Mrs. Mann was a champion ballroom dancer? She still has some of her old costumes. Gorgeous."

Noah slid a glance at her while she talked. God, she was amazing when she was passionate. Whether it was in bed or talking about her work.

Her cheeks flushed and eyes brightened. He picked up her hand and brought it to his lips.

She smiled. "What was that for?"

"Because I wanted to." Because Sabrina made him happy to be himself. When they were together, he wasn't the mayor or a boss or a son or an uncle. He was just Noah. He liked it. "Do I need a reason?"

"No." She leaned toward him, though the bucket seats and gearshift prevented her from getting as close as Noah would have liked. "But if I knew the reason, I could do it again."

He kissed her palm. "There's no reason." He kept her hand tucked in his the rest of the drive.

Would have kept it even afterward had the kids not commanded all their attention as soon as they pulled up to the house. Their little bodies spilled over the front steps in a jumble of arms and legs and shrieks of delight, demanding attention and affection as if it was their right.

"Sabrina!" Daisy hugged Sabrina's knees almost knocking her over. Noah put a steadying hand on Sabrina's back. "Hi. Let's play. Can I wear your boots?"

Sabrina was wearing the famous red boots. A couple of weeks earlier, Noah had noticed Marissa sporting an awfully similar pair in pink.

Paul was quieter than his sister and stood slightly

behind her, waiting while Daisy finished what seemed to be a long and involved tale of dinner.

"Hey, Paul. Ready for the game tomorrow night?" Noah asked.

Paul nodded, his face lighting up. "Mom washed my jersey today." He edged closer to them.

Noah had bought some tickets to the preseason junior hockey game playing in the neighboring town and they were making a boys' trip out of it. Kyle, Paul and Noah. It was nice, just hanging out with the guys. In a few years, Scotty would join them, then Timmy. Maybe eventually Noah's own kids.

He felt a warm glow fill him at the thought. His kids. He looked at Sabrina who was holding her own under Daisy's exuberant greeting. She'd be a great mom.

He noticed Paul turn to look at her, too. The poor kid had a massive crush on her. Always hanging around, watching with moony eyes. Noah couldn't blame him. The kid had good taste. While Daisy announced her ideas for the games they could play, Paul moved another half step close to Sabrina.

"Hi, Paul." She noticed his approach and pulled him in for a hug, which Paul pretended he didn't like. "Where's Scotty?"

"Getting his diaper changed," Paul said and then ducked his head.

"He made a stinky," Daisy overshared. "It was

gross. Daddy said they should leave it for you, but Mommy said no."

"Remind me to buy your mother something nice," Noah told her as the toddler in question came out the door holding his mother's hand.

When Scotty saw Noah and Sabrina his eyes opened wide and his thumb popped out of his mouth. "Sabby." He reached out for her. Noah didn't even rate a glance. It appeared that Sabrina had won the hearts of everybody in the Barnes clan.

She picked Scotty up, planting loud kisses all over his face which made him laugh. "Me, too," Daisy insisted, still hanging on to Sabrina's leg. Sabrina bent down and kissed Daisy a few times, too. Paul sidled closer and allowed her to kiss him once on the cheek.

Marissa gave her a one-armed hug which was all she could manage with three of her kids draped over Sabrina. "Kyle's just putting Timmy to bed."

"He has to go to bed early because he's little," Daisy said. "But I'm a big girl so I get to stay up late."

"Eight isn't late," Paul told her.

"It is, too." Daisy put her hands on her hips and glared at him.

Noah intervened before they could get going. He'd rather not spend the night breaking up arguments over who said what and the meaning behind it. "Why don't you two go inside and figure out what we should play first?"

Happy to have a goal, the pair ran off. Noah noticed that Paul let Daisy beat him to the front door though he could easily outrun her. He'd probably let her choose the first game, too. Noah made a mental note to let Paul pick the first game. It was good for Daisy to learn that being louder and more demanding didn't always mean getting her way.

Sabrina and Marissa chatted away on the front step while Scotty stood at their feet looking perfectly content to be there. Noah did, too.

The women were still feeling their way around their old friendship, building a new bond even as they polished up the old one, but they both seemed better for it. He couldn't help counting it as a point in favor of Sabrina staying. Surely, she saw the same things he did. How the townspeople had opened up their arms and welcomed her back as one of their own. How she'd given them a piece of herself in return.

Marissa said something and the two of them broke into peals of laughter. Scotty chortled along with them and Noah smiled.

Sabrina was a part of Wheaton. She was happy here. She must see that.

CHAPTER SIXTEEN

SABRINA FROWNED AT George Cuthbert even as a laugh burbled up inside her. But really. George was the kind of man who took a mile with or without that first inch. It was important not to let him think he was getting away with something. That only fired him up.

"George. Do you want to do this interview or not?"

"Of course I do." He ran a hand over his bald head, buffing the shiny top. "You think I got dressed up for the ladies here?"

She eyed him steadily, perusing the war uniform he was proudly sporting. "Yes."

He cackled. "You got me, girlie. You know what they say about a man in uniform."

She did, but she didn't want to hear about it from George. Again. She pressed the tip of her pen to the notebook in her hand, having found the visual aid of taking notes seemed to keep George somewhat in line. "All right. Tell me what Wheaton was like before you left."

As she'd told Noah, she hadn't started her new

series with George. But that hadn't stopped his chest from puffing out with pride when she did ask him. Even now he was practically popping the buttons on his jacket.

"You told my boy how you feel yet?"

Sabrina's pen stalled without writing a single word, and her breath was suddenly lodged in her throat. She maintained her calm front or did the best she could. "Pardon?" She met George's gaze even though she wanted to look anywhere but at him.

"Noah. You sure you don't got potatoes growing in those ears?" George shook his head at her. "You going to tell him how you feel or just pussyfoot around it?"

Tell Noah how she felt. She swallowed. "I'm here to interview *you,* not the other way around." But there was a slight tremor in her voice that no manner of calm breathing could dispel entirely.

George snorted. "You at least told him you're staying?"

Some of the banding around her lungs eased. This was something she could answer, easily and without delving too deep. "I'm not staying, George."

He snorted again. "'Course you are."

"No." Sabrina swallowed, ignored the little button of pleasure that popped at the idea. Staying.

Here. With Noah. With everyone. "I have a life in Vancouver," she reminded George and herself.

A life she was dying to get back to, right? Of course she was. She was a city girl at heart. She only wore the red boots and casual jeans because she wanted to fit in while she was here. But really, her sky-high heels, late nights and glittery life were where she truly felt at home.

"You have a life here," George said. He reached out a gnarled hand and placed it on her knee. For once, there was no attempt to grope or pat her in inappropriate places. "Don't tell me you're too blind to see that."

"I'm not the one who needs glasses." But her chest was tightening again. A long, hard squeeze that made it hard to catch her breath, hard to remember what she really wanted, what she'd fought for.

George patted her knee again. "Noah's a good man. You could do worse."

An understatement and one she didn't want to analyze. "Thanks for the insight. Now let's talk about you."

With the threat that she'd interview someone else or place him on the third page instead of the cover like everyone else, Sabrina managed to bring George back around to talking about his time in Wheaton before and after the army. But the lingering discontent remained with her, tarnishing her good mood and making it difficult to focus. She even let George get in a butt pat as she left.

If that wasn't the sign of a distracted mind, she didn't know what was.

George was wrong, Sabrina told herself as she drove back to her apartment post-interview. Not about Noah, but about her staying. Out of the situation, freed to really think about it, she knew that now. She swallowed the burn rising up her throat. Probably had too much coffee today. Nothing more. Nothing more at all.

She knew she couldn't stay. Yes, she'd made some changes to her life since she'd come back, but those were only temporary. And she and Noah knew where they stood. They would enjoy each other's company while she was in town. Nothing more.

But her mind felt no calmer when she got home and she paced around the apartment unable to sit still or concentrate. Even the power of her soothing decor couldn't ease the restlessness. She'd barely arrived and already everyone was assuming that she'd stay. Seriously. How long had it been? A couple of months? She mentally counted back and then paused. Four? Four *months?*

And when was the last time she'd called her editor or Big Daddy? She swallowed. A couple of weeks? She rushed to her computer on wobbly legs and powered it up.

According to her Sent file, it had been a month. Sabrina sank into the chair. An entire month. And she hadn't called them, either, because if she'd called she would have emailed to follow up. Her head began to throb. She'd let everything slip. Everything she'd worked so hard for. Released as though she'd never had it at all.

Sabrina shook her head, forced back the headache. There was nothing to get upset about. She'd been caught up in the simplicity of small-town life. It had been easy to rest, to lie back and just let things happen to her. No more. She opened up a new message and typed quickly before any of the self-doubt or confusion could take root and stop her. Then she pressed Send. Now all she'd have to do was wait.

But even after the email was long gone and the nerves battering her insides had quieted, she still worried whether she'd done the right thing.

SABRINA HADN'T EXPECTED the call when it came the final week of September, three weeks after she'd sent her last-ditch email to both her editor and Big Daddy. She'd resigned herself to the idea that life wasn't going to work out exactly as she'd planned, and though she wouldn't say she was content, she could deal with it. It wasn't as if she had much choice.

She told herself she could be satisfied here. Trish

was giving her more assignments at the paper; she actually had come to enjoy her part-time work at the coffee shop; she loved her apartment; and of course, there was Noah. It wasn't the city, but maybe it was time to grow up and recognize that part of her life was over.

And then she answered the phone and everything changed.

Sabrina swallowed her nerves. Well, it was done now. Her emailing and badgering and persistence had paid off. Everything was working out. So why did she feel sick inside?

Her apartment was quiet. Too quiet. Noah was still at work and she'd turned off the music an hour ago, finding it distracting. She turned her attention back to the computer screen to the article she was writing for Trish. To the last article she'd probably ever write for the *Wheaton Digest* and shook off the melancholy. She wasn't leaving forever. She'd come back. Things had changed and she wouldn't forget about her little hometown so easily.

But she still jumped when she heard the telltale crunch of Noah's tires turning into the driveway, the sound of the front door opening, the thump of his footsteps as he came to her place instead of his own and slid the key she'd given him into her lock.

Excitement and apprehension warred within her and made the back of her neck tingle. She wiped her hands on her jeans as she rose to greet him.

Noah smiled as he set his briefcase down on the floor and strode straight to her, gathering her into his arms. "Mmm." He buried his face in her hair and inhaled. "I missed you today."

Sabrina's hopes sang even as they sank. She loved it when he said things like that, letting her know that he thought about her, that she was part of his life. But today the feeling was bittersweet. She clung to him, her hands holding his shoulders, wishing she could put off her news for just a little while. Just long enough to enjoy the moment with Noah wrapped around her, whispering in her ear and following up his sweet words with tiny nibbles that made her entire body quake. But she would only be putting off the inevitable conversation, and she sensed that doing so would make things worse.

She pulled back, painting her face with a cheerful smile. "I got some news today." News she'd hardly dared to hope for.

"Oh?" He kissed the side of her neck again.

She forced herself to lean farther back. He stopped nuzzling, a puzzled expression on his face. Sabrina kept her smile bright. It was good news, so there was absolutely no reason for the twinge in her stomach. "I heard from my editor at the Vancouver paper."

His fingers spasmed at her waist, but he didn't let go. He didn't say anything.

Sabrina tried to ignore the sense of foreboding.

There was nothing wrong. This was good news, and exactly what she'd been chasing for the past few months. Finally, her hard work had paid off. "They've offered me my old job."

Noah stilled. His mouth grew tight, but he remained silent. It was up to her to fill the quiet that had invaded the room. His hands still held her, but she felt cold, as if she'd been abandoned.

She cleared her throat. "I know. I was surprised, too." She reached up to stroke his face, but he didn't get that usual sleepy, sexy look in his eyes. He just watched her.

"When?"

"When did they call me? Today." She longed to press herself against him, but didn't. Something in the tilt of his head warned her she might not like his response. She was glad she'd held back when his hands dropped to his sides and he took a slow step away.

"And you're going." His voice was calm. But not the normal sort of Mr. Mayor calm. No, this was a dangerous calm. Like the air before a lightning strike, full of static and the acrid scent of burning ozone.

Her lungs felt swollen, taut, like a balloon that would burst at the slightest pressure. She pressed a hand to her chest. Why was he watching her with those forlorn eyes? A sadness that went so deep she feared there was no bottom to it. They'd both known their relationship would end like this. Right? Sabrina brushed off the memory that every once in a while, when the night was dark and quiet and there was no one around to see her, she'd thought about staying forever. With him. "Yes. I am."

"And you didn't think to talk to me about it first."

The truth was she had. When the job offer came over the line, her gut instinct had not been to say yes and ask when she could start, but that she needed to talk to Noah. Except she knew what Noah would say. That he didn't want her to go, that he wanted her to give up all her big dreams and stay in this tiny town where she would never reach those lofty goals. So she'd forced down the apprehension and hastily agreed to the terms. "We did talk about it, Noah. You knew I was trying to get my job back."

His nod was stiff, unfriendly. As if they were strangers. As if she was supposed to have done something different. But what option did she have? Noah couldn't come with her. His life was here. He was the mayor and up for re-election in two months. He loved this town. And Sabrina couldn't stay. Not really. She had to see this through.

Her throat felt scratchy. He hadn't even said he loved her. And she hadn't said it back. Exactly what did he expect from her?

"How did this come about?"

She clasped her hands together and tried to re-member that this was a good thing, that she hadn't done anything wrong, hadn't given him false hope. "Actually, I probably have to thank you for it." When he only looked at her, a quizzical lift to his brows, she continued. "The article I wrote about you at the festival. I sent it off to my editor and to Big Daddy. A sample of what I can do." With the written promise that she'd be happy to do a simi-lar feature on Jackson and Big Daddy if it meant they'd lift her ban. And they'd bitten.

"The article on me." There was an angry slant to his mouth.

Sabrina flipped her hair over her shoulder, a gesture that was all nerves straining to break free before she broke down. "Yes. It was a great article. Everyone thought so."

"I see." But his icy eyes didn't look like they saw anything. "So you used me."

What? "Of course not."

But Noah was nodding, already judge and jury. "You said it was for the local paper."

"It was." That's all she'd intended it to be. A great piece on a great man. She'd done it for him. Didn't he know that? "Noah."

He cut her off with a short wave. "When are you leaving?"

She sucked in some air. "Wednesday." Two days,

which probably wouldn't give her enough time to pack everything, but she needed to get back to the city. She had to find an apartment to rent, drop in at the office and talk to her editor, get in touch with her old contacts and friends to see if they had any leads for future interviews. She reached out to put a hand on his arm, to touch him.

He stepped away so that her hand fell back to her side. "Did you even think about staying?"

Sabrina swallowed. "Noah. I..." She didn't know what to say. "I have to go."

"Of course you do." The eerie calm disappeared, replaced by the composed, cool mayoral stance. He didn't look like Noah anymore. He was all Mayor Barnes displaying polite authority and cool logic. "This is what you wanted."

Sabrina nodded and prayed the indecision wasn't shining in her eyes. Because she'd already accepted her old job. Already decided that she had to go back, if only to prove that she could. On Monday, she was expected in the office as though she hadn't been missing these past eight months. "I can't stay."

"I understand." His lips curved up in a semblance of acceptance, but his eyes looked flat, as washed out as the lake on a foggy morning.

Sabrina swayed on her feet. Part of her wanted to go to him, hold him close and whisper how much she was going to miss him and make him promise that he'd come to see her in the city. But she was frozen, a morass of indecision because Noah didn't look like he wanted to be touched, had already backed away from her once. "Noah, we talked about this."

"I said I understood." For a moment, fury flashed out again and cracked through the room before he schooled his features in a composed expression.

She stared, feeling her own anger rise to meet his. Where did he get off using that snippy tone? She'd been completely up-front and honest about her desire to return to the city. He'd known that when he'd pushed for all those nights together, pushed her to come to his family dinners. So why was he now acting like she'd betrayed him? "I haven't done anything wrong. I don't appreciate you treating me like I have."

Emotions crackled between them, but when he spoke his tone was measured again. "I apologize if it came across that way." But his hands clenched at his sides, flexing and releasing like he was practicing strangling something or someone. Probably her. "I hope you're very happy in the city."

A flicker of disgust rang through his final word, as though the city was something bad or dirty, so much less than the purity of life in Wheaton. Sabrina curled her fingers into her palms. The city wasn't perfect, but neither was this place. But rather than tell him that, she offered a fake smile. Noah wasn't the only one who could put on a front for others. "I will be. The city is my home."

"Then it's best you go back."

"I agree." Back to her old life full of nightclubs and high heels, weekend trips to Vegas and Whistler. A place where people didn't force their way into her life and want to know every detail about her. Where she could move on if things got boring or hard and no one would get bent out of shape about it. Where no one would walk in her front door and tell her they missed her.

Oh, God. She sucked in some air. She had to go back. There was no place for her in Wheaton. She'd worked at Vancouver's largest broadsheet for almost nine years. She'd made a place for herself in the city.

"Good luck." His words were quiet and her anger washed away as quickly as it arrived.

She wasn't mad at him. Not really. She was scared and worried. But she wasn't allowed to turn to him for support anymore. Not now.

Sabrina hadn't wanted things to work out this way. She'd known Noah wasn't going to be thrilled. To be honest, she didn't feel much like celebrating, either. But things didn't have to end like this. With anger and hurt coloring all the joy they'd shared.

She longed to tell him they could still see each other. He could come and visit her in the city. She'd be back for holidays and other times during the year. But her mouth felt glued shut and her throat was tight.

Still, she reached for him as he began to move, to turn for the door, to walk out of her apartment and out of her life. "Noah."

But he didn't pause, simply walked out of her apartment, crossed the hall and closed his door behind him with a final click.

It was only then that the reality of her situation set in. She was going, leaving Wheaton in her rear-view mirror just as she'd planned. Only instead of celebrating, Sabrina wanted to cry.

CHAPTER SEVENTEEN

NOAH DIDN'T LEAVE his apartment for two days. He'd heard Sabrina knock on his door, the light tap of her hand and call of her voice. He hadn't responded, hadn't moved, hadn't answered; he just sat there, stewing.

And she hadn't pushed, hadn't demanded that he let her in so they could talk. He didn't know whether he should be grateful for that or not. Because if she'd fought, it would have meant that he was important to her, that what they had was more than a summer fling. Instead, she just gave up and slipped an envelope under his door. It still sat there. He couldn't be bothered to get up and look at it.

He watched from the couch Wednesday morning as she loaded up her SUV and drove away. He thought she might have glanced at his windows, a wistful look on her face, but that was probably his imagination. Wishful thinking.

Noah drank a beer and told himself it was five o'clock somewhere.

His body ached. He'd trusted her and she'd used him. He'd let her in. Welcomed her into his life, his family. Let her see the real him, the man behind the mayor and she'd used it to accomplish her goal of getting away from this town, away from him. She hadn't even really asked if he'd go with her. No, she'd forgotten about him, about all of them, just as soon as she got what she wanted.

Noah was still sitting on the couch, watching the same sports highlights he'd been watching all morning when Marissa came by with the kids. He gave them the silent treatment, too. But Marissa was made of sterner stuff and used the key he'd given her to let herself in. She wrinkled her nose at the sight of him.

He glanced down at himself. He didn't look that bad. His clothes were rumpled and hadn't been changed in a few days, but they were relatively clean. That small spot from the burrito he'd eaten last night and the splotch where the beer had dripped were hardly noticeable.

"Hi, Uncle Noah." Apparently, unaware of his current state of mind, Daisy flung herself at him with abandon. He caught her with an *oof*. She wrinkled her nose, too. "You smell funny."

Marissa opened the French doors. Chilly air blew in and Daisy jumped down from the couch and complained she was cold. Noah didn't care about the drop in temperature. He hadn't noticed until Daisy said something.

Arms now unencumbered by busy five-year-old,

he picked up his beer, ignoring the unpleasant taste it left on his tongue and sipped. If he was going on a bender, he needed to do it right.

"Enough." Marissa swooped in and plucked the beer from his hands, dumping it down the sink. "You need coffee."

Coffee, which made him think of Sabrina. Damn. Would it always be like this? Would coffee, or at least the coffee shop in town, always remind him of her? Was the sweet joy of caffeine now ruined forever?

He crossed his arms while Timmy chortled in his mother's arms. Scotty stood by the side of the couch watching with big eyes and sucking his thumb. Daisy jumped on the couch.

Noah zeroed in on his niece. She was a good distraction from the painful path his thoughts were taking. "Aren't you supposed to be in school?" She'd been very proud to enter grade one this fall and had shared that piece of info with him over and over. And over.

Daisy jumped some more. "No school today."

He listened to Marissa banging around in the kitchen, then heard the click of his coffeemaker. He should let her know that this was his private domain and he'd make coffee if he wanted it, but it seemed like too much work. Instead he watched Daisy bounce off the couch and land on the floor with a thump. She started to twirl. Scotty copied her, thumb still firmly planted between his lips.

"Why don't you go take a shower?" Marissa laid a friendly hand on his shoulder.

Noah shrugged. He was fine here on the couch. He watched the kids spin in front of the open doors. He could see the corner of one of the chairs Sabrina had put out there. He remembered the day Sabrina had painted the pair of them. He'd come home from work and found her on the lawn in front of the porch, cherry-red paint slopped on the grass, her shorts and a dab on her nose. Of course she'd suckered him into helping.

She hadn't needed to try very hard. He'd wanted to help her and to test them out. To his great enjoyment, Sabrina had found the chair too hard, and determined that it was much more comfortable on his lap. After that, whenever they sat out there, she'd snuggle in and twine her arms around his waist and tell him all the amusing parts of her day.

Damn. He didn't want to remember. He pinched the bridge of his nose until it hurt and then pinched a little longer.

Marissa squeezed his shoulder. "Seriously, Noah. You smell like a brewery."

His jaw tightened. Could he not take one day for himself? Okay, a little more than a day. But did a man not deserve forty-eight hours to right himself when his legs had been slashed out from under him? "I'm fine."

He wasn't fine. Where was the numbing comfort from all the beer he'd imbibed since he'd walked out of Sabrina's apartment on Monday night and into his now bleak future? The painful clamp around his heart told him it was nowhere to be found.

Sabrina had taken everything he had to offer, everything he'd always feared giving, worried that it would be too revealing, the bits of himself that he tried to tamp down so no one would ever see anything but the thoughtful, intelligent man he wanted them to see. Well, she'd seen and she'd gone, slicing him out of her life without a thought.

Noah could never allow that to happen again. Never give anyone reason to question his goodness, how much he cared for the town and its residents. Never give them any cause to ask him to leave, to bounce him out on his ear or politely nudge him aside.

But he needed today for himself.

"Noah. Shower." Marissa poked him. "Or I'll sic the kids on you."

He opened his mouth to tell her to forget it, that he hadn't holed up to practice his hygiene and if she didn't like it she could leave, and then stopped. "Fine."

Marissa would leave more quickly if he just

went ahead and showered, and he was feeling a little grimy. Not that he'd admit it.

He left the four of them in the main room and walked to his bedroom, purposefully shutting the door behind him and flicking the lock. It was the first time he'd ever engaged it, but one couldn't be too careful with Daisy in the house.

By the time Noah came back out, hair wet, skin soaped and rinsed, he was feeling marginally better. The hot cup of coffee Marissa poured for him helped, too.

"What's that?" She pointed to the envelope she'd collected from the door and set on the kitchen table, propping it up on the decorative silver bowl that always sat in the middle.

Noah's place was furnished, but didn't have a homey, lived-in look. He'd gone to a big-box furniture store in a town an hour away, and ordered all the matching pieces, which left him with a slightly sterile effect that was missing the warmth that people with natural style achieved effortlessly. Like Sabrina—her place welcomed visitors with open arms.

He carved the thought out of his brain with surgical precision. He wasn't going to think about her anymore. Hadn't he decided that in the shower? And last night? And the day before that?

He picked up the envelope. His name was on the front in Sabrina's handwriting. "I have no idea."

And he had no plans to open it up and find out. He moved to toss it in the trash.

"You should read it."

No way. Absolutely not. Noah already knew what the letter would say. That she hoped they could be friends. That she hoped he was happy for her. That she hoped he understood why she had to go.

Marissa sighed. "Okay, my attempts at subterfuge and manipulation are a dismal failure. I recognize Sabrina's handwriting. You need to read it."

"I don't. I'm fine."

Marissa snatched the envelope out of his hand before he could crumple it into a ball. She started to tuck it into the bowl then paused. "You promise not to throw it away when I leave?"

"No."

She put a hand on her hip. Daisy ran up and followed suit. Noah was unmoved. He didn't want to read what Sabrina had written. There was nothing she could've written that would make any of this better. "You'll want to read it when you're feeling better."

No, he wouldn't. He stared at her.

"Promise you won't throw it away."

He considered refusing, but Marissa would argue with him and quite frankly it wasn't worth the trouble when he could just chuck it as soon as she left. She'd never know. "Fine."

He picked up his coffee and sipped. Marissa smiled at him. He eyed his sister-in-law more closely as a thought about someone other than himself, other than Sabrina, crawled into his brain. Marissa appeared normal, no signs of aggravation or upset, save when Daisy demanded a cup of coffee.

Noah frowned. Odd. He'd thought she'd be hurt by Sabrina's desertion, too, but she seemed fine. "Aren't you mad?" he asked.

Marissa blinked at him. "That you aren't reading the letter? No, you'll do that in your own time."

Noah shook his head. Not the letter. He didn't care about the letter. Much. "That she left again."

Understanding colored Marissa's gaze and made one corner of her mouth turn down. "No, I'm not mad."

Noah humphed. So he was alone in this. Alone in his hurt and disappointment. But then he was the only one whose life had been upended. The only one whose satisfaction with the status quo had been rattled and removed, leaving him lost.

Had it only been a few months ago that his life had seemed satisfactory? That he'd been content to tag along with his brother's family, go on the odd date and fill his life with the duties of town leader? He didn't feel like the same man. But maybe he wasn't. Before Sabrina. B.S. A bitter smile curved his lips. How fitting. Maybe if he'd realized, he

wouldn't have been so quick to agree to her interviews, to allow her to use him because he offered
a means to an end.

Marissa finished her coffee and put the cup in
the dishwasher. "Make sure you eat something and
don't lock yourself in again. Kyle told everyone
that you'd be back at work tomorrow."

Noah winced. Work. Where everyone would
know that he'd been missing and that this tied in
rather conveniently with Sabrina's departure. He
didn't know if he could take their well-meaning
solace and advice. The humiliation that he'd been
taken in and fooled might make them question his
ability to lead.

"He told them you had a cold."

"They won't believe it."

"They will." She gathered the kids. "They care
about you, Noah."

He wasn't so sure about that. They cared about
the jobs he created in the community. They cared
about him acting as a shield to prevent the likes of
Pete Peters from turning their undeveloped green
space into a strip mall. They cared about what he
could do for them. But did they care about him?

For so long, he'd been Noah Barnes, mayor.
Philanthropist. Giver. Caretaker. But he no longer knew if that was really him, or if they were
just characteristics he'd slipped on, like a good suit,
to create a persona that he'd thought he needed.

Because if he was just Noah, former hockey player, brother of Kyle and son of Ellen, would they still want him? Would he still be welcome?

He shook the confusing thoughts off. It didn't matter. Because he wasn't leaving and now that his free time was open, he could rededicate himself to them. Show them that they needed him, that their town wouldn't be the same without him.

It would be enough. It had to be.

CHAPTER EIGHTEEN

SABRINA STARED AT the walls of the dank basement suite she'd managed to rent on a day's notice, agreeing to the lease before she even left Wheaton. Actually, calling the place a suite or an apartment was an insult to apartments and suites everywhere. It was more like a cave.

The space was mainly below ground level, so the only windows she had were small and placed high on the wall. She couldn't even see out of them without tilting her neck up and then the only thing she was likely to spot was the feet of the residents who lived on the level above her. And she'd heard plenty from them already. Stomping around, morning, noon and night.

She reminded herself for the millionth time that her residence in The Cave was only temporary. She didn't have to live here the rest of her life and if she missed the large windows and cheerful colors of her apartment in Wheaton, all she had to do was recall how it had looked before her redecoration project. She could do the same here.

Okay, maybe not here in The Cave, but here in Vancouver.

Sabrina rubbed her forehead and chalked up the ache to the strain of moving and her noisy neighbors. She'd only moved in four days ago and she was already intimately acquainted with their walking patterns. Even so, she was sure she'd made the right decision to return. She had her job back, she'd already heard from some of her old friends and had plans to meet them for Sunday brunch tomorrow morning.

She had begged off hitting the clubs tonight, claiming exhaustion and lack of clothing options since most of her belongings were still in boxes. She probably should have gone, returned to the swing of city life to remind herself why she'd chosen Vancouver. Put on a pair of cute heels, styled her hair, put on some makeup and hit the dance floor. Only she didn't feel like caking on a pound of eyeliner and mascara. Her hair was just fine down with no hairspray or styling products. And the only shoes she wanted to wear were her red cowboy boots.

Sabrina eyed the water stain on the wall. A hot air balloon? Sunflower? No, mushroom cloud. Like the one that had tried to detonate her life in January. She exhaled, the only sound in The Cave since her upstairs neighbors were currently silent. Luckily, she'd avoided the destruction and

her life was now firmly back on track. She refused
to allow it to be derailed again.

Even if that meant writing a suck-up piece on
Big Daddy and his dilettante son.

The article would run in next week's paper. She
should probably write it tonight, but that made
her think about how sad it was to be working on a
Saturday night. And what had happened the last
time she'd done so, when Noah had shown up and
kissed her on the couch. No hope of that happening now.

Sabrina moved her hand to her stomach, rubbing
the ache that resided there. She should probably eat
something, whip up a masterpiece or just something edible on the scratched stove and cracked
countertop.

She didn't move from her reclined position on
the couch.

It hurt that Noah claimed she'd used him, written that article with the explicit goal of leaving.
That had never been the plan. Never.

Part of her wished she could go back and not
write the article, not move in across from him, not
flirt with him or kiss him or love him. But even
as she wished for the hurt to ease, she couldn't
regret the memories they'd created and the feelings they'd shared. Those had meant something.
Even if they were only temporary. She just wanted
the whole thing to be easier. But then if it were

easier it wouldn't have meant as much. A nice little quandary.

Sabrina stared harder at the water spot on the wall. She was just being a conscientious renter. It was important to keep an eye on the spot, to note any new darkness so she could alert the landlord. Because, you know, he clearly took such good care of the place.

And it meant she didn't have to think about how Noah hadn't said goodbye, hadn't answered her knock on his door and hadn't contacted her about the letter she'd left. According to Marissa, he'd refused to read it. She didn't understand why he acted like she wanted things to end this way. She hadn't. But what were their options? She was a city girl, he was a country boy. She had to come back to Vancouver for her job and he couldn't leave Wheaton.

She'd tried to be angry, to work up a self-righteous fury at his complete shutdown. He'd known she planned to come back to Vancouver. He'd encouraged her to get her job back. And then when everything worked out just as expected, he got mad?

But no matter how tight her grip, Sabrina couldn't hang on to that desire to fight, to rage against him. She tucked her hands around herself and curled onto her side. Maybe if she warmed herself the ache would go away. Maybe if she had a nap. But lately sleep was as elusive as her appetite. She closed her eyes anyway.

Minutes later, the sound of stomping feet overhead roused her from her attempted rest. The Stompson Twins were up and alert and pounding around. Sabrina shot a glare at the ceiling and followed the sound with the bird though they couldn't see her. Her attempt to send the message psychically fell on deaf ears, too, as a second pair of feet joined the first and then the thump of bass from the stereo.

Sabrina closed her eyes and swore. Great. So much for a peaceful night of moping. She was not willing to lie around if it meant she had to listen to people storming around all night.

She dragged herself off the couch and into the bathroom. Her hair was knotted on one side. She ran a brush through it, slicking it back into a ponytail, then slipped on a light coat since the nights were getting cold, put on her red boots and headed out.

She bumped into a couple carrying a bottle of wine coming in. They had thick-framed hipster glasses, tight jeans, plaid shirts and an air of good cheer that annoyed her. She clomped down the front steps of the building in her boots. She could hear laughter coming from her neighbor's place, and see shadows of people moving around. Obviously they were having a party.

If this had been a few months earlier, Sabrina would already know the neighbors. She'd have invited them over for nibbles and a drink; they'd be on a first-name basis by now and she'd have been invited to the party.

She tucked her chin into her chest and headed down the sidewalk. She didn't have the energy. She wasn't staying in The Cave for longer than necessary, so what was the point? She'd make friends with them and then they'd be upset when she left. She didn't want to do that anymore.

Sabrina walked around the neighborhood until her legs were tired and she thought maybe she'd be able to sleep even through the noise of the party upstairs. When she returned she brushed off the greeting of a group on the front steps, acknowledging them with a short nod, and slipped into the overwhelming grayness of The Cave. But her plan to lie on the bed and wrap herself in a cocoon of blankness eluded her.

The fresh air had put her brain on alert and though her body wanted to shut down, her mind refused, bouncing from thought to thought until Sabrina wanted to scream. She hadn't hooked up her TV, and she didn't feel like streaming anything on her laptop. She didn't have the energy to start the article on Big Daddy and son. She didn't want to read, didn't want to listen to music, didn't want to go back out, didn't want to stay in.

She picked up her phone, opened her contact list and scrolled through, then put her phone back down. She shouldn't call Marissa tonight. But Sabrina picked the phone back up and scrolled through again. This time her thumb hit the call button. Once it rang, it was too late to hang up.

"Oh, no," Marissa said in lieu of hello, "you are not calling me at ten o'clock at night."

"I am." Some of Marissa's attitude seeped through the phone line and into Sabrina's bones. She felt a little better, a little stronger, a little more herself. Marissa's support of her decision to return to Vancouver had been a balm to her soul. If Marissa wasn't hanging on to her grudge and accusing her of being a bad person for leaving, then maybe she wasn't. "And don't you dare hang up."

A part of her expected Marissa to hang up anyway, just because she'd told her not to. Marissa could be contrary that way, but she only sniffed loudly. "This better be good. The kids are in bed and so am I."

"Would I call if it wasn't good?"

"Yes."

Sabrina grinned. True, Marissa hadn't been thrilled that Sabrina was going and had vocally and without reservation stated her opinion that Sabrina should consider staying in Wheaton. But when Sabrina made it clear that her mind was made up, Marissa had acknowledged the legitimacy of her choice. It proved to be a big step forward in their relationship and one Sabrina hadn't known she'd needed until it was there. "So how are things?"

Marissa snorted. "We talked earlier today and I told you all about how things were." She paused. "Since I know you couldn't have forgotten, I can only assume that you're asking about other things. A certain town mayor?"

Sabrina let her eyes close. She'd done her best not to bring Noah's name into her now daily conversations with Marissa because she didn't want Marissa to feel obligated to act as a go-between and she didn't want to hear that Marissa thought she should come back and see for herself. Marissa stated that often enough without Sabrina giving her an opening. But the truth was she did want to know, to have the guilt weighing her down assuaged. No matter what had happened between them, she wanted to know that he was okay. "How is he?"

Sabrina did her best to achieve a neutral tone. She knew she'd failed by Marissa's sad sigh. "He's okay." Marissa blew out a breath of air. "No, that's not true. He's not okay. I think you broke him."

"Don't say that." As if she didn't feel awful enough? Now she had Marissa adding to it. Sabrina twirled her fingers through her hair, but the soft slip of silky strands did nothing to ease her guilt. "I wasn't important enough to break him." Not even enough to rate a goodbye. "He'll be fine."

"You were important to him." Marissa's quiet voice said more than if she'd shouted the words. "But you're right. One day he'll meet a nice woman who will recognize what a catch he is and she'll stay."

Displeasure jolted through Sabrina. She didn't like the idea of another woman moving in on her man. Then had to remind herself that Noah wasn't hers. She'd given up that claim when she'd moved away. But the irritated buzzing remained under her skin. "Well, I hope he'll be very happy with her. Whoever she is."

Marissa laughed. "No, you don't. Which should tell you something." It did, just nothing that Sabrina was ready to consider. "Anyway, why are you calling me on a Saturday night? Shouldn't you be out living your fabulous life with the wannabes?"

"They're not all wannabes." Some of the tension slipped from Sabrina's shoulders. This was safer ground. One that wouldn't require her to dig through the morass of emotions that she preferred to stuff down. "Also, I'm not feeling particularly fabulous at the moment."

Not even the red boots had done the trick. They were the one tangible thing she'd taken with her from Wheaton and she'd taken to wearing them constantly. She kicked her feet out and admired them now, even though the sight always sent a pinch through her stomach. Noah had loved the boots. Almost as much as she did. Of course, neither of them loved the boots as much as Daisy, who, after wailing over the news that Sabrina was leaving, had begged her to leave the boots. Sabrina had actually considered it, but Marissa had told her daughter to forget it because Aunt Sabrina needed them.

Sabrina wasn't sure which had pleased her more, that Marissa saw she needed that tie to the town or that she'd called Sabrina the kids' aunt.

The one thing that had given her true happiness since her return was wandering down Fourth Avenue and seeing a pair of kid-size cowboy boots in red. She'd walked in, plucked them out of the window and shipped them off the same day. Some things were necessities in life—like a great pair of boots.

"If you're so unhappy, come home," Marissa said. "We miss you."

"You miss me," Sabrina corrected. "Singular." But she held her breath just in case Marissa said that Noah missed her, too. Sabrina didn't know what she would do with that information, but she wanted to hear it anyway.

"We," Marissa insisted. "Kyle and Ellen and the kids." There was no mention of Noah and Sabrina felt her initial hope deflate. "And by the way, can

you see if you can find another pair of red boots for Scotty? I'll pay." She sighed. "He keeps taking them from Daisy's room and wearing them around until she realizes what's happened and loses it. I've had to start keeping them in our room on the closet shelf so that no one gets the boots unless I say so."

Sabrina could picture the scene in perfect detail. Scotty's happy smile as he wandered around, thumb in mouth. Daisy busy chattering away about something and only noticing that Scotty was wearing the boots after he'd been in the room for ten minutes and then flying into a fit about it.

"I tell you, it's been quite a trial."

Sabrina laughed. "Yes, because you so desperately hate to be in charge."

"It's true. I do." Then they both laughed. "I mean it, though, Sabrina. Come home."

"I am home," Sabrina said.

"Are you? Really? Because you're not acting like it."

Sabrina's knee jittered. She watched the rhythmic bounce of her boots. Up, down, up down. "I'm just getting back into the swing of things," she told Marissa. "It takes time."

It wasn't unreasonable to take some time to get back in her zone. She needed to find an apartment she loved where she wouldn't feel that unpacking was a waste of time. She needed to resettle into her job. Her stomach jumped at the thought of returning to the office on Monday after eight months away. She needed to adapt to the lifestyle of her city friends where eleven at night meant it was time to go out, not settle in for the evening.

"It didn't take you any time here," Marissa pointed out.

"That was different." Sabrina ignored the niggling feeling that Marissa was right. She could easily have taken some steps to settle in already.

"How?"

Sabrina didn't have a good answer. "It just was."

"Yes, because your home is here. With us."

Sabrina felt a prickling behind her eyes. She'd thought about it many times and just as quickly discarded the idea. She hadn't fought so hard to get her job and life back here to give it up. She couldn't go back. She just couldn't.

Not even for Noah.

"I can't," she said, as she said every time Marissa mentioned it.

"Fine, but I'm going to keep asking."

"Why?" Sabrina really wanted to know. "Not that it doesn't make me feel incredibly loved, but why is it so important? You hated me only a few months ago and you took Noah's side."

"I miss you," Marissa said.

The prickling sharpened and Sabrina blinked,

though there was no one to see if she let the tears roll down her cheeks.

"You sold me a false bill of goods, wheedling your way back into my good graces. I barely got to make you pay for that article. I feel I didn't get all my punishing in. And now you've added the cowboy-boot situation to the mix. Really, Sabrina, how can I make you pay when you live so far away?"

"If anyone can find a way, it's you." She swiped the back of her hand across her eyes and coughed to clear the thickness in her throat.

"Are you crying?" Marissa wanted to know. "Stop it. I like it better when you get all snarky and bossy."

"I do not get bossy."

"You do. You *so* do."

"And you don't?"

"Of course I do. How do you think I so easily recognize the trait in others?" Marissa sighed. "Quit being stubborn. You're not happy there."

She wasn't, and fear that she'd once again made the wrong decision bubbled up. Sabrina fought back, breathing in and out slowly until her lungs felt normal and her leg stopped bouncing. "I will be happy," she told Marissa, hoping she sounded more certain than she felt. Thinking negatively was doing her no favors.

She had her job. Her health. She'd won her job back, and that hadn't been easy. It was something to be proud of. Just as soon as she found her place, literally and figuratively, she'd be back to feeling like herself.

Even if she wasn't sure who that was anymore.

CHAPTER NINETEEN

NOAH SPENT THE DAYS after his minibender busying himself with work and his ignored campaign. Since there was no longer anyone to fill up his free time, he filled it himself. Calling meetings with his campaign advisory committee and discussing his platform, getting new photos taken, his poster and other marketing materials printed, finishing his budgets for the dealership and driving back and forth between his two locations.

He'd barely been to the dealership located outside Wheaton over the summer. Too often he had plans with Sabrina or other events that pulled at his time. He should have handled his schedule better, should have made time. He vowed to address the problem immediately.

Plus, it got him out of Wheaton. He drove over on the following Tuesday and booked himself into a hotel with the intention of staying until the weekend. There would be meetings to hold, sales numbers to run, problems to solve. He looked forward to immersing himself in everything. Only they didn't need him.

He'd staffed the dealership well. His new manager, the one he'd hired just before the heat of summer, was fantastic. Engaged and observant, she had the dealership running like a well-oiled machine. Coupled with his competent team of sales professionals and the best mechanics in town, the place turned a profit and ran smoothly even in his absence. They were happy to see him, of course, to show off their successes and plans for future ones, but they didn't need him. Noah stayed anyway. Because no one at this dealership watched him with sympathetic eyes or asked how he was feeling.

He was fine. Perfectly fine. Better than fine.

And when Noah drove back to Wheaton it was with a renewed dedication to winning the upcoming mayoral election. Not just because Pete wasn't a good candidate for the town, but because he needed the community's vote. A vote that told him that they wanted him to stay.

SABRINA STARED AT THE marked-up papers sitting in her in-box in her newly regained cubicle. Her editor was a traditionalist and still preferred to make revisions on paper, fearful that something might get lost electronically. This wasn't the article on Big Daddy and son, which had run last week, but her latest article. Clearly, her editor had not been as enamored of the words as she had.

She swallowed her irritation and, if she were

completely honest, the hurt. Back in the day—
okay, a year ago—her articles had only received
the lightest edits. But all of the pieces she'd submit-
ted since her return had received the same bright
red critique.

Her sleek messenger bag felt heavy on her shoulder and she slipped it off and hung it over the back
of the rolling chair at her desk. The sounds of the
newsroom clacked around her, louder than she remembered.

She sat in the chair, pulling the pages from
her plastic tray and flattening them on her desk.
Slashes and question marks, notations in the mar-
gins stared back at her, but she barely noticed them
over the one word that jumped out at her from the
bottom of the page.

Crap. In block letters and underlined twice.

A low rolling boil started in her blood. Her work
was not crap. The article was insightful and charming and fresh. The complete opposite of crap. This
would have been gold in Wheaton. Sabrina reminded herself that she wasn't in Wheaton anymore and scowled at the page when she read what
was written below the underlined crap.

You've gone soft?

As if she'd gone soft. She'd fought and clawed
and badgered anyone linked to her job for nearly
a year looking for a toehold to come back. And
she'd found it. How was that *soft?* Not to mention

the fabulous red boots she was wearing. Given the right trajectory and force the tips could draw blood. Not even a little soft.

In fact, she felt like kicking something right now. Or someone.

The noise of the cubicled office added to her ire. Fingers hammering across keyboards like they were trying to communicate in Morse code, phones with the ringers turned up full blast and, worse, the conversations that followed, every person seemingly unaware that she could hear every detail being shared. No offense to any of them, but Sabrina didn't want to know that Nerissa had slept with a guy who had a hair sweater hiding under his dress shirt last night, that Shirley's niece was refusing to enter rehab and that Marvin's wife had given the entire family food poisoning on the weekend.

She thought longingly of her Wheaton apartment where the only sounds were the birds outside or Noah knocking on her door. But this wasn't Wheaton.

Sabrina wasn't used to the cacophony of city living yet. Last night she'd actually woken up when a fire truck siren had roared past The Cave. She told herself that she just needed a little more time to settle in and ignored the tiny voice that asked if three weeks wasn't long enough.

Apparently not. It had probably taken her two months to get used to the quiet of Wheaton, so it made sense it would take at least that long to re-acclimate to the bustle of Vancouver.

And she was doing better. She'd gone out with her old city friends twice last week. So she'd gone home early the second night. She'd been tired and what was wrong with admitting she needed a little beauty rest? She'd even glanced through the vacancy listings in the paper yesterday, though most longtime Vancouverites knew the only way to find a good apartment was through word of mouth or to call apartment management companies directly. By the time listings reached the public, the good ones were long gone.

Still, she was making an effort.

Sabrina shoved down the irritation threatening to spill over when the occupant of the cubicle next to hers—someone new who hadn't been around when she left—answered his cell phone while already talking on his landline and thought it was reasonable to carry on conversations with both parties at the same time. Ridiculous.

Well, she couldn't stay here. How could any sane person work in this kind of environment? Without glancing around, she gathered up the papers and crammed them into her messenger bag. She'd deal with them, with everything, back at The Cave.

Sabrina's boots slammed against the sidewalk all the way home. She felt marginally better when she entered the dim apartment. For once, the space was blessedly quiet. Just a wash of sunlight trickling through her high windows and the squeaks that were common in older buildings. The Stompson Twins were probably still sleeping off their carousing from the night before. She'd heard them arrive home just after one in the morning, clomping around in their hard-soled shoes, turning on the stereo and walking back and forth until she felt like screaming. Though the noise only lasted about thirty minutes, Sabrina had stared at her water-marked ceiling until four.

As she plunked her laptop onto the kitchen table—she hadn't gotten around to setting up an office area—she considered making some noise herself to give them a taste of what it was like to live with ignorant neighbors, but hitting the ceiling with a broom seemed petty and like a lot of work. Not to mention she feared bringing down a rain of plaster on her head and who knew what else. Asbestos? Mold? A dead mouse? She shuddered and pushed aside the desire for revenge. She wouldn't be here much longer, and she could put up with anything, even the Stompson Twins, temporarily.

Her laptop hummed to life, and Sabrina pulled out the notes and read through them again. There were a lot. No easy fixes, but that was okay. She'd proved that she could handle tough assignments. Still, a cup of coffee wouldn't go awry. She made a big pot and after pouring herself a jumbo cup, she sent off a quick email to the editor and staff, letting them know that she'd be working from home today. She didn't worry that it would get lost electronically. Then she got down to work.

The overriding tone of the notes was that she'd been too easy on her subject, a sweet nineteen-year-old actress who'd been working in Vancouver since she was a kid but had recently landed a role in a Hollywood blockbuster due to film this winter. Movie reviewers and bloggers believed the film would be the next *Twilight* or *Hunger Games* and would catapult the young actress and her costars into the celebrity stratosphere. Sabrina's editor wanted her to be tougher. Everyone was writing fluff pieces—they'd stand out by being hard-nosed.

But seriously, there was nothing hard about the girl. She'd been unfailingly polite, well-spoken, cheerful and quite funny. Charm and charisma were the hallmarks of any successful actor, Sabrina knew that, but this girl was the real deal. Exactly what was Sabrina supposed to write? She took a sip of her steaming coffee even though it scalded her tongue.

Fine. They wanted snarky cattiness? She'd deliver. And she'd show everyone, her editor, her friends, her colleagues that her time in her hometown hadn't turned her soft. Not even a little. That she was more than capable of handling anything the city might throw at her.

The morning disappeared while Sabrina slaved over the words. She referenced her interview notes over and over, looking for pauses, phrasings that could be twisted to suit her purpose. She stopped only twice to refill her giant red coffee mug.

The Stompson Twins arose, stormed around awhile and then left. Sabrina noticed only when their matching spindly legs caused a shadow to fall through her window. How two people with so little body fat could manage to make so much noise was a mystery. Other building residents came and went, their footsteps thumping on the concrete stairs outside. The coffee pot emptied. The sun passed its apex and began to descend.

Sabrina remained glued to her laptop, writing, deleting, rewriting. She polished, revised and tightened. She checked her notes against the material she'd derived from other sources—the actress's publicist, other news articles from reputable sources. Then she checked them again. As the last bit of daylight drifted away, she sat back, leaning against the hard wooden slats of her kitchen chair.

Her butt was numb, her stomach churned from too much coffee and not enough food, her shoulders and forearms were tender from typing, but she was done.

Her masterpiece was complete, and it was worthy of the title. She smiled as she read the lines. Sharp and clean and bitchy. Her editor would love it. So would all her city friends. Sabrina could imagine them now, laughing wildly over Sunday brunch as they repeated a particularly ruthless sentence.

It would be her grand reintroduction. Her statement that this time she wouldn't be leaving and that no one could take her place.

But instead of soothing her, the laughing faces of her city friends changed and morphed into those of her friends in Wheaton. Marissa and Kyle. The kids. Ellen, Trish, Mrs. Thompson. George and all the friends she'd made at Cedar Oaks. Her customers at the coffee shop. Her parents.

Noah.

Only none of them were laughing. Their eyes didn't shine with schadenfreude or approval. They didn't smile or nod. Instead, they looked downright disappointed in her.

Sabrina shook her head to clear it. Why was she thinking about them? The chances of them even reading the article were slim. Okay, fine. Maybe she'd received some emails and texts from town residents complimenting her on her article last week. Maybe they would read it. No big deal. They'd know that she was being facetious, that she didn't really think poorly of the actress, right?

But her stomach twisted and even when she

poured the rest of her coffee down the sink and drank some water instead, it wouldn't stop churning.

This was crazy. She wasn't soft. The actress would understand, if she even bothered to read it. It was just business, a way to sell papers. Nothing personal. And sometimes these snarky articles did more to increase the subject's profile than the softball pieces their publicists were always angling for. Wasn't that what the actress and her team were after? Coverage to increase name recognition, building her brand so that she could demand a higher salary and more perks in her next contract?

Sabrina rinsed the cup out and stuck it in the rack to dry. Or would the actress feel like Marissa? As though she'd been betrayed by someone who'd acted like a friend. The churning grew more aggressive. Was this how Noah felt when she told him that she'd used her article on him to get her job back?

Sabrina told herself it wasn't the same situation at all. She and the actress had no personal connection and if the girl was naive enough to think that they were friends, then that was her fault. It would be a good lesson. She shouldn't be so trusting with the media because there were plenty of jackals out there who wouldn't pause to consider her feelings. They'd jump all over anything she said; some would even create rumor and supposition if they thought they could get away with it. Sabrina would be doing her a favor because her article wasn't that nasty, just a little reminder of what the actress could expect from others if she didn't protect herself more carefully.

The taste of coffee lingered in her mouth. Sharp and bitter, even after she brushed her teeth. This wasn't just about the coffee. She put her tooth-brush away and returned to her computer. Maybe she could ease up on some of her snarkier obser-vations a tad.

But when she clicked on the menu to open her recent documents, a different title caught her eye. George Cuthbert. It had been the last article she'd written for the *Wheaton Digest* and had run the week after she left.

No one had taken over the series. Sabrina knew because she checked the paper online every Tues-day, Thursday and Saturday. She knew she should be a bigger person, but she was glad the series had folded. It was hers, her idea, her baby and she didn't like the idea of someone else putting their grubby paws all over it.

Those interviews had been fun. There had been no publicists in the background ready to put a stop to the proceedings if they didn't like the way the questions were framed or the answers their client gave. There was no hedging of words or spinning of stories. Of course people had wanted to show themselves in their best light. That was human nature. But no one had lied or obfuscated, refused to comment or claimed that a particular subject was off-limits.

The young actress hadn't, either. And Sabrina wondered who she herself had become. Was she really the kind of person who repaid someone's openness and honestly with a vicious, baseless article?

She blew out a breath, but the roiling inside her didn't abate. Did she want to be the kind of reporter who attacked through words? Who made someone else feel bad to make others feel better?

For the first time, she saw her article on Jackson through his father's eyes. She'd gone after his boy with guns blazing and his father had fought back. And he'd been right. No, his son wasn't a civic-minded, charitable member of society, but he wasn't evil, either. Just shallow and self-centered.

What she'd done to Marissa had been worse. Sabrina closed her eyes. So much worse. And yet Marissa had forgiven her. Had acknowledged her hurt and moved past it. And what had Sabrina done with all the goodwill that had been shown to her? Used it to get out of Wheaton, away from the kind hearts that had surrounded her and back to the cold, unforgiving city lights.

She reopened the article on the actress. Then

she highlighted the entire piece and clicked delete. Done.

The corners of her mouth turned up even before the page blinked into a blankness. She wasn't that kind of reporter anymore. Maybe she never had been. She'd just been fooling herself to think she could keep up the charade forever.

The pain that had attached itself to her over the past weeks loosened. She wasn't high-rise condos and metal furniture. She was a shared duplex with fuzzy couches and warm rugs and a lush garden out back. She wasn't experimental theater and night clubs. She was concerts in the park at the annual Northern Lights festival. She was dinner with friends, not brunch after a night of heavy drinking. She wasn't Jimmy Choos and Manolo Blahniks. Okay, wait, she could still be those things. But she was also cotton dresses and bandannas for her hair, jeans and plaid shirts. She was red cowboy boots.

Relief at finally admitting the truth trickled through her. Her arms no longer hurt and her stomach finally settled. Even that persistent ache behind her heart that she'd come to believe would be a constant companion eased, replaced by a radiating warmth. This was who she was, and she was okay with it. She didn't have to prove anything to anyone. Not anymore. And she refused to spend another minute being someone she wasn't. The deleted article was only the start.

Sabrina Ryan was going home.

CHAPTER TWENTY

THE SOFT TAP AT THE dealership office door irritated Noah. A lot of things irritated Noah these days. Hadn't he told the staff that he wasn't to be disturbed this morning unless it was an emergency? Since there hadn't been a loud boom indicating an explosion, there was no smoke sneaking under his door hinting at an inferno already ablaze, nor was there the splash and rush of water pouring from a pipe, he saw no explanation for why his orders had been ignored. Which meant they were bugging him over nothing. As usual.

"Come in." He was careful to keep the snappish tone out of his voice. No one at the office had done anything wrong and it wasn't fair to take his irritation out on them. Still, he didn't understand why they couldn't grasp that he didn't want to be bothered.

The election was in one month and his campaign was in full gear. He and his team were going around this evening, putting up signs and posters around town. He noticed Pete had done so last night, which was illegal. Candidates had to wait until the election was thirty days away before posting election materials, but Noah wasn't going to report the man. He'd beat him despite it.

"Got a minute?" Kyle walked in without waiting for Noah to answer and shut the door behind him.

"Just one." Noah found that if he kept busy or gave the illusion of looking that way, people left him alone. It made the days easier to get through.

"Make it two." Kyle sank into the chair across from him.

Noah met his brother's gaze and tamped down his annoyance. Kyle wasn't one to wander in for a chat or to ask a simple question. In fact, his brother had done a good job of running interference for him at the office by taking on a greater amount of the responsibilities and training the staff to come to him for certain questions. But Noah crossed his arms over his chest as encouragement for Kyle to state his business and then leave. "What is it?"

Kyle paused to crack his knuckles. An old habit he'd had since he was a kid and a sign that Noah wouldn't like what he was about to say.

Tension coiled around Noah's chest. He didn't move. Just stayed silent. Watching and waiting. Knowing the hammer was about to drop.

"I just got off the phone with Marissa."

Oh, hell. Was she pregnant? Again? Noah bit back the nudge of jealousy that rose. His baby brother already had four kids and a loving wife while he had none.

Kyle kept talking. "She talked to Sabrina this morning."

The pressure flowed from Noah's chest, up his neck and intensified along the line of his jaw. He could feel the muscle twitching, practically threatening to pop through the skin and did his best not to let the strain seep into his voice. "I've told you I don't want to hear this."

Kyle leaned forward, hands on his knees. His blue eyes pinned Noah. "She's coming back."

For a second, Noah thought Kyle was playing a joke on him. A sick, cruel joke that would have any logical person filing for emancipation from his family. But the worried look in Kyle's eyes told Noah this was no joke. He was telling the truth. Sabrina was coming back.

He forced a shrug though it pained the muscles in his neck, which regularly felt like concrete when he got up in the morning. He rubbed at them now. "And?"

"And I didn't want you to hear it from someone else."

Noah started to shrug again, then realized that it probably looked like he was trying to project an image of disinterest. He was, but if he saw through it, so would others. Even his sweet, good-natured, look-for-the-best-in-others brother. So he converted the movement midshrug into an awkward shoulder roll that probably wouldn't fool anyone, either.

Kyle was polite enough not to mention it. But he watched. His kind eyes taking in everything. Everything Noah wanted to keep hidden.

"So now you've told me." Noah forced the words through the tightness in his throat. They scratched and clawed as they fought their way free. "Anything else?"

So casual. As if this wasn't a blow. As if he didn't curse himself every day for letting Sabrina past those barriers he'd erected over the years. As if he hadn't let his life twine with hers, twisting and merging together like the ivy that grew up the sides of the porch at the house. As if he hadn't believed they were building something special together.

He should have known. She'd told him she wasn't staying. Not even implicitly with suggestions and hints. She'd been clear that she was in contact with her old editor, that she wanted her old job back. If he'd believed that her actions spoke louder than words, that with every turn of her head, every coy glance over her shoulder and stretch of her leg she was letting him know that she wouldn't leave him, he had only himself to blame.

Sadly, this bit of insight didn't make the knowledge easier to bear.

The fist of pain that had been Noah's constant

companion since she'd walked out of his life punched him in the chest, then followed up with a crosscheck to his lungs. He might look okay on the outside—sure, he was a little pale, but he could blame that on his long days of campaign planning—but inside he was a mass of bruises. He breathed through the attack.

Sabrina was coming back.

"Maybe you should take the rest of the day off," Kyle said. "We'll go to the lake, do some fishing."

Trout Lake would close for fishing at the end of the month, but Noah didn't feel like taking advantage of that. "Can't. Too much to do."

"Noah."

He didn't look at his brother. Not really. He gave the impression of paying attention, looking in Kyle's direction and pasting on a polite expression. He could even nod and murmur if necessary. But he couldn't look at him. Couldn't bear to see the compassion shining out of his brother's eyes.

He was the big brother. The one who was supposed to have everything figured out. Who didn't call on others for help just in case he became a drain on them. Just in case he did something that caused them to push him away.

That might be the thing that hurt most about Sabrina. That he'd let himself believe he didn't have to pretend around her. That he could just let go. Except when he had, she'd pushed him away, too.

The edges of his vision darkened. He blinked and sucked in some oxygen until the darkness receded. Never again. It was a hard lesson to learn, but best he learned now while he still had the opportunity to change. The next woman he dated would see only the perfect, mayoral side. The public side he showed to the world. And maybe she would stay.

"Marissa thinks you need to talk." Kyle held up a hand when Noah opened his mouth. "I told her to leave you alone, but you know how she is."

Noah did know. Kyle had managed to allow Noah some privacy in his professional office life, but his personal family life was a different story. Marissa had been a regular visitor to his apartment since Sabrina's departure. Often with a kid or two in tow. Sometimes she brought dinners for him to stick in his freezer and heat up when he was hungry. Sometimes she came to help with the campaign. Occasionally she told him the kids needed some bonding time with their uncle and escaped, leaving them behind. But Noah knew those were all ruses. She was checking up on him to see if he was improving. And pushing—always with the pushing—urging him to talk about his feelings. "If she shows up, I'll handle it."

"You sure?"

He nodded once to let Kyle know he was okay, and waited until the door clicked shut behind his brother before he exhaled softly. Slowly, just in case anyone was listening.

Sabrina was back. For a visit? Permanently? He realized those were questions he should have asked his brother. He could call him back and ask now, but the thought left him icy cold. Maybe it was better not to know. He should continue on with life as though her appearance made no difference to him. Because it shouldn't.

She'd left. Her position was clear. She didn't want to be with him. He wasn't good enough for her to stay.

Noah hoped like hell she wasn't planning to stay, wasn't moving back into her old apartment. It would be much easier to ignore her presence if he wasn't forced to live next door to her, the entryway filled with her perfume, her music acting as a soundtrack to his evenings.

He had too much on his plate to let Sabrina's return and the reasons behind it twist him up again. No, he was done with that phase of his life. A youthful indiscretion that would soon be a distant memory.

Noah pushed up his shirtsleeves and got back to business.

BY THE TIME NOAH LEFT for home, he was beat. He'd stayed late on purpose, keeping his campaign team longer than necessary because he didn't want

to go home. His reasons would have been obvious to anyone who knew, but he'd heard no comments about Sabrina's return, which had relaxed
him a little.

But as he neared the house, his anxiety reappeared. What if she was there already? What if
she was waiting for him? He didn't know what he
would say. He didn't want to talk to her, but how
could he avoid her if she was living right beside
him?

He turned off his headlights before he turned
up the driveway, hoping to slip in under the cover
of night. The moon was high and bright and gave
enough illumination for him to park without running into anything.

When he saw her SUV sitting in its spot by the
house, he gritted his teeth. So she was here. Or at
least her car was.

Noah crept up the porch steps, careful to hold
the door tight to absorb the sound of his key turning in the lock. He could hear the drone of her
TV before he had the door fully open. Lamplight
spilled into the hallway from her apartment where
she'd left the door propped open. Her red boots
acted as the doorstop, a cheerful bastion greeting
his arrival.

Noah ignored the low pull in his belly at the
sight of those boots. He should see them as a har-
binger of doom, not great sex. He shut the front

door behind him and told himself not to peek into her apartment. She might see it as a welcoming gesture, and that wasn't something he was willing to give.

But he couldn't help a hurried glance. He told himself it was simply preparation. If she came barreling out, he wouldn't be caught off guard. But that wasn't the only reason.

He wanted to see her. Wanted to see that sweep of dark hair, those big green eyes and those pretty red lips. Did she look as tired as he did? Had she been sleeping well? Did she regret her decision to go?

What he saw was her crashed out on her couch, one hand tucked under her cheek, hair curled over her neck while the TV played in the background. She looked so angelic, a tiny smile on her lips as she dreamed. No one would ever guess she was the kind of person who could rip a man's heart out, stomp all over it and then come back, expecting he'd simply ask for more.

Noah quelled the urge to walk in and cover her with the blanket off the back of the couch. If she got cold, she'd wake up and do it herself. He didn't owe her anything. Not even a warm blanket. And one night of shivering wouldn't kill her.

But once safely inside his own bed, he wasn't able to sleep. He couldn't help thinking of her sleeping over there, door wide open, with nothing and no one to protect her.

Cursing, he got up and marched over. He didn't take as much care with noise this time. If she wanted to talk, he had a few things to say. Namely that a man should be able to sleep in his own bed without worrying about his neighbor catching a cold or worse.

Noah whipped the blanket over her. Sabrina didn't rouse, didn't even move as the blanket settled. He turned off the TV and locked the door behind him. Yes, he'd kept her key. He hadn't meant to hang on to it. He just hadn't been thinking about those kinds of details when she'd told him she was leaving. Once he realized he still had it, she'd already been gone for a week. He'd planned to give it to her parents when they came around to close up, but he hadn't seen them. He should have dropped it in the mail or contacted them, but he hadn't. He didn't stop to think why that might be. The fact was, he still had it and it had come in handy.

Noah climbed back into his own bed and closed his eyes, but sleep remained elusive. So when dawn rolled around, followed by a pounding on his door, he felt as cranky as a grizzly bear.

He snarled as he flipped the lock. He knew who was behind it, making all that racket with her fists. Did she think he was deaf? He yanked the door open, forgetting that he was supposed to act as if he didn't care. "What?"

God, Sabrina looked good. Noah didn't want to notice. Didn't want to drink her in from her head to her toes. But he did anyway, gorging himself on her fresh-faced, bright-eyed appeal. Even her hair, messy with sleep, looked glorious to him, just begging a man to wrap his hands in it. He'd barely been able to stop himself from touching it last night, and he curled his fingers against his palms now.

He didn't want to think about how he looked. Exhausted and beat up, like he'd spent the night tossing and turning in between bouts of punching his pillow into a different shape as though that might be the culprit for his insomnia.

Sabrina smiled and his heart thumped. "Hi."

Hi? Just a couple of neighbors saying good morning? "Hi." He returned the greeting, curt and abrupt. The tone of a man who didn't have time for simple pleasantries because he had bigger and better things on his schedule. "Need something?"

Her smile dimmed. Good. Noah reminded himself he had no reason to feel guilty. He hadn't done anything wrong, and if Sabrina regretted her choices, she could learn to live with them, the same way he was doing. She clasped her hands in front of her. "I...I hoped we could talk."

She hoped they could talk. How nice for her.

How nice to think that a brief little chat was part of her plan today. Too bad—it wasn't part of his. "I don't have time today."

Her brow wrinkled slightly. "Tonight then?"

"Busy." And if he wasn't, he'd find something to do.

"Okay, tomorrow. I'll take you out for coffee. I know you have time for that."

Noah's resolve didn't waver. He couldn't be weak around this woman, the one who'd gotten behind his defenses and made him think that she would stay. That he was worth staying for. "It's not a good time right now." He stopped short of saying her name, afraid that hearing it slip from his lips would shatter the thin shield of protection around him.

"Oh." He saw the realization register. She tried again anyway. "When would be a good time? This is important."

"Not to me."

Surprise then pain flashed across her face. He schooled his features into polite boredom. He would not crumble, would not let her know she still had the ability to dig into his heart. He had to protect himself. "Noah."

"I need to get ready for work," he told her. His hands were clenched so tight that he wouldn't have been shocked to find the nails had broken skin.

"But…"

But nothing. Noah stared at her. She didn't finish her sentence.

"Well, I wanted you to know that I'm back." She slowed and took a breath. Her eyes met his and her voice quieted. "I quit my job in the city."

Goodie for her. He didn't say a word.

"I wanted you to know that."

"And now I do." He didn't shift, not even a millimeter. What did it matter if Sabrina was back? Nothing had changed between them. Nothing at all.

"Okay." He saw her throat bob as she swallowed. "Then I guess I'll let you get back to dressing."

Noah looked down at his bare chest and boxers. Hell, he hadn't even thought to grab a pair of sweatpants or a shirt. It was her. Sabrina confused him, made him disregard the image he'd worked so hard to create. He hated that. More than ever he needed to cloak himself in that armor of perfection. And in less than twenty-four hours, she'd already managed to make him forget.

"Noah?" He didn't want to look at her. Did his trick of looking just past her, letting his gaze fix on something in the distance. "I hope you'll be willing to talk to me soon. I know that things..." She shook her head. "I'd like to talk. When you're ready."

Like he just needed a few more days to get over it. That everything would be well and good if she gave him another day, a week, a month. Noah didn't think it would ever be well and good between them again. But he didn't say that. He didn't say anything. Just mumbled something noncommittal and watched as she headed back to her own apartment.

She still had that swing in her step. The one that made her ass look absolutely delectable. He knew he shouldn't be watching, shouldn't be punishing himself by viewing what he couldn't have. But he did, not closing his own door until she was safely behind hers.

He let his head rest against the cool wood. Sabrina had quit her job. The hope he'd been fighting tried to blossom. He hoed it back. She hadn't said she'd quit for him, hadn't said she'd come back for him. She'd just said she was back. Maybe all she wanted to talk about was how they could move forward as friends, so that living beside each other wouldn't be horribly awkward when she wanted to bring someone new home.

Noah's stomach roiled at the thought. He swallowed the burn working its way up his throat. She could bring back any man she wanted, and do whatever she wanted with him. It had nothing to do with him if she wanted to ride some new sucker like a cowgirl on that beautiful big bed of hers.

But she'd better not wear the boots if she did.

CHAPTER TWENTY-ONE

WELL, THAT HADN'T gone as planned. Sabrina rubbed at the numbness creeping up her neck and over her ears. Not that she'd expected Noah to throw open his door and invite her in for a cup of coffee. Okay, that would have been nice, but she was reasonable.

She just hadn't anticipated the crushing coldness. The flinty look in his eyes and small sneer on his mouth as though he couldn't believe she was wasting his time. She wasn't wasting his time. Didn't he understand he was part of the reason she'd come back? That he'd shown her all she'd missed out on for the past nine years and she didn't want to miss the next nine?

She sighed. She was back now and she wasn't going anywhere. She'd made sure of that, telling her Vancouver editor that she wouldn't be party to a fabricated story about the young actress and when he threatened her with dismissal, she'd told him not to bother because she quit.

But it meant she was unemployable at her old paper and probably any other in the city, too. The industry wasn't large and word of her difficult behavior would certainly make its way around. She shoved the thought away. She didn't care. She had no intention of going back.

Although she'd been here less than a day, arriving yesterday afternoon with the furniture and boxes she'd never bothered to unpack, Sabrina already felt more at home than she had the past few weeks in Vancouver. Even that little pinch behind her heart was gone. Yes, she'd done the right thing.

Now she just had to convince Noah.

Satisfied that at least their reconnection hadn't devolved into painful accusations, she turned on her coffeemaker. If spending the night on the couch didn't earn her a strong pot, she didn't know what would. Then she hurried to the shower, shedding clothes as she went. She sang a little as she turned on the spray and waited for it to heat up.

Yes, coming home had been the right move. Of course, it would be better if Noah were with her right now, kissing the side of her neck and telling her all the delightful areas he planned to wash for her, but all in good time.

He still cared about her. She was sure of it. Why else would he have taken care of her last night?

Sabrina might have dragged the blanket off the back of the couch and wrapped herself up in it while still sleeping. She might have even woken up long enough to turn off the TV and then fallen back asleep without remembering. But there was no way she'd climbed off the couch, traipsed over to the door, moved her red boots and locked up. Her boots had been placed neatly beside the door, toes pointed toward the wall, heels perfectly even. No, that was all Noah. Which meant that icy facade and brusque manner had just been an attempt to hide his real feelings.

She hurried through her shower. She was due at the coffee shop in twenty minutes. Her parents had been thrilled when she'd called to tell them she was coming back and had happily agreed to let her move back into the apartment, which they had yet to rent out. Then they'd happily informed her she could start at the coffee shop as soon as she arrived.

She yanked a comb through her wet hair. Not because she was so desperate to get to the kitchen, the rich aroma of the now ready coffee filling the apartment, but because she couldn't wait to start her new life.

Sabrina gave herself a quick hug. Today, she would reintroduce herself to Wheaton and show them that she meant to stay.

"HE'S BEING DIFFICULT," Sabrina complained to Marissa over coffee two days later. She'd spent the morning at the newspaper office and was covering the afternoon shift at the coffee shop, but she'd decided she needed a break. The shop was slow between two and three anyway. "He wouldn't even accept a coffee from me this morning."

And after she'd made him a cup to go. Didn't he know that not everyone was treated to a morning cup of coffee, Sabrina style?

She'd waited by her door, travel mug in hand, until she'd heard Noah's door open. Then she'd walked out, too. He'd thanked her for the thought, but declined the cup.

"It's frustrating."

"I know." Marissa had one eye on Scotty who was rolling a toy truck across the wooden floor a couple of tables over, unaware that the other patrons had to step over and around him. Timmy slept against Marissa's shoulder. Paul and Daisy were still at school. "I told you, you broke him."

"I did not break him." Sabrina took a sip of the latte in front of her in hopes it might calm her nerves. It didn't. She put the cup down hard enough that the liquid splashed up and over the rim. "Aren't you supposed to be on my side?" she asked as she mopped up the mess.

"I am?"

"Yes." Wasn't it obvious? "You didn't let up on me when I was away. 'When are you coming back? I miss you. The kids miss you.'" She crumpled the soiled napkins into a ball.

"We did miss you."

"Did Noah?"

Marissa blew out a breath and rocked the baby. "I think so. But, Sabrina, this isn't about being on a side. I'm on both your sides."

"You *think* so?"

Scotty, alerted by the change in their voices, wandered over, truck in hand. He dropped it when he spied his hot chocolate still sitting on the table. His earlier attempts at drinking had landed the majority of it on his shirt, but he didn't seem to care. He reached for the cup now. Sabrina helped him guide the cup to his lips.

He drank and grinned at her, then lifted his arms to be picked up. The contents of the cup spilled out onto Sabrina.

"Scotty," Marissa said, juggling Timmy with one arm and grabbing napkins with the other. "Be careful."

Scotty popped his thumb in his mouth and stared at Sabrina with worried eyes.

"I know it was an accident," she assured him as she blotted the liquid off her jeans. He nodded, his thumb securely fastened between his lips. He pointed to her lap even though it was still damp. Sabrina lifted him up. He turned and curled against her, content to be held. "People make mistakes," she said, her eyes on Marissa.

"You make a lot of them."

"I'm a slow learner." They were both quiet for

a moment. The sounds of the coffee shop filled the silence. The bubble and hiss of machines. The low conversation of the few other patrons. None of them held the answer Sabrina was searching for. "He's going to forgive me, isn't he?"

Marissa considered the question. "I think so. He's just worried."

"About what?" Sabrina wrapped her arms around Scotty, who wriggled closer, his warm body snuggling into hers. There was comfort in holding a child. A protective instinct curled through her, warming her in a way coffee never could.

"Well, I'm only guessing since he won't talk about it, but I think he's afraid you won't stay."

"What? That's ridiculous." Had she not quit her job in Vancouver? Given up her apartment? "What am I supposed to do? Write up a contract proclaiming that Wheaton will forever and always be my home?"

Marissa snickered. "Not that you're dramatic or anything."

Scotty giggled, too, and the cheerful noise rumbled through Sabrina, chasing out the tension. He reached up to pat her face. "Pretty," he said shyly.

"Handsome." She patted his cheek back and then hugged him, squeezing until he giggled again. This time, the sound wormed its way into her heart and planted a seed. No, that wasn't true. Scotty, his siblings, Marissa and Kyle. Ellen, Mrs. Thompson,

Trish. Her parents. They'd all carved out a place in her heart, lain down those roots of home, before she'd ever come back. She just hadn't been able to admit it.

But she no longer saw Wheaton as nothing more than a pit stop in the race of life. It was home and she wasn't leaving. No matter what Noah thought. Even if they couldn't be together. She swallowed and lowered her chin to rest on Scotty's head.

What if they didn't get back together? What if she was forced to stand by while Noah wined and dined some other woman? Asked her to marry him? Moved her into his apartment and let her redecorate?

"Aunt Sabby?" Scotty tilted his head to look at her. She tickled him until he laughed and then hugged him hard. This was her home. The place she felt whole. Scotty gave her a sloppy kiss on the cheek, no doubt leaving traces of hot chocolate behind.

If only relationships with grown men could be so simple. A tickle and a hug and they were yours for life. As if to prove the point, Scotty kissed her again, then he pushed out of her arms and toddled off to play with his truck. So maybe a little more than a tickle and a hug were required.

"Are you glad you came back?" Marissa asked.

"Yes." The answer came without thinking. Sabrina had missed out on all of this. The joy of seeing friends settle down and start families. Settling down and starting one of her own. Not that she'd been ready nine years ago to become a wife and a mother. No, she'd had some living to get out of her system, to become the person she was. Or grow up enough to admit to herself who she really was. She sighed and let her head loll back. "He doesn't think I'm going to stay."

"Well, you haven't exactly built up a reputation for loving the town."

"I had things to do." Sabrina threw her arms wide to encompass all she'd done. The last-minute trips to Vegas, dancing at the club all night and going for brunch before bed, flirting, kissing, living. But it had all been leading her back to Wheaton. "I was young."

"And you're such an old hag now."

Sabrina's head shot up. "If I am, then so are you. In fact, you're older and haggier by an entire six weeks." She snickered at Marissa's narrowed gaze. "Good thing I'm here to help you maintain the remnants of youth that you haven't destroyed."

Marissa's eyes narrowed farther. "You know, I've changed my mind. I didn't miss you at all. In fact, I think you should go back to Vancouver."

Sabrina snorted. "Nice try. You've realized now that you can't live without me. That I'm integral to all your future happiness. Also, here to make sure your hygiene is up to public standards." She reached out and plucked what looked like a piece of cereal from Marissa's hair.

Marissa looked down at Sabrina's open palm and shrugged. "Kids."

Sabrina wiped her hands with one of the remaining dry napkins. "So if Noah thinks I'm going to leave, I need to show him I'm staying." She looked at her friend. "Any bright ideas?"

"I haven't slept through the night in eight years," Marissa said and took another slug of coffee. "I'm lucky to remember to put makeup on in the morning."

"Or wash your hair."

"Very funny." But the edges of Marissa's lips twitched. "You've always been good at getting what you want. How do you do that?"

Sabrina thought about it. "Usually, I just keep going until things work out, but I don't know if that will work this time." She tapped a finger against her lip. She feared that pushing Noah would make him back off more. That he'd start outright ignoring her. And then what? She'd have to break into his apartment and refuse to leave until he talked to her?

"Why not?"

She pursed her lips. "He won't let me in. There's this polite reserve that I can't penetrate."

"It's only been two days," Marissa pointed out.

"I know. But he's never been like this before." She rolled her shoulders. "Not with me."

"Maybe give him some time. He probably just needs to come to terms with his feelings."

Sabrina nodded slowly. She hoped Marissa was right.

CHAPTER TWENTY-TWO

IT TOOK TWO WEEKS for Sabrina to realize that her tactic of giving Noah his space was having the opposite effect from the one she intended. Rather than realizing how much he missed her and that she was right there, he took advantage of the distance to make sure they saw even less of each other.

She only knew he was living next door to her because she saw his car outside in the mornings. Most days he got home after her and didn't leave until she'd already gone. When he came into the coffee shop he was distant and always tried to time it so that he was served by whoever she was working with. She doubted anyone else noticed, but then they weren't watching their esteemed mayor like a hawk, either.

He was there now and Sabrina studied him, counting the number of customers between him and the front of the line. It wasn't a scientific process. Some orders were quicker than others so she might serve two while her partner served one and Noah was sneaky enough to do his own tabulating and kindly allow the person behind him to go ahead if it meant he could avoid her.

So maybe it was time to try something different.

When there was only one other person in front of him, Sabrina turned to the twenty-year-old college student working beside her who was taking a semester off from school to find himself. "It's slowing down. Take a break."

He glanced at the line still extending halfway to the door, then peeked at Sabrina's face and shrugged. "You sure?"

Oh, she was sure. She was very sure. Her entire body snapped to attention—finally she was doing something instead of waiting for something to happen. Nothing too grand, nothing that would embarrass Noah in front of everyone. That wouldn't serve her purpose, either. But a little nudge to let him know that she was on to his tricks and she wasn't going to stand back anymore.

Noah barely looked at her when he ordered. She almost laughed. Did he know who he was dealing with? She wasn't the type to sit by and let things happen to her, the past two weeks notwithstanding.

"Did you say a double shot espresso?" she asked as though he hadn't spoken clearly and she didn't already know the beverage was his lifeblood of choice. But it forced him to look at her, to speak to her since everyone was watching. Wouldn't be very good for Mr. Mayor's campaign to be seen deliberately ignoring one of his constituents. She stood, waiting, blinking her green eyes at Noah as if she was truly unsure what he'd ordered.

His eyes narrowed when he turned to face her. Good. Sabrina smiled. But aside from the brief whitening of his lips when he pressed them together there was no other indication of his irritation. "Yes." His voice was calm, modulated. All kindly town leader and authoritative statesman. "Please."

Oh, that "please" was a nice little touch. Sabrina could see the older generation looking proudly on their golden boy. So polite. So well-mannered. His mother had raised him well. Little did they know the true Noah. How he would look at her with demanding eyes, strip her clothes off and take her up against a door. Or when he'd lay back and let her take charge. Sabrina wasn't sure which one she liked better. Good thing she didn't have to choose.

She upped the temperature on the machine to ensure the water would be close to scalding. Not to burn Noah—the coffee would have cooled enough by the time she served it—but extra heat would give the coffee that lovely burned taste. Not very nice, but ignoring her wasn't very nice, either. And since her sweet-as-pie act wasn't getting her anywhere, maybe being a little more demanding would.

She stood watching Noah while the machine

steamed and popped. There were other drinks she could make, counters to wipe, pastries to box, but they could wait. In truth, no one would mind. All eyes were glued to them, waiting to see what would happen next.

Noah appeared unaware or unmoved by the attention. He chatted to Mrs. Fields about her garden, assisted Mr. Rae to a seat and made sure the man's cane was securely hooked on the table. Wasn't he just the perfect and attentive soul? To everyone but her.

Sabrina called him when his drink was ready. Made sure to wrap her hand fully around the cup so that Noah had to touch her when he took it. Just the smallest of flinches before he thanked her and left the shop. Small and only a flinch, but it was something. Better than the polite veneer. And way better than pretending she didn't exist.

But Sabrina wasn't satisfied with her victory, though it did cause a sweet warmth to fill her. This was only the start, the first shot in their personal war. She spent the rest of the morning plotting as she poured drinks, made small talk and assured everyone that, yes, this time she was staying for good.

Once home, she placed a pair of small potted evergreens on the porch. Staking her claim. Then she waited. Tonight, she would wait until Noah showed up. There were only so many places in Wheaton that stayed open after ten. So what if she had the early shift at the coffee shop tomorrow? Bleary, gritty eyes were worth it.

By ten-thirty there was still no sign of him and she was growing sleepy. Worried that she'd doze off if she stayed inside where it was cozy and comfortable, she pulled on her winter coat, gloves and a hat, wrapped herself in the couch blanket, and headed to sit on the porch.

The air was bitter outside and slipped through her layers like they were nothing. Sabrina shivered. She was definitely going to have to invest in something warmer before winter actually arrived. She'd grown used to the mild seasons of Vancouver, where temperatures rarely dropped below freezing and snow was a treat, not a test of fortitude.

At least she wouldn't fall asleep. She hunkered down in one of the red Adirondack chairs, curling into herself to conserve as much heat as possible and keeping her eyes trained on the driveway.

After what felt like a year, headlights finally appeared. She heard the spin of the tires on pavement, the hum of the engine as Noah drove past her and parked. She tried to stand, realized her muscles had seized and quickly rubbed them with her hands before climbing to her feet.

He was halfway up the porch steps before he noticed her. "Sabrina? What are you doing out here?" She heard the note of concern in his voice. Oh, how she needed this little bit of warmth. Of course, that was sort of like saying that rainforests needed precipitation.

"What does it look like I'm doing?" She refused to be ignored for one more minute. Not even another second. "I've been waiting for you out here for over an hour."

Even in the dim light, she saw the frown mar his features as he checked his watch. Good—she hoped he felt guilty. Forcing her out here to freeze to death. If he'd just come home at a normal time, like a normal person, she wouldn't have been forced to resort to such measures.

"You've been sitting out here since nine forty-five?"

"What?" Her self-righteousness melted away. It couldn't be ten forty-five. "That's not right. It's got to be midnight. At least." Sabrina moved forward to see for herself, her gloved hands gripped his arm to see that it was indeed ten forty-five. A whole fifteen minutes of sitting. "Well, it felt like an hour." She pulled the blanket more tightly around herself. "Since you refuse to talk to me I had to take drastic measures. I could have hypothermia."

"I haven't refused to talk to you. I just have nothing to say." He reached out to touch the exposed part of her wrist between glove and coat. "Jesus.

You're freezing." He wrapped an arm around her. "Get inside."

Since his arm was around her and felt awfully nice there, Sabrina was inclined to do as he said. "See? Hypothermia."

"You don't have hypothermia." Noah unlocked the front door and hustled her into the warmth of the entryway. Sabrina had never noticed how cozy it was before. "But you should take a hot bath."

She put her hands on her hips, but the effect was probably ruined when she shivered again. "You're just trying to get rid of me."

"Sabrina." He held up a hand. "I'm tired. Another time."

"No. I want to talk now." She followed him to his door, wiggling under his arm when he pushed it open. Rookie mistake on his part.

"I'm serious," he told her.

"So am I. Noah." She heard the crack in her voice and tried to cover it with a cough. "Please."

He closed his eyes. He probably wasn't lying when he said he was tired, but that didn't mean he wasn't using it to get rid of her, either. Well, she wouldn't be so easily shaken. She'd risked hypothermia for him. Did that count for nothing?

Quietly, she let the blanket slide off her shoulders and peeled off her gloves. Then shifted so she was directly in front of him. Practically on top of him. "Noah?"

His eyes flashed with surprise, then pleasure and then worry.

She'd take the first two and do her best to eliminate the last. He needed her. He just wouldn't admit it. She wrapped her arms around his waist, curved her body into his. "The best way to combat hypothermia is to share body heat." Reminiscent of their picnic by the lake and dip in the cool water.

"Sabrina."

"It's true." His body relaxed. For one long, glorious second, he sank into her. "I'm not going anywhere," she told him.

Which was the wrong thing to say. He put his hands on her shoulders. Not to push her away. No, Mr. Mayor would never be so rude. But to hold her in place while he stepped back. "I'm not up for this tonight."

She eyed him, careful to keep her gaze steady. "You don't fool me."

He moved back a little farther and removed his hands. "I don't know what you're talking about. I'm not trying to fool anyone."

"Yes, you are." She'd seen that light of hope that flashed across his face before his old fears got in the way. Marissa had been right. He was afraid she was going to leave. "I'm not leaving and I don't mean just tonight." She took a step forward to close the distance between them. "I'm not leaving Wheaton. It's my home."

Her announcement didn't ease the tension in his shoulders or erase the lines around his mouth. Instead, he dared to cock an eyebrow at her. "Is it? Until when?"

Sabrina flinched. A direct hit and one she probably deserved. "Ouch."

Immediately, the smirk disappeared from his face. "I shouldn't have said that." He shook his head. "Sorry. I'm tired."

She blew out a breath. "It's okay." And strangely it was okay. Even though his anger had been directed toward her, at least it wasn't his picture-perfect mayor face. She could work with anger and irritation and annoyance. What she was handcuffed by was his insistence on presenting a false front. Time for a little more nudging. "I think you missed me."

Noah jerked, as though he'd been hit by lightning, and frowned at her. "What are you playing at?"

"I'm not playing." She dared to place her hand on his chest. "I think you missed me."

He picked it off and put it by her side. "You're wrong."

Now she was the one to cock an eyebrow. "Then why won't you talk to me?"

"The two have nothing to do with each other."

"No?" She put her hand back on his chest. His heart was pumping faster than usual.

"Sabrina." His voice rolled over her, delightful even when deepened in irritation. "Stop it."

She took off her hat and ran her hands through her hair. She knew how much he loved touching the strands, letting them slip slowly through his fingers while she rested her head on his shoulders. How he liked to wrap it around his palm when he kissed her. How he sighed with deep pleasure when she drew the ends across his naked body.

Noah's hands clenched at his sides, but he resisted the urge to touch. Clearly, he had superhuman willpower.

She twirled a lock around her fingers. "I just want to talk."

"I don't."

She untwisted her finger, letting her hair bounce back into place and lifted a hand to his face. His cheek was warm and a little rough. She loved the feel of that stubble. She let her thumb run over the tight seam of his mouth. She couldn't get enough of the feel of him. He felt it, too, she knew. He was just too stubborn to admit it.

"Sabrina." Noah didn't raise his voice, but the command was all the stronger for the lack of volume. "Enough."

She ignored the warning. "See how nice it is to talk?"

He caught her wrist, pulled her hand away, the movement sharp and short. When she looked into his eyes there was no hint of play there. No sign that he was hiding some deeper feeling or desire. There was just pain before he shuttered it with a cold blink.

Fear lanced through Sabrina's belly in a cold arc that made her evening outdoors seem like she'd been tanning on a Hawaiian beach.

"We're not talking."

"Why?" She tested his grip. Loose, but firm.

"Because you didn't want to stay. You don't want to be here and I do. There's nothing else to talk about."

A low heat crept up the front of her chest, but did nothing to warm her inside. "I came back."

"For now," he said and dropped her arm. Like an exclamation point.

"I'm staying this time." She started to reach for him and then paused when he shook his head at her. Heat crept up her neck to her face. Noah didn't believe her. He thought she was lying.

"That's what you say, but what if you get an offer from another paper?"

"I won't, Noah. I'm staying." She'd never lied to him and she wasn't planning to start now. They'd talked about her job in the city and she'd been very clear about her intention of going back. She realized she should have talked to him about the offer before taking it, but she hadn't lied. Not about anything. So when she told him she was staying, he should realize she was sincere.

"Really? What if L.A. calls? Toronto? New York? You're telling me you wouldn't even consider them?"

Even as Sabrina told herself these were impossibilities—newspapers were laying off reporters, not hiring them, as their audience was carved away by bloggers and other online sources—excitement lit within her. She'd been satisfied in Vancouver, but she wouldn't have been averse to more. Bigger cities, more readers, better pay. She shook off the thoughts. Dreams. Fantasies that had no basis in reality. She was here in Wheaton. For good.

"You'd consider them." A dullness crept into his voice, scarier than any aspect of his cold demeanor. She wouldn't let him go down that rabbit hole. She wouldn't lose him to something so ridiculous.

"Of course I'd consider them." Sabrina put her hands on her hips. "That would be a perfectly reasonable reaction." Push and push and nudge and nudge.

"You'd leave." His tone was a like a gray fog, sucking the life out of everything in the room.

She blinked and felt everything slow. "Noah."

"You wouldn't stay." Her eyes met his.

She opened her mouth, wanting to deny it, her brain screaming at her to deny it, but she couldn't. She would consider them and she wasn't going to lie to him. "I didn't say I'd leave. I said I'd consider them. The two have nothing to do with each other."

Noah closed his eyes, as though he'd been steeling himself to hear her words and now that he had, all his energy was gone. "I understand."

"No." She was desperate to explain. "You don't. I wouldn't just leave. I'd think about it. Talk to the people who were important in my life and then make a decision."

"The way you talked to us last time?" His gaze was calm now. Mr. Mayor was back in the house.

Her arguments faded on her tongue. He was right. It was exactly what she'd done. Why wouldn't he assume she'd do the same thing? It was her pattern. But she was breaking it. Slashing through the pastel stripes with some flashy red snakeskin. Only she didn't get a chance to tell him.

"Sabrina. It's fine." His tone was gentle, understanding. He had it all under control, while she felt like she was spiraling downward with nothing to grab on to, no one to hold. "I understand your career is important to you and has to come first."

She watched as his Mr. Mayor persona slipped into place. A smooth, unflappable mask. She wanted to tear it off and rail about the injustice of arguing with someone who wouldn't argue back. But she felt frozen.

"I encourage you to pursue any opportunity that might come your way." He smiled, like she was some supporter clamoring for his attention and he was too polite to pawn her off. "We had a good run."

A good run? Fear and anger surged through her. No, she wasn't going down. Not without a fight. She'd see how long he could keep up under her onslaught, even as she locked her knees to keep them from trembling. "You can't shake me, Noah."

"I'm not trying to."

Sabrina stepped toward him, not stopping until their bodies bumped. She saw the emotion flare in his gaze before he blinked it away. "Then stop talking like we're over."

"We are—"

"No." She clamped her hand over his lips to keep him quiet. His lips were warm under her palm. She rose onto her tiptoes so she could look him directly in the eye. "I'm. Not. Leaving." She said each word slowly, distinctly, just in case he'd misunderstood her earlier. "Get that through your skull."

Noah raised an eyebrow at her, but that was the only indication he'd heard her at all. She waited until she started to feel foolish and slowly lowered her hand.

"Done?"

No, she wasn't done. She was barely getting started. "You're being very passive aggressive."

"I'm not being anything. You just don't want to hear what I have to say."

"Because you keep saying the wrong things." Sabrina scowled up at him. "Stop acting like what we had is finished."

"Sabrina." She wavered under that cool, collected authority, but remained in place. "You left, remember? I just got on with life."

But a life without her? No, she couldn't imagine it. Her lungs tightened. "I made a mistake. I'm trying to fix it."

Noah's smile was gentle, like the one he gave Daisy when she was getting overwrought and needed to be calmed down. "There's nothing to fix, Sabrina. It's fine."

He could speak for himself because she was not fine. Not even a little. "But, Noah." Her breath caught and the edges of her visions grayed out. She blinked as her pulse thundered through her ears. It felt so final, like he was really saying goodbye. Forever. "I love you."

She had to say it. She couldn't hold back any longer. What was the point anyway? She did love him and he needed to know everything before making a decision that could affect the rest of his life. Affect the rest of both of their lives.

Sabrina held her breath and watched as Noah absorbed her information. The veil he protected himself with lifted. Only for a moment, but she saw it. The warming of his gaze, the tilt of joy on his lips and the way his hands automatically reached out to clasp her elbows and pull her even tighter into him.

Then he let go and stepped back, cleared his throat and tried to blink the hope away, but she saw it. Hiding beneath the surface, wanting desperately to appear but afraid. "If you really loved me, you would have stayed."

"People make mistakes, Noah. You have to forgive me for being human."

But he just shook his head. "I can't do this right now, Sabrina. The election…" He trailed off.

"I love you," she repeated.

"No." And this time there was nothing lurking below the surface, he just looked sad. "You only think you do."

CHAPTER TWENTY-THREE

NOAH FELT LIKE AN ASS watching Sabrina slowly blink and then turn and walk out of his apartment. Out of his life. But things would be better this way. The two of them would go on leading their separate lives. She would figure out what she wanted and go out and do it. He would survive. Because he'd be a fool to think that this time she really was staying.

She wasn't a small-town girl. Wasn't that what she'd told him? He rubbed the heel of his hand against his chest. Better that he lock down all those feelings and hide them away where they couldn't get him into trouble again.

His chest continued to ache even when he rubbed hard enough to leave a bruise. Nothing left to do but get on with things.

Noah forced himself into motion, closing his door once he saw Sabrina was safely in her own apartment, then putting one foot ahead of the other until they led him to the kitchen table. He thumped down in the chair, looking at the bits and pieces of his campaign scattered across the table and told himself that this was enough. The town would remain and he a part of it.

He slept poorly. If what he did that night—namely, looking at the ceiling, counting to one thousand, practicing his talking points—could be called sleeping. The last time he'd looked at his alarm clock it had read five in the morning, which he already knew from the slow lightening of the sky. The next time he opened his eyes was when the clock started wailing at him. He stumbled to the shower, hoping that the spray would do something to refresh him.

It didn't. Even after a vigorous toweling, his brain remained groggy, his body lethargic. He needed coffee, but he'd forgotten to set the timer on his machine last night. Now he didn't have time to make any. He was going to have to stop by the coffee shop, go caffeine-free or drink the swill that passed for coffee at the dealership. He suspected the staff of making bad coffee on purpose so that he'd continue to bring them the good stuff on Mondays. He should probably tell them that they'd get the good stuff regardless.

There was no choice. Noah needed the caffeine to function and he wasn't drinking swill. He hoped Sabrina wasn't working this morning. Or, at least, wouldn't be making his coffee. She'd burned it the last time. On purpose. Not that he'd said anything.

Resigned that he was going to have to run the

risk of seeing her, he ran a comb through his hair, threw on a suit jacket and headed for the door. Briefly, he thought about leaving by way of the French doors, but that would be like running scared. And he wasn't scared. He just wasn't looking for any contact.

So, of course, Sabrina was standing in the entryway, leaning against her door, one leg crossed in front of the other, waiting for him. She straightened, smiling as he stepped out. "Good morning."

Noah didn't know what was so good about it. He grunted. And tried not to notice her red boots. Those things were like Kryptonite. He never should have told her about that fantasy of her wearing them with a smile and nothing else. She was shamelessly using them against him now.

Sabrina fell into step beside him as he headed for the front door. "Coffee?" And there in her hand, like nectar from the gods was a steaming cup of what smelled like the most delicious, strong, unburned coffee.

He'd declined last time, able to lift the travel mug he'd made himself, but his hands were empty now. It would be petty not to take it. Also, he was desperate. "Thanks," he said and drank half the cup in one swallow. He shouldered the door open and held it open for her to exit behind him. He wasn't a total ass.

But rather than detour toward her own car, she

followed him to his. Her boots crunched across the pavement. He stopped short and turned to pin her with a gaze. "Is there something else we have to discuss?"

Her smile was wide and bright, no indication of the falling out they'd had last night. And why did she look as though she'd spent her night in full REM sleep, not even waking up to roll over? "I need a ride." She raised an eyebrow when he didn't nod or give any other indication that this would be fine. "You're going past the coffee shop, right?" She took a step toward him. So close. Like last night.

Noah's body hardened at the memory as her scent wafted over him. How tempted he'd been to kiss that gorgeous mouth and tangle his hands in her hair. It would be so easy to push the troubling thoughts aside and kiss her now.

Even better pick her up and carry her into his bedroom. But then what? He could fall again. So, so easily. And Sabrina could—no, she *would*—leave just as easily. He remembered why it was a bad idea. He couldn't put his heart, his trust, in someone who wouldn't stick around. He didn't think he could handle the pain.

"You have a vehicle," he pointed out, refusing to take one step closer or farther away. Either might give her an indication of the inner turmoil currently making the coffee into a whirlpool in his stomach.

"It's out of gas." She fluttered her lashes at him and laid a hand on his chest. Noah felt the touch like a brand, forced himself not to react.

"Really." He didn't believe her, even before that silly batting of the eyes routine. "Call Vic at the station. He'll swing by with a jerrican for you."

"I'll be late."

"You're the boss's daughter."

Sabrina pouted at him. Damn, he loved that little jut of her lips. Made him want to run his tongue over them. "I try not to abuse nepotism," she explained, seemingly unaware of the fact that he was holding on to his control by a thin thread. "You'd understand."

"Me?" Why would he understand? His father had died long before Noah was ready to enter the workforce and Ellen had never been in a position to offer him or Kyle a free ride. Unless he wanted all the prune juice he could drink.

But Sabrina nodded as though this made perfect sense. "Yes, you. You're the mayor, but you never use that to your advantage. Even when you should, you don't trade on your position in this town to make your life easier."

Her assessment stunned him into stillness. He could still hear the bird songs in the trees around them and still see the leaves fluttering under a gust of morning wind. But for one long moment he didn't move.

"Don't look so shocked." She lifted her hand to pat his cheek. "You're a good man, Mr. Mayor. The type of man who would give a stranded woman a ride to work."

Her blatant attempt at manipulation made him smile. Not a large, open smile like hers, but he could feel the corners of his lips tilting up. Even when he told them to stay down. *Bad lips.* "Is your car really out of gas?"

Sabrina looked over her shoulder at the offending vehicle in question. "It could be."

They both knew it wasn't. "Let's check."

She put her hand back against his chest when he started to move. "Let's not and say we did."

"Sabrina."

"Noah." She mimicked his tone. The way she had of taking over a space, swamping it with her energy, washed over him.

Again, Noah wondered why he was putting up a fight. Whose battle was this? And then he thought about how it would feel if he let her back in and she left him again. The air in his lungs vanished. He inhaled slowly, cautiously. The way he'd always lived his life until her. The way he should return to living it. "You don't need a ride." Very carefully, touching as little of her as possible, he removed her hand and placed it by her side.

"I could."

"You don't." And he needed to get out of here, away from her. "I'll follow you to make sure you don't run out of gas." Once she was safely parked, he'd leave.

And from now on, Kyle could be responsible for getting coffee.

CHAPTER TWENTY-FOUR ·

SABRINA KNOCKED ON Noah's door causing her new friend to yip.

"Oh, God, Chester. Do not pee all over me," she whispered to the puppy and was rewarded with a lick from neck to ear. Not quite as good as if it were Noah doing the licking, but there was comfort in the warmth of the wriggling body and the joyful look in the puppy's eyes when she petted him.

She hugged the little guy, glad that her current landlord allowed pets. More glad that the current landlord was her.

She smiled. Yesterday, she and her parents had finalized the particulars of transferring the title of the apartment into her name. They'd wanted to gift it to her, told her to consider it an early inheritance, but Sabrina wanted to buy it herself.

The amount in her bank account was paltry—wouldn't even afford her the likes of The Cave in Vancouver—but Wheaton wasn't Vancouver and housing prices were far more reasonable. Especially when she factored in the daughter discount.

Sabrina had had a busy couple of weeks since

the late-night conversation with Noah. Every morning, she waited for him with coffee. Every morning, he accepted. But he still declined her invitations for dinner or an indoor picnic since the weather had turned or just hanging out and watching a movie. Still, she felt like he was starting to believe her when she said she was staying.

He just needed a little more encouragement. She hoped today would provide enough.

Chester burrowed his cold nose into Sabrina's neck. Good thing he was so cute. She'd adopted him from the animal shelter yesterday and already they were besties. His tags jingled as he wriggled in her arms and she fussed with the extra tag she'd added making sure the "Vote for Barnes" sticker was visible. It was election day and she wanted Noah to know she was fully behind him.

She felt a little faint when she heard the click of the lock and she squeezed Chester, which caused him to bark again. "Hi." Okay, maybe she should have thought out her greeting.

Noah stared at the pair of them for a moment. Chester tried to jump into Noah's arms, but Sabrina held him tight. "Good morning."

"Big day." Sabrina nudged her way past him into the apartment and put Chester down. He immediately barked and scrabbled across the wood floor, on the scent of something.

"What is that?" Noah's gaze tracked the dog,

who had his head jammed between the couch and a side table, his tail wagging madly.

"That's a dog. Don't get out much, do you?"

"You know what I meant." He pinned her with a look, those beautiful blue eyes finally focusing on her. Not through, not around her. On her. Sabrina might have melted right there if she hadn't feared that Noah would simply mop her up and put her outside. "What is the dog doing in my apartment?" His eyes narrowed. "Sabrina, he'd better not be a gift."

"Chester is my dog. Mine. He's simply here for a visit." She clasped her hands together when Noah ran his fingers through his hair. She wanted to do that for him. "Consider him a mascot of sorts."

Noah studied her, only looking away when Chester, apparently bored with his investigation, ran over and slid into his legs.

"He's still working on stopping," Sabrina said. Chester, more paw than dog, leaned against Noah's leg until Noah finally gave in and bent down to scratch him behind the ears.

Chester whined in puppy ecstasy. Sabrina told herself not to be jealous. Not even when Noah crouched down to give the dog a full-body scrub and tell him he was a good boy. His fingers danced over the collar fit for a diva. "Nice collar."

Sabrina had picked up a pretty, sparkly red one studded with diamonds before heading to the

shelter. Daisy had helped. It wasn't until they got
there and Chester stole her heart that Sabrina realized she should have bought something neutral. Oh, well. It had looked sparkly and pretty in
the store, and it looked just as sparkly and pretty
around Chester's neck. "He's comfortable with
his manhood," Sabrina told Noah.

A smile quirked the corner of his mouth. Her
heart, which had been living in the vicinity of her
toes these past few weeks lifted. Only to her knees,
but it was a noticeable improvement.

"I wanted to wish you good luck, though I'm
sure you won't need it."

"Thanks." His smile flickered again.

Sabrina wanted to hug him, but she held back.
Marissa had said she needed to let Noah come to
her now. She'd made her position clear and after
today, everyone in town would know it. Her pulse
raced a little when she thought about what she'd
done, but she shoved the trickle of fear away. Trish
wouldn't fire her. Probably. No matter the outcome, it would be worth it. It had to be. "Have
you read the paper yet?"

Noah pointed to the folded-up edition sitting
on his table. Her unopened envelope sat beside it.
She felt a slice of pain lance through her, but kept
her smile in place as she walked over to pick up
the envelope and wave it at him. "Not much for
reading, I see?"

He had the grace to look embarrassed. "Yeah. I've been busy."

He'd had time to read her letter if he'd wanted to. Then again, he hadn't thrown it away, either. The rest of the house was immaculate. No old papers or mail waiting to be tossed. Everything neatly filed and in order. So perhaps this situation wasn't as bad as it first appeared. "Well, maybe you can read it later. After the election."

He nodded.

"You should read the paper, too. The online edition."

His brow furrowed. "Aren't they the same?"

"Usually." Sabrina paused, but Noah didn't ask for an explanation. Neither of them said anything for a moment. Why didn't he say something? Recognize the significance of Chester, who would not be easy to take to the city? Ask how her career at the paper was coming along? Mention her red cowboy boots? Instead, he just watched her, those blue eyes as silent as his lips. "Well, I should get going. You've got a busy day and I need to vote."

Noah nodded and gave Chester one final pat. Chester, who'd rolled onto his back, stopped wagging, looked up and yipped.

"Come on, buddy." Sabrina patted her thigh to call Chester. She scooped up the bundle of energy and prepared to leave. Perhaps this would be their future. Casual conversation that never delved beneath the surface, a good rub for her dog and then they'd go off on their separate ways.

"Sabrina?"

His voice pulled her back. She held her breath and squeezed her dog until he yelped. She loosened her grip from death to chokehold and tried to look like nothing had happened. Nope. No dog barking here.

"You look good."

Thank God for red cowboy boots.

NOAH SAT IN HIS OFFICE while his supporters mingled outside on the floor of the dealership. They'd closed down sales and turned the floor into the campaign war room for the day. No one was going to buy a used truck or a new car with all the election excitement anyway. Large-screen televisions were set up around the floor space, tables loaded with campaign paraphernalia. Nets holding streamers and balloons were hung overhead ready to be opened when, or if, Noah was announced as the winner. Supporters mingled around, nibbling from the plates of food set up, proudly sporting their "Vote for Barnes" buttons.

It had a different feel than the previous elections when Noah had run unopposed. Those years, they'd thrown the same party but there had been no sense of urgency. He would be the mayor, and that was that. They'd spent more time debating the merits of the other mayoral races happening across the province, since by law every city and town held elections on the same day.

This year the mood was high. Noah was the only one not enjoying the buzz, which was why he'd excused himself and taken up residence in his office. Why had Sabrina decided to invite herself into his apartment on this morning of all mornings? And what was with the dog? Noah wondered who'd care for the dog when Sabrina inevitably left. Perhaps he should offer. He could use a companion.

He fiddled with her letter, which for some reason he'd grabbed before exiting his apartment. He'd gotten as far as opening it, but hadn't yet pulled out the pages. Did he really want to do this? Especially today, when he had other things on his mind?

"You need to see this." Noah looked up to see his brother walking through his office door, waving an iPad at him. Kyle had downloaded an app that kept track of the votes as they were reported and was proudly showing it off to everyone at the dealership.

"Is the vote close?" Noah put the envelope down, glad to push it aside for the moment, and focused on his brother. Although no one said it, this was no ordinary Election Day. It was the first time Noah had faced competition and though early polls suggested an easy victory, Noah had learned not to take anything for granted. His muscles tensed.

"It's not about the vote." Kyle placed the tablet on Noah's desk and angled the screen to face him.

Noah glanced at the screen, which displayed an article about the election. Why did Kyle want him to read this now? The election was under way. Half the votes were probably already cast. He frowned and looked back at his brother. "Can this wait? I'm a little busy."

"No, you're not. Read." Kyle maintained his position. "Marissa sent me in here. And Mom. You know I can't leave without making an effort."

"Wimp," Noah said. As though he'd have done anything different. But he picked up the tablet. "Happy?"

"I'll wait." Kyle crossed his arms over his chest.

Noah huffed out a breath. His brother knew him too well. He'd planned give a cursory examination to the article, then return the tablet to his brother and do his best to forget all about it. Apparently that would not be permitted. Slowly, he scanned the paper and found Sabrina's byline. His lungs seized. He didn't know what she'd written, but he was sure he'd prefer to read it later. In the privacy of his own home.

When people talk about a home, they usually mean a building. A place to lay your head. A place to eat. A place to raise your family. For me, home is something different.

It's a person.

And his home is here in Wheaton.

Noah inhaled slowly.

He gives this town all of himself. He protects the residents. He makes the hard decisions. He asks for nothing in return. In short, he's the heart of this town.

I could go on extolling all his virtues, of which there are many, but that would probably embarrass him. He likes to pretend that he doesn't deserve any special treatment or accolades, that he's just a regular resident. But he's so much more. His opponent? Well, my mother always said that if I had nothing nice to say I shouldn't say anything.

Trish wanted this to be a balanced article, highlighting both candidates. She's not going to be too pleased when she sees this. But if this means that just one of you, one single person who didn't plan to vote, will now head to your polling station and vote for Noah, then I'm satisfied. Even if it means I'll never work in this town again. (Well, except for the coffee shop. Love you, Mom and Dad.)

There's only one candidate who's right for

this town. And one candidate who's right for me.

Noah Barnes. Go vote for him.

Noah blinked, read the article again, his breath caught in his chest. Sabrina had written this. For him. Potentially putting her job at the paper at risk. She loved that job. He looked up at his brother.

"Well?" Kyle asked.

But Noah didn't respond. Thoughts churned through his mind. Would she stay? Really? Could he trust her not to leave this time? "She's just trying to help me win."

Kyle shook his head. "No, that's not the only reason. You know she bought a dog."

"Chester."

Kyle nodded. "She bought the apartment, too. I think she's serious when she says she isn't leaving."

"She bought the apartment?"

"That's what she told Marissa." He smiled. "You should talk to her."

He wanted to. Badly. His eyes strayed to the envelope. But what would he find inside? Another viewpoint? One where she told him that she had to go? And which one was real? Noah rubbed the back of his neck. "I'll come join you in a minute," he told his brother.

He handed back the tablet, but remained seated at his desk, waiting until the door clicked shut before picking up the envelope again. The paper smelled like her. Did he really want to know what she'd written? He tapped the corner against the desk.

"Hell with it." He slipped the pages out and flattened them. Whatever she'd written couldn't be as bad as not knowing.

Noah,
I don't know what to write.

I want you to know this was a difficult decision for me. I'm used to being on my own. Not that my parents aren't fully loving and supportive, but I haven't had to answer to them or anyone in years. It's always just been me. What do I want? What works best for me? (Only-child syndrome. Me, me, me.)

But I thought about you when I made this decision. Your kindness. Your smile. The way you look at me. The way my chest squeezes when you walk into my apartment. The way you make me feel like I belong. The way I'm not sure I'll be able to let you go.

Because I know that if I stayed, it would be forever. That scares me. I'm not ready to give up my career dreams yet. I feel like I've still got something to prove. And I want to know that when and if I come back, it was my choice.

I thought about rewriting this, cleaning up

the bits I crossed out and polishing it until it was worthy of publication. As you can see, I decided against it. This is me. Mistakes, crossed-out sentences, poor word choices. Poor life choices? Probably.

I'll probably regret this decision one day. I'm sorry. I wish you could come with me, but your life is in Wheaton. I couldn't ask you to leave the town you love so much. That wouldn't be fair to you. I love you too much to ask that of you.

No, scratch that. I love you.

Sabrina

Noah's lungs contracted. This wasn't what he'd expected. Sabrina had wanted him to come with her? He reread that line to make sure he hadn't seen what he wanted to rather than what was there. But no, that was what she'd written. A flush of heat stole through him. And now she was back, according to her letter because she'd chosen to return.

She'd chosen him.

Noah didn't stop to think about what he was doing. A floating sensation filled his limbs. For the first time since she'd left he felt light, as though the weight of life wasn't wearing him down.

He didn't stop to shake any hands or kiss any babies on his way out. Not that he needed to. Based on the joking comments directed to his back, everyone in the war room knew exactly where he was racing off to. Obviously, they were regular readers of the paper's online edition.

He made one stop and sped the rest of the way to make up time. The wheels of his car kicked up dust as he peeled into the driveway. He jumped out, not bothering to lock the car door or even close it and hurried up the steps. To Sabrina. To home.

He hammered on the door, then hammered again when she didn't answer fast enough. Chester yipped a greeting. Noah smiled. She'd gotten a dog. Whose paws were the size of a corn field. She'd never be able to afford an apartment big enough for him in Vancouver. No, Chester would need the wide open space of Wheaton.

Noah heard Sabrina shushing Chester, so he thumped on the door again. Let the dog make some noise. He needed to see her. Now.

"Noah?" Her eyes widened, warmed and then shuttered closed. As if she was afraid. The thought punched him in the gut. He'd done that to her. Well, he'd just have to make it up to her. Starting now.

He walked in, scooping Chester up under one arm when the dog accidentally butted him in the shin in excitement. "I read the article."

Chester barked happily. Sabrina didn't. "I see."

"And the letter." Noah breathed slowly, reverently. "You're staying."

"Which I've been telling you for weeks."

He shut the door behind him, stepped toward her. Her hair looked like silk, felt like it, too, when he smoothed a hand over it. "I was stupid."

The light reappeared in her eyes. "Really?"

He nodded, slowly pulled her forward until she was pressed up against him and the puppy. Okay, the puppy was not a part of his planned seduction. He carefully placed Chester on the ground and gave him a pat. "Good boy. Go play."

Chester woofed and scrabbled off to the corner of the room where something new held his attention.

Noah straightened and faced Sabrina. "I need to tell you why." He gripped her hands. "I know I didn't listen to you, but I'm asking you to be a bigger person and listen to me."

"Of course." Her smile could have lit the entire town.

He pulled her close and hugged her. Just hugged her, long and hard.

Every night when he'd gone to sleep—on those occasions when he wasn't staring at the wall thinking about her—she'd drifted through his subconscious. Always smiling, laughing, dragging him into the middle of whatever caught her interest. She flitted through his dreams, close enough to touch if only he wasn't afraid to reach. He'd be lying if he said he wasn't afraid anymore. He was.

Life held no guarantees. Noah was well aware of that and had been from far too young an age, but he was more afraid of losing her forever. Of seeing that bright light focused on someone else. Someone who wasn't afraid to accept what she offered so generously. Of living the rest of his life on the sidelines because he hadn't taken the opportunity when it was handed to him.

Hell, not even handed to him. When it hunted him down, waited on his porch steps and bought a dog. He gave her another squeeze. "I'm afraid to leave this town. I'm afraid that if I'm not their mayor or if I leave them, they won't let me back in."

Sabrina pulled away to look at him, but didn't speak. Her arms circled more tightly around his waist.

"My biological mother died when I was a baby. I was too young to remember her and by the time I was old enough to ask, my dad was gone, too." He gritted his teeth. He didn't like talking about this, which was why he usually didn't. "I'm not from here. Not like you. I can't trace my ancestors back to the town founders. I can't even trace them back a single generation. But when I needed this town, when I thought they would send me away, they didn't. They took care of Mom and Kyle and me."

Sabrina lifted a hand to cup his cheek. The gentleness of her touch, the silent support almost undid him.

Noah swallowed. "I don't want to lose them." He couldn't imagine life without them, but he'd lived it without Sabrina and he knew which was worse. "But I can't lose you." He looked down at her, "If you got a job offer somewhere else. Toronto, New York, London. I'd want you to take it. And I'd want to go with you."

"Noah."

"I mean it." He brushed her hair back, letting his fingers slip through the long, silky length. She'd hurt him when she left. He wouldn't deny that, but she'd also come back. She'd risked everything. For him. "Thank you for not giving up on me."

She pretended offense. "As if you could shake me so easily."

Noah smiled. God, he was lucky. "I missed you so much." And he had some time to make up for. He took her by the hand and led her toward the bedroom. Chester tried to follow, but was resoundingly denied. He stopped crying when Noah gave him a chew toy.

"Where did you get that?" Sabrina wanted to know.

He ushered her into the bedroom, locked the door and stripped off her white button-down shirt. "I stopped at the grocery store on my way over."

"What?" Her hair brushed across his forearm. "You mean you didn't just come straight here when you realized the error of your ways?"

Noah nudged her onto the bed and slipped off her boots. He'd missed these boots. He wondered if she'd wear them with nothing else one day. He'd have to ask. But not today. Today was about her. Not him. Loving her, showing her everything he'd kept bottled up inside, too afraid to tell her how he felt.

He rose from his crouch and undid her jeans, working them over her hips. Her bra and underwear were the same shade of fiery red. He toyed with the lacy edges and pressed a kiss to her shoulder. "I thought a gift might be required."

"For the dog."

Noah pressed a kiss to Sabrina's other shoulder, then trailed his tongue across her collarbone. "That was just the start." She shivered in his arms. "Let me show you the rest."

Her only response was a smile.

CHAPTER TWENTY-FIVE

SABRINA COULDN'T STOP smiling as she and Noah walked into the dealership. He'd have been happy to stay in bed all night, but she insisted. This was the first time she'd be in town when he won and she wanted to see it firsthand. Chester was with them.

"The puppy!" Daisy's scream drew the attention of anyone who hadn't already seen the two of them enter.

"Daisy." Marissa snagged her daughter's shoulder just before she launched herself at Chester, who took one look at the screeching Daisy and promptly peed.

Daisy stopped, then jerked back making sure the pee didn't touch her red boots. "Ew. He needs a diaper. Like Timmy and Scotty."

"He was scared." Sabrina crouched down so she was eye level with Daisy. "Remember how we talked about gentle voices and pats."

Daisy nodded and stroked Chester's soft fur. "He's a nice puppy." Chester tried to crawl up her.

Noah bent down holding a roll of paper towel

someone had handed him. When Sabrina attempted to take it from him, he shook her off. "He's my dog now, too." Since she didn't really want to clean up puppy pee, she let him.

He looked so handsome, mopping up the mess, gently chiding Chester, who clearly did not understand he was in trouble and kept trying to lick Noah's face. Sabrina smiled as he balled up the paper towels and walked over to a nearby garbage can. He looked pretty hot in his suit, too. She thought about how she'd get him out of it later.

"Why are you smiling?" Daisy asked.

"Yeah, why?" Marissa chimed in with a knowing grin.

"I'm happy." She shot a glare at Marissa who only laughed.

Daisy laughed, too, as though she was in on the joke. "I'm glad you're here." She put her arms around Sabrina's neck and hugged. "Where are your boots?"

Sabrina had decided on a simple gray dress and sleek black heels. The fitted skirt and straps around her ankles were very film noir chic. Appropriate for the mayor's partner. But she'd had to promise Noah to wear the boots for him later. Apparently he had some fantasy about her and boots and nothing else.

She hugged Daisy back and then stood, still carrying the little girl. Daisy responded by wrapping her arms and legs around her.

"Nothing for me, Daisy?" Noah asked, coming back over. "This is my party, you know."

Daisy frowned at him and clung to Sabrina more tightly.

"Your niece knows how to hang on to a good thing when she finds it," Sabrina informed him. "You could take lessons." Of course, if Daisy wanted to ease up on the hugging just a smidge, Sabrina wouldn't be upset.

Noah's fingers curled across her hip, sending a bolt of pleasure up her spine. He leaned down to whisper in her ear. "Already have."

"No whispering," Marissa said. "Daisy, let go of Aunt Sabrina."

"No." Daisy had staked her claim and wasn't giving up without a fight. "You said she was my aunt and we had to show her how much we loved her because Uncle Noah might not." She turned her miniscowl on her uncle. "You love Aunt Sabrina don't you?"

"Daisy." Marissa's eyes were enormous. Embarrassment warred with laughter on her face.

Sabrina felt her own cheeks heat. Noah looked like he wasn't sure whether he wanted to hug his niece or pretend she didn't exist. Sabrina's lips twitched. She tried to turn her laugh into a cough. Marissa did the same, then the two of them were laughing hysterically as if it was eleventh grade all over again and they'd just driven off with Ed's parking sign. Who needed a personalized street sign anyway?

Noah sighed. "You're supposed to let me mention that in my own time, Daisy."

"What does that mean?" Daisy peered at him and then at Sabrina and Marissa who were still laughing. "What's so funny?"

The question set Sabrina off again with Marissa right behind her. "Daisy," Marissa finally choked out. "We need to go."

"Where?"

"Anywhere." She took her daughter's hand when Sabrina set her on the ground. "We'll come chat later."

"Later when?" Daisy asked as she was dragged away.

Noah ran a hand through his hair. "My niece knows how to ruin a moment."

"No." Sabrina looked up at him. He looked so adorable, slightly confused, a little rumpled, but all hers. "It was perfect."

She saw someone coming toward them, waving a sheaf of papers. No doubt the polls on how Noah was doing and what the likely outcome of the election was. But Noah seemed uninterested. He turned to face her, ignoring the rustle of news. "When did she start calling you her aunt?"

"A couple of months ago." Right around the time she'd left, foolishly believing that her place was in the city.

"I see. My family has been going behind my back for a while then."

Sabrina nodded. "It was for your own good." She peeked at the young man who remained stationed a few feet away, shifting from one foot to the other. Kent someone. He'd been a few years behind her in school so they hadn't run in the same circles. "I think people are waiting to talk to you."

"Mmm-hmm." Noah's eyes stayed on hers. They made her feel hot and cold at the same time. Maybe she shouldn't have been so insistent that they leave her bed. They could have watched the coverage on TV tomorrow morning. "They can wait."

He lowered his mouth to hers and Sabrina forgot about the election. About the man with the sheaf of papers. About her niece who was probably watching somewhere.

"I love you, Sabrina Ryan." She could only clutch his shoulders and hang on for dear life.

She didn't get a chance to respond before Kent interrupted by clearing his throat. Noah's mayoral face dropped into place as he turned to listen.

God, that was sexy. The authoritative way he took charge. She shivered, remembering the way he'd done so in bed only an hour ago. She'd have to get him to show her again later.

But first she had to answer to Trish who was heading over with a not-so-happy look on her face. Clearly, she'd seen the online article.

The rest of the evening passed in a whirlwind of conversations about scrutineers, a mobile poll and how long Sabrina planned to stay in town. Her preferred answer of forever got some lengthy laughs. Trish forgave her the online article, but told her not to pull a stunt like that again.

Her parents, Ellen, even George had all come out in support of Noah. And the only time the excited chatter quieted down was whenever the news channel broadcasting the province-wide election results flashed Wheaton across the screen. Then there was a collective intake of breath and silence as everyone read the latest numbers. All except for Daisy who could be heard asking for more juice or singing about puppies.

Each update showed Noah further and further in the lead. Any tension eased as it became apparent that Noah would be elected to his third term by a considerable margin. Kyle continued to show the room the wonders of his election app. Sabrina noticed a number of other people put the app on their own phones.

When the results were finally called by the pundit sitting on a panel, a wild cheer filled the room and a waterfall of balloons rained down on them.

Noah turned and kissed her amidst the celebration. "Thank you."

Then he was tugged away to give his victory speech. She watched along with everyone else, so full of love and pride that she was amazed she didn't float up to the rafters. Chester barked happily and tried to chew a balloon. Then scared himself when he succeeded in popping one. This time she convinced Daisy to clean up the pee by telling her it would be good practice if she wanted to get her own puppy.

"First the red boots and now a puppy?" Marissa asked as she oversaw her daughter's cleaning attempt. "Remind me why I wanted you to come back?"

Sabrina simply laughed and hugged her best friend.

The crowd was in the mood to party, but lucky for Sabrina, that meant everyone was gone by eleven instead of nine. She helped Noah sweep up some of the mess while Chester roared around the room.

There were still a few stray streamers and some balloons that had gotten wedged in the rafters when Noah walked over, carrying Chester under one arm and plucked the broom from her hands. "I think we've cleaned up enough. We're done for now."

The night was clear and cold. Sabrina snuggled

into Noah's free arm as they walked through the empty lot to his car. He'd already laid a blanket in the backseat for Chester. Sabrina had a feeling it wouldn't be long before Chester, who'd already gone from her dog to their dog, would soon be his dog. She hoped Noah knew that meant he was on early-morning walking duty.

"Well, now that you're mayor again, what's next?"

He draped his arm more securely around her, protecting her from the gust of wind that blew past them as they walked around to the passenger side. "Let's go home."

She leaned her head against his shoulder and smiled. "I'm already there."

* * * * *

LARGER-PRINT BOOKS!

GET 2 FREE LARGER-PRINT NOVELS PLUS
2 FREE GIFTS!

⬧HARLEQUIN®

Romance

From the Heart, For the Heart

YES! Please send me 2 FREE LARGER-PRINT Harlequin® Romance novels and my
2 FREE gifts (gifts are worth about $10). After receiving them, if I don't wish to receive
any more books, I can return the shipping statement marked "cancel." If I don't cancel,
I will receive 4 brand-new novels every month and be billed just $4.84 per book in the
U.S. or $5.24 per book in Canada. That's a savings of at least 19% off the cover price!
It's quite a bargain! Shipping and handling is just 50¢ per book in the U.S. and 75¢ per
book in Canada.* I understand that accepting the 2 free books and gifts places me under
no obligation to buy anything. I can always return a shipment and cancel at any time.
Even if I never buy another book, the two free books and gifts are mine to keep forever.

119/319 HDN F43Y

Name	(PLEASE PRINT)

Address	Apt. #

City	State/Prov.	Zip/Postal Code

Signature (if under 18, a parent or guardian must sign)

Mail to the **Harlequin® Reader Service:**
IN U.S.A.: P.O. Box 1867, Buffalo, NY 14240-1867
IN CANADA: P.O. Box 609, Fort Erie, Ontario L2A 5X3
Want to try two free books from another line?
Call 1-800-873-8635 or visit www.ReaderService.com.

* Terms and prices subject to change without notice. Prices do not include applicable
taxes. Sales tax applicable in N.Y. Canadian residents will be charged applicable taxes.
Offer not valid in Quebec. This offer is limited to one order per household. Not valid for
current subscribers to Harlequin Romance Larger-Print books. All orders subject to
credit approval. Credit or debit balances in a customer's account(s) may be offset by
any other outstanding balance owed by or to the customer. Please allow 4 to 6 weeks
for delivery. Offer available while quantities last.

Your Privacy—The Harlequin® Reader Service is committed to protecting your
privacy. Our Privacy Policy is available online at www.ReaderService.com or upon
request from the Harlequin Reader Service.

We make a portion of our mailing list available to reputable third parties that offer products
we believe may interest you. If you prefer that we not exchange your name with third
parties, or if you wish to clarify or modify your communication preferences, please visit
us at www.ReaderService.com/consumerchoice or write to us at Harlequin Reader
Service Preference Service, P.O. Box 9062, Buffalo, NY 14269. Include your complete
name and address.

HRLP13R

LARGER-PRINT BOOKS!

HARLEQUIN *Presents*

PASSION GUARANTEED SEDUCTION

GET 2 FREE LARGER-PRINT
NOVELS PLUS 2 FREE GIFTS!

YES! Please send me 2 FREE LARGER-PRINT Harlequin Presents® novels and my 2 FREE gifts (gifts are worth about $10). After receiving them, if I don't wish to receive any more books, I can return the shipping statement marked "cancel." If I don't cancel, I will receive 6 brand-new novels every month and be billed just $5.05 per book in the U.S. or $5.49 per book in Canada. That's a saving of at least 16% off the cover price! It's quite a bargain! Shipping and handling is just 50¢ per book in the U.S. and 75¢ per book in Canada.* I understand that accepting the 2 free books and gifts places me under no obligation to buy anything. I can always return a shipment and cancel at any time. Even if I never buy another book, the two free books and gifts are mine to keep forever.

176/376 HDN F43N

Name	(PLEASE PRINT)	
Address		Apt. #
City	State/Prov.	Zip/Postal Code

Signature (if under 18, a parent or guardian must sign)

Mail to the **Harlequin® Reader Service:**
IN U.S.A.: P.O. Box 1867, Buffalo, NY 14240-1867
IN CANADA: P.O. Box 609, Fort Erie, Ontario L2A 5X3

**Are you a subscriber to Harlequin Presents books
and want to receive the larger-print edition?
Call 1-800-873-8635 today or visit us at www.ReaderService.com.**

* Terms and prices subject to change without notice. Prices do not include applicable taxes. Sales tax applicable in N.Y. Canadian residents will be charged applicable taxes. Offer not valid in Quebec. This offer is limited to one order per household. Not valid for current subscribers to Harlequin Presents Larger-Print books. All orders subject to credit approval. Credit or debit balances in a customer's account(s) may be offset by any other outstanding balance owed by or to the customer. Please allow 4 to 6 weeks for delivery. Offer available while quantities last.

Your Privacy—The Harlequin® Reader Service is committed to protecting your privacy. Our Privacy Policy is available online at www.ReaderService.com or upon request from the Harlequin Reader Service.

We make a portion of our mailing list available to reputable third parties that offer products we believe may interest you. If you prefer that we not exchange your name with third parties, or if you wish to clarify or modify your communication preferences, please visit us at www.ReaderService.com/consumerschoice or write to us at Harlequin Reader Service Preference Service, P.O. Box 9062, Buffalo, NY 14269. Include your complete name and address.

HPLP13R